Broken Bones and Shattered Spears

Book Three in the Tenochtitlan Trilogy

Edward Rickford

ISBN: 978-1-7351319-3-1

Glossary

Mexica: the most powerful people in pre-Hispanic Mexico. Also known as the Aztec, an erroneous demonym popularized by 19th century historians.

Great Speaker: term that refers to the highest-ranking political figure in the Mexica Confederacy.

Totonacs: disgruntled vassals of the Mexica.

Tlaxcala: an independent nation in the basin of Mexico. Avowed enemies of the Mexica.

Motecuhzoma: leader of the Mexica Confederacy. The Anglicized version of his name is Montezuma and the Hispanicized version of his name is Moctezuma.

Spanish League: about 3 miles. Similar in length to a long-run, a Mexica unit of length.

Malintze/Doña Marina: indigenous woman who translates for the Spanish. Enslaved for most of her childhood, she speaks Nahuatl, Yoko Ochoko, and Spanish.

Teteo: Nahuatl term that roughly translates, in English, to powerful, mystical people. Singular of this word is *teotl*.

Mexico 1519

Central Mexico 1519

Pronunciation Key

In Nahuatl, x is pronounced the same way that English speakers pronounce sh in shell.

In Nahuatl, tz is pronounced the same way English speakers pronounce tz in ritzy.

In Nahuatl, i is pronounced the same way that English speakers pronounce ee in seep.

List of Old World Characters

Vitale: New Christian of Jewish descent. Hails from Granada area.

Hernando Cortés: Old Christian. Hails from Medellín in Extremadura. Considered a minor hidalgo on account of family connections. Has benefitted from a formal education, has limited experience as a battle commander. Captain-general of the Spanish forces.

Pedro de Alvarado: Old Christian who hails from Badajoz in Extremadura. Has not had the same educational opportunities as Cortés, does have more military experience in the New World. High-ranking officer, trusted confidant for Cortés.

Juan Garrido: New Christian of African descent. Hails from Kongo. Served Cortés' one-time rival.

List of One World Characters

Malintze/Doña Marina: Distinguished translator. Hails from Painalla area. Speaks Nahuatl, Yoko Ochoko, and Spanish. Serves as a translator for the Spanish. Will be freed if campaign is a success.

Cuauhtemoc: Distinguished warrior. Hails from Northern Tenochtitlan. Has led numerous campaigns throughout the One World. Kin to Motecuhzoma Xocoyotzin.

Xicotencatl the Younger: Distinguished warrior. Hails from Tlaxcala. Has been heavily involved in military efforts to repulse foreign invaders from Tlaxcala. Could one day become the Speaker of Tlaxcala.

Chichi: Distinguished warrior. Hails from Tlaxcala. Served as deputy to Xicotencatl the Younger.

Synopsis for The Serpent and the Eagle, Book One in
The Tenochtitlan Trilogy

In early 1519, Hernando Cortés sails for the New World with a Spanish army as factious as it is rapacious. They arrive in the Yucatan Peninsula expecting to be welcomed by friendly Indians—only to discover the local war chiefs are keen on battle.

Shortly after landing, the weary explorers must decide if they will abide by a distasteful ultimatum or if they will engage a numerically superior foe. The Spaniards choose the latter and crush the local forces. Chastened by defeat, the war chiefs bend the knee and inform Cortés of a mysterious people far to the north that live in magnificent cities far grander than any in Europe. These people are known as the Mexica, some today call them Aztec, and they have amassed a fortune of Biblical proportions though trade and battle.

To march upon their cities will invite conflict with a fearsome monarch who commands a military machine unrivaled both in power and brutality. Undeterred by the prospect of war, Cortés leads the Spaniards northward.

The Spaniards reach Mexica lands in short time, but the sheer might of the Mexica polity deters them from launching an immediate attack. Instead, they begin dialoguing with local envoys. The Mexica strive to be generous hosts and the Spaniards are quite pleased to be greeted with lavish presents rather than a hostile army. Their hosts, however, are far from pleased by Cortés' persistent entreaties for a personal audience with the Mexica monarch. Hoping to put an end to such impetuous talk, the Mexica terminate all trading relations with the "pale people" and the Spaniards are forced to fend for themselves in a harsh, alien environment. Many Spaniards clamor to return home as disease takes its toll. Desperate to save the expedition, Cortés enters into an alliance with aggrieved Mexica vassals. His would-be allies soon prove they are not above treachery or deceit, but Cortés insists they play a vital role in the prospective march on the Mexica capital. His fellow countrymen harbor serious reservations about the fledgling alliance; some fear the Mexica cannot be defeated. Battling mutiny and desertion, Cortés sinks the ships that could be used to escape the mainland. With no option of retreat, the Spaniards must commit to a grueling campaign that could lead to unimaginable wealth or gruesome death.

Synopsis for The Bend of the River, Book Two in the
Tenochtitlan Trilogy

The pale people are making an inland march, a journey that will take them through scorching deserts, freezing mountains, parched grasslands, and lush forests. Their tenacity comes as a great surprise to the Mexica, as does their willingness to ally with enemy nations. Perhaps most surprising, however, is their brutality.

Shortly after entering into an alliance with Tlaxcala, the pale people launch a vicious attack on the altepetl of Cholula. The wanton violence sparks heated discussion in Tenochtitlan. Should the Mexica rally an army to make war on the pale people?

Many nations have tried, but none have been able to triumph over the pale people. Hernando Cortés has proven himself an able commander, and his knack for exploiting long-standing rivalries makes him a formidable enemy. Convinced a direct confrontation would be disastrous, Motecuhzoma opts for a more cautious approach: he will lure the pale people and their allies into Tenochtitlan and lull them into a false sense of safety. Then, once they have let their guard down, the Mexica will launch a surprise attack and kill the pale people. It is a risky strategy, but it is preferable to a direct confrontation. So long as the pale people are inside the city, they can be controlled. Outside the city, they are an unchecked menace.

The Mexica play the part of the generous host well, but the pale people do not make for easy prey. For the most part, they keep to themselves and do not stray far from their redoubt in the center of the city. Reluctant to make a head-on attack, the Mexica bide their time by gathering materials for a mass poisoning. Unexpected developments upend these plans, and a bloody struggle for Tenochtitlan ensues.

Unable to overcome the Mexica forces, the pale people and their allies beat a hasty retreat from Tenochtitlan. The retreat is an unmitigated disaster, and they lose hundreds of soldiers, along with a fortune in gold and silver. Emboldened by victory, the Mexica give chase and engage the combined forces of the pale people and the Tlaxcalteca on an open field of battle. The decision proves to be a terrible mistake, and Cortés helps cinch a victory for his beleaguered army with a daring cavalry charge.

The stunning rout leaves a profound impression on Cuauhtemoc. A high-born warrior destined for command, Cuauhtemoc has come of age in a world defined by Mexica supremacy. Following the battle at Otampan, he is convinced the Mexica can defeat the pale people only by allying with other nations.

Cortés retains command of the army following the victory at Otampan, but his grip on power is tenuous. So, too, is his health. Before the army can reach the capital of Tlaxcala, Cortés collapses in full view of his men. With Cortés out of his wits and his prospects for recovery dim, the entire future of the campaign is thrown into doubt.

Part One
July-September, 1520

Chapter 1

Cuauhtemoc shaded his eyes against the lake's harsh glare and glanced back at the Chalco settlement as it melded into the war canoe's wake. The *altepetl* wasn't all that large, about fifteen thousand people called it home, and had not been absorbed into the Mexica Confederacy until his father's lifetime. The Chalcans probably resented their loss of independence, and Cuauhtemoc had taken great pains to be courteous with his Chalcan hosts. To his surprise, they gave little outward appearance of hostility. On the contrary, they had been pleased to receive him, cloying almost.

Whether they could be counted on in battle, Cuauhtemoc did not know. He hoped so. If Chalco defected, others would do the same. He ground his teeth. The Mexica Confederacy had always been beset by rifts and faults, but he had never fully understood how dangerous that could be. At least, not until the *teteo* arrived.

The *teteo* first arrived in the One World almost ten years past, but they had done little to merit serious attention then. For the most part, they stayed inside their water-houses and made few attempts at communication. However, they had become much bolder in recent years, and the ones who had landed with Cortés had proven boldest of all. The *teteo* weren't just bold, though. They were also cunning. Worst of all, they were powerful.

The canoe knocked against a submerged obstruction, and the rowers shouted at one another. He paid little attention to their yelling. The collision had not done serious damage to the canoe, but the unexpected juddering had reignited an old pain in his back. He grimaced and waited for the discomfort to pass. Many of his wounds from the Battle at Otampan had yet to fully heal. Simply bending over could rob him of breath, but what hurt most was his pride.

Otampan should have been a great victory, should have been the battle that eliminated the *teteo* threat once and for all. Instead, it was the battle that proved the *teteo* were most deadly when backed into a corner and that a charge of hornless stags could devastate an army.

A memory of anguished screaming came rushing back to him, and he closed his eyes. After the Battle at Otampan, recriminations abounded. Most of them had been directed toward Great Speaker Cuitlahuac, but some *pilli* had the temerity to blame the warriors who fought at Otampan. Just thinking about it made his blood boil. Those who didn't fight always made the harshest assessments.

He took a deep breath but kept his eyes closed. Gradually, his other senses came into focus. The melodious plashing of the oars filled his ears. Off in the distance, he could make out what sounded like a flock of horned grebes. He drew air in through his nose, filling his nostrils with a heady mix of lake odors.

First came the pleasant ones: blooming flowers, wood smoke, and fresh-cut sedge. Then came the unpleasant ones: rotten egg, musty soil, and the tang of fresh sweat. Thankfully, it would not be long before the day began to wane. When that happened, the unpleasant odors would fade and the afternoon's unrelenting heat would finally give way to the cool of evening.

Having achieved a modicum of peace, he opened his eyes again. The warrior in front of him, Ollin of Northern Tenochtitlan, snapped his head forward and focused on the watery horizon. Cuauhtemoc pursed his lips. Ollin had much to learn when it came to subtlety.

Cuauhtemoc folded his hands together and waited for Ollin to turn around. It did not take him long to oblige Cuauhtemoc's silent demand. Realizing he was the object of Cuauhtemoc's staring, Ollin froze in mid-turn.

"Do you have a crick in your neck?" Cuauhtemoc asked.

Ollin flushed. After a moment, he recovered his wits. "Indeed, I do. Your powers of observation are most impressive."

Cuauhtemoc nodded. "Strange that should happen. Perhaps it is an issue of posture. Should I ask one of the rowers to switch places with you? The boat master is very good at enforcing proper posture amongst his charges."

Ollin held up both his hands. "Let us do without the needless punishment; I am a warrior, not a rower." Grinning, Ollin turned so he could look Cuauhtemoc in the face. "Have I given offense?"

Cuauhtemoc shook his head, careful to keep his smile in check.

"Good," Ollin said, his voice warm again. "My powers of observation are not as sharp as yours, but it seems as if you are deep in thought. Do you care to unburden yourself to me?"

Cuauhtemoc stiffened. Sharing his thoughts was not as easy as it used to be. His countrymen still respected him, as much for his blood relations as his courage in battle, but the debacle at Otampan had shaken Cuauhtemoc's once supreme confidence. The stain of defeat was not easily washed away, and he did not wish to admit to weakness. Not to the enemy, and not to his own men.

Then again, if he could not speak candidly with the men in his service, men like Ollin, there was no one he could unburden himself to. More than fifty men had crowded into the canoe with him—rowers, warriors, and diplomats—and he trusted all of them as he would his own kin.

"That is most kind of you." Cuauhtemoc gazed out at the watery blue expanse that surrounded him on every side. He could make out the outline of various settlements on both sides of the lake, but they were too far away for him to pick out any unique features. "Look around you, Ollin. What do you see?"

Ollin tapped his thumb against the thwart. "I see a lake."

Cuauhtemoc allowed himself a small laugh. "My, what powers of observation you have. What do you see when you look at the shore?"

Ollin peered off into the distance. "Stone houses—"

"How many?" Cuauhtemoc asked.

Ollin shifted in his seat. "I cannot say with any confidence. It has been some time since a census was conducted."

"Indeed it has," Cuauhtemoc said, surprised by the sadness in his voice. It could be months or years before the next one was conducted. Like so many other important tasks, it would be delayed until the *teteo* were finally exterminated. "But we can both agree there are many, right?"

Ollin nodded.

"Good," Cuauhtemoc said. "Tell me, do you think those people see us as their allies or their masters?"

Ollin scratched his hairless chin. Like most of his countrymen, Ollin detested facial hair. So soon as a hair germinated, he plucked it. Cuauhtemoc had yet to meet a *teotl* who did the same. For whatever strange reason, the *teteo* took great pride in not being able to see their chins or their cheeks and let their facial hair grow in thick ugly patches. "They see us as their masters, of course," Ollin said.

Cuauhtemoc sighed. "I fear you may be right."

Some of the warriors exchanged confused glances. The rowers, had they been close enough to hear, probably would have done the same. "Our fathers, and our fathers before them, fought countless battles to expand the Mexica Confederacy," Ollin said. "Should we not take pride in their accomplishments? Tenochtitlan is the most powerful *altepetl* in all the One World, and people from every province humble themselves before us."

"No nation aspires to servitude," Cuauhtemoc said. "If our subjects see us as their masters, they must also wish to see us humbled. We should hope they see us as their allies. Otherwise, they will betray us at the soonest chance."

A wistful look passed over Ollin's face, and he touched the braid tucked behind his ear. It signified to all the world he was an elite warrior and conferred upon him benefits no ordinary warrior would ever enjoy. Cuauhtemoc had earned his fighting braid many years prior, back when he was on campaign in the Near South. "Great Speaker Cuitlahuac has sent out many diplomatic envoys to nations all throughout the valley," Ollin said. "Do you think these efforts will bear fruit?"

Cuauhtemoc traced the lines of his palm with his thumb. Ollin did not know the half of it. Not only had the Great Speaker sent out diplomatic envoys to almost every *altepetl* in the Valley of Mexico, he had sent a great many outside the valley also. Even Michoacan would receive one, despite their long history of enmity. Perhaps most important of all, the Great Speaker agreed to send a diplomatic envoy to Tlaxcala.

If those efforts succeeded, the *teteo* would lose more than just a safe haven; they would lose their best allies. They would be more vulnerable than hatchlings, and the Mexica would finally be able to revenge themselves for Otampan.

"Let us hope so," Cuauhtemoc said. Unable to hold Ollin's gaze any longer, Cuauhtemoc broke eye contact. Without the aid of other nations, victory would not come easy. If at all.

~ ~ ~

Xicotencatl shivered. Like all the fine houses in Tlaxcala, Father's house was built with thick stone slabs, and the cool interior could not have contrasted more harshly with the blazing heat outside. The unnatural chill unsettled him, and he itched to step outside. Being inside brought back too many memories of his forced confinement in Tenochtitlan.

How many of his countrymen had died trying to escape that accursed city during the Sad Night? He honestly could not say, nor did he want to think about it. He would die a happy man if he never spent another day in Tenochtitlan.

Noyollo, a long-time servant in Father's household, brushed past Xicotencatl and laid a bowl of pitted cherries on a low table with a deliberate clatter. In any other household, doing so would have been considered rude. In Father's household, all servants were expected to do such. Blind in both eyes, Father relied upon such cues so he could carry on with life the same as anyone else.

Father, seated in front of the table, reached for the bowl, guided by sound alone. He missed by only a finger span and swept his hand out in both directions. When he finally found the bowl, his fingers latched onto the clay rim like an eagle's talons. Using his other hand, he plucked a cherry out by its stem and brought it to his puckered lips. He sucked it into his mouth with a small whoosh and munched slowly on it.

"May I have some, Father?" Xicotencatl asked.

"Of course."

Xicotencatl leaned forward on his stool and grabbed the nearest cherry. It dissolved in his mouth like a honey ball, but he did not reach for another. Weeks of privation had shrunk his stomach, and he could no longer relish food the way he once did. He had been most surprised by the change, did not even know if it was normal. All he knew was that if he tried to gorge himself, like he did the first night he returned to Tlaxcala, he would spend all night ejecting everything he had eaten.

"Father, can you please dismiss the servants?" Xicotencatl asked.

Father narrowed his eyes. "Do you think I keep gossips in my household?"

Xicotencatl shifted in his seat. Father liked to think of his servants as insensate, unthinking beings that never gave in to idle talk, but Xicotencatl knew better. Servants were always listening, even when they weren't.

"Father, please," Xicotencatl said.

Father said nothing and reached for another cherry.

Xicotencatl reached across the table to squeeze his hand. Father did not pull his hand back, but he did not take hold of his hand either. Instead, he moved his jaw back and forth slowly as if he were trying to grind a seed down. Xicotencatl's lip curved upward. Father always did that, whenever he was deep in thought.

After a moment, Father lifted his free hand and flicked his fingers toward the door. The servants quietly filed out of the room, and Noyollo shot him a confused glance as she exited the room. Xicotencatl flushed and glanced away. They had been intimates once, and her dismay discomfited him. All the same, he needed privacy to speak candidly with Father.

"Thank you, Father—"

"What happened in Tenochtitlan?" Father asked, his voice cold and imperious.

Xicotencatl stiffened. *I had forgotten how gruff you can be, Father.* Months had passed since they had last spoken, but Father had not changed at all. "When we first arrived in Tenochtitlan, the Mexica treated us as honored guests," Xicotencatl said. "We were sequestered to a palace at night, but they gave us free roam of the city during the day. For months, they treated us as their honored guests. They might have continued doing so, but we raided Motecuhzoma's household. After that, everything changed."

"Did the raid fail?"

Xicotencatl shook his head. "We lost some warriors in the raid, but we gained possession of Motecuhzoma's children. Soon afterwards, Motecuhzoma surrendered himself to our possession."

Father's face brightened. Motecuhzoma had been consecrated as Great Speaker eighteen years past and had done his utmost to grind the Tlaxcalteca into dust. No one in Tlaxcala would ever recall his reign with fondness.

"Cortés was confident the Mexica would not attack so long as we held their sovereign and left the city to deal with a political matter," Xicotencatl continued. "Most of us stayed in Tenochtitlan while we awaited his return and kept to the palace for safety's sake. We began to worry, however, the Mexica would attack us before Cortés could return. Since victory favors the bold, we launched a surprise attack during the Toxcatl Festival."

"Did you take many hostages during the battle?" Father asked.

Xicotencatl winced. "Only a few," he said, his voice clipped. He did not like thinking about the Toxcatl Festival overmuch. Many of the men they had killed that day had been warriors of the highest order, men who would not have hesitated to carry war into Tlaxcala. But they were also unarmed, and there was no honor in a victory like that. "Father, it wasn't truly a battle. They were trapped and unarmed, and we cut them down like stalks of corn."

He waited for Father to say something, sure that he would upbraid him for his lack of honor. To his surprise, Father stayed silent. Was he thinking about the suffering the Mexica had imposed on Tlaxcala with their sanctions and invasions? Or was he simply too disgusted to speak? Xicotencatl did not know either way.

"Once word of the massacre spread, the Mexica attacked the palace we were staying in. Were it not for the bravery of our warriors and the tools of the *teteo*, the Mexica would have overpowered us. They ambushed us anytime we tried to leave the palace, and we had no choice but to stay inside at all times. We were confined to the palace for weeks on end, and water became so scarce we had to dig wells and collect rain with buckets."

Xicotencatl shivered. The weeks had been most trying and haunted his dreams still. He sometimes came to in a cold sweat, sure that he was back in Tenochtitlan.

"When Cortés returned from the coast, he brought many reinforcements, and we forced our way out of the city. We underestimated the resolve of the Mexica, however. They harassed our column relentlessly, and we lost many good men during our retreat. That night alone, we lost two hundred times twenty Tlaxcalteca."

Father blinked and craned his head toward him. The sight of his rheumy eyes had always unsettled him, and Xicotencatl quickly looked away.

"Not all of them were warriors. Many of them were porters, but I grieve for all of them," Xicotencatl added. "It was so senseless. We died because our men lacked proper armor, because the *teteo* could not bear to leave their gold behind."

A flash of anger passed over Father's face. "Our people lack proper armor because the Mexica forbid us from trading with our neighbors. Do not forget why you marched to Tenochtitlan with the *teteo*."

Xicotencatl pursed his lips. The Mexica sanctions had caused a great deal of suffering in Tlaxcala, he could not deny that. However, he had no interest in continuing to fight them. Enough blood had been spilled at Otampan and Tenochtitlan and so many other places.

"Tell me more about the retreat," Father commanded. "If it was so terrible, why are you uninjured?"

Xicotencatl huffed. No use telling Father about the way his ankle ached if he ran more than half a long-run, the way his stomach roiled whenever he tried to eat more than a few handfuls of food at a time, the way his nightmares made him relive the worst moments of the campaign; those would not count as battle injuries to Father.

"The Mexica followed us from Tenochtitlan with a small force and attacked us anytime we stayed in one place more than a night. We didn't know it then, but they were herding us to Otampan Valley. Once we reached the valley, they attacked us with their main force. I do not think I have ever seen an army that big. It was like something from a..."

He trailed off, unsure what to say. Like something from a nightmare? Father would just scoff. Maybe there wasn't a good word for it. Xicotencatl had traveled through enough of the One World to understand that people naturally clustered together. Sometimes for trade, sometimes for security, sometimes for both. Until Otampan, he had never known so many people could cluster together for the sake of killing, though.

"Victory should have gone to the Mexica," Xicotencatl said. "But we refused to yield, and the horse charge did great harm to the Mexica army." Xicotencatl stopped. In times past, he had referred to the horses as hornless stags, and he was surprised at how easily the word horse came to him. He had spent too much time with the *teteo*. They were corrupting him with their language and their strange customs. "Father, the fighting was very intense. At one point, Cuauhtemoc took me captive—"

Father's eyes widened. Xicotencatl gritted his teeth. He had said too much. He had not meant to tell Father everything, not yet at least.

"Did you fight your way free?" Father asked.

Xicotencatl ran his way free as much as he fought his way free, but he was not going to tell Father that. "Yes, but I had the help of a mastiff."

Father quirked an eyebrow.

"Mastiff is what the *teteo* sometimes call their dogs," Xicotencatl explained. "Father, the *teteo* are very... different from us. Do you ever wonder if we are making a mistake by allying with them?"

Father scoffed. "What does it matter that they are different? Their weapons are most powerful, and they want the same thing as us."

"What if they don't?"

Father rapped his fingers on the table. "Do they still wish to see Tenochtitlan brought low?"

"Of course they do, Father," Xicotencatl said, exasperation coloring his voice. "But what if they want more than that?"

Father went quiet. Sensing an advantage, Xicotencatl pressed the offensive. "Not so long ago, the *teteo* were our enemies. They killed many Tlaxcalteca people when they invaded our lands."

Father waved his hand dismissively. "They were our enemies for a few days; the Mexica have been our enemy for generations. Allying with the *teteo* allows us to secure a future for Tlaxcala, to step out from the shadow of Tenochtitlan once and for all."

"The Mexica might be able to offer a better future than the *teteo*," Xicotencatl replied. He held his breath, waiting for Father to answer.

He expected Father to fly into a rage, to remind him of all the terrible indignities the Mexica had foisted upon the Tlaxcalteca. Instead, he rubbed his fingers together and reached for another cherry.

"Interesting you should mention that," Father said. "Envoys for the Mexica suggested much the same. They would like us to receive an official delegation from Tenochtitlan so we can discuss terms for an alliance."

Xicotencatl grinned. Cuauhtemoc had made good on his word! Knowing it would be unseemly to sound too excited, Xicotencatl forced himself to speak in a slow and measured tone. "What would an alliance entail?"

"The Mexica will lift all sanctions and exempt us from any tribute payments. They say they will also ask their vassals to send tribute to us. In exchange, they ask that we kill the *teteo* in Tlaxcala."

"Do you favor their proposal?"

"No." Father wiped his lips with the back of his hand. "But we will hear what they have to say. Perhaps they may surprise us and offer better terms when we parley."

A warm feeling blossomed in Xicotencatl's breast. In the past, the Tlaxcalteca had made war against the *teteo* and lost, but he was confident that his people could prevail over the *teteo* if they joined forces with the Mexica. "A shame that Cortés is out of his wits with fever. He'd probably eat dirt to keep us from dialoguing with the Mexica."

"Do not fret for his health," Father said. "He will recover soon enough."

Xicotencatl sobered. "What makes you say that?"

"The gods have big plans for that Christian. Soon, he will wake. When that happens, it may be necessary to reconcile your differences."

Xicotencatl glowered at Father. "Why?"

"Because most of our countrymen have no wish to abrogate our alliance with the *teteo*. And if it is decided we will honor our pact with the *teteo*, we will go on campaign with them again."

"We?" Xicotencatl asked, an edge to his voice.

"You will go on campaign with them again," Father clarified. "And you will not dishonor Tlaxcala again. Either you will return victorious, or you will return not at all."

Chapter 2

Vitale arched his back and tapped the edge of the crate. It did not make for a comfortable seat, but he preferred a splintery crate to an Indian stool. Their stools were much too low to the ground and made him feel as if he were sitting on a chamber pot.

He took a deep breath. Compared to most sick rooms, this one smelled rather pleasant. A faint trace of sweat permeated the air, but it was masked by fresh-cut flowers and burning incense. The captain-general was fortunate to be receiving such care, not that he was in any state to appreciate it.

Still bedridden, Cortés was pale as parchment and weak as a newborn. He could neither feed himself nor stand and was wholly dependent upon his retainers. To see him so reduced was odd, like seeing a star matador beg for plaudits, but it was also humbling. For so long, Cortés' name had inspired fear and awe. Now it evoked only pity.

Vitale volunteered for guard duty solely to gain more information regarding Cortés' condition, but he had gained precious little information thus far. Sometimes Cortés shivered like a man with palsy, sometimes he sweated as if he were trudging through desert. What that meant, Vitale could only guess. Vitale's most serious brush with fever happened long ago, long before he sailed for the New World.

Nonetheless, it was comforting to know that a man as well-to-do as Cortés was also susceptible to malady. It made the social chasm between them less daunting, even if they would never be equals in any real sense of the word. They knelt before the same king and spoke the same language, but Cortés came from the better family and nothing mattered more than that.

The sound of light footsteps reached his ears. He turned as Doña Marina entered the room. She carried cotton blankets under one arm and cradled a flower-filled vase in the other. The march from Tenochtitlan to Tlaxcala had been trying for everyone, but she still carried herself with a remarkable sense of grace. Whether that was a testament to her strength or her ability to pretend, he did not know.

"Where is Olea?" Doña Marina asked. She set the blankets down on a long table and smoothed out the wrinkles. "He should be helping guard."

"He's taken short," Vitale replied.

Doña Marina scrunched her lips together.

"Went to find a chamber pot," Vitale explained.

"Taken short," she repeated. "I will remember that one. I still have much Spanish to learn about."

Vitale laughed. "You speak Spanish better than half the men in the company."

"Thank you." Doña Marina drew back some of the curtains to allow in more natural light. "I try very hard to be good at your language."

Vitale scratched his chin. He wasn't all that sure he could call Spanish his language. True, he had more familiarity with it than any other tongue, but it had been forced on him from an early age. All so that he could blend in, not that he was much good at it. Despite the best efforts of family, he spoke with a Ladino lilt and often felt ill at ease amongst Old Christians.

Malintze placed some fresh flowers by Cortés' pallet and sat on a stool next to him. She laid her hand on his forehead and frowned.

"How is he?" Vitale asked.

"Still hot," she said. "I think he's getting cooler, though. He said a few words yesterday."

Vitale nodded. It had been four days since Cortés collapsed, and he had been bedridden ever since. If he did not recover in the next few days, he probably never would.

"Were you a healer back in Potonchan?" Vitale asked.

Doña Marina stiffened. "I was a slave in Potonchan."

As far as Vitale could tell, her condition had not changed much. Cortés granted her many liberties, she had her own guards and wore only the finest cloths, but Vitale doubted that she would stay with the company any longer than she had to. He certainly had no intention of pledging his life to the company. Vitale had done enough marching and killing and maiming to last a lifetime.

Doña Marina dipped a compress into a bucket of water, wrung it of excess liquid, and laid it across Cortés' forehead. He exhaled but made no sound otherwise. She dried her hands and emptied a bag of shriveled leaves into a mortar. After inspecting each one, she picked up a pestle and began grinding the leaves into small pieces.

Vitale massaged his forearm. He had injured it during the Battle at Otampan, but he knew better than to expect ministrations from anyone of importance. He would have to trust that his arm would heal in time.

"What do you think happens if Cortés don't get better?" Vitale asked. He knew it was wrong to ask, but he couldn't help himself. He had never been alone with Doña Marina before and did not imagine another opportunity would soon present itself.

Doña Marina turned toward him, pestle and mortar still in hand. "It is not worth thinking about." Her tone brooked no disagreement, and Vitale wondered if he had overstepped his bounds. "Why are you here?" Doña Marina asked. "You never guarded for Cortés in past."

Vitale cracked his neck. "Some of Cortés' guards are with Saint James now, so I volunteered for watch duty."

Doña Marina nodded. She kept her dark eyes fixed on him as she continued to grind the leaves. "There are a lot of men you could kill and fight for. Why do you care so much for Cortés?"

"Cortés offered more than the others." Vitale glanced at his mud-stained boots. He had no more honor than a harlot; there was a time when he was so desperate to escape poverty he would have pledged himself to the Sultan's army.

Those days were behind him, but not because he now enjoyed great wealth. Joining the campaign had done precious little to improve his fortunes. He still had his health, however, and he intended to keep that.

He fixed his gaze on Doña Marina's fine footwear. Some of the poorest drudges had to go barefoot after the Battle at Otampan, but not her. She was too important for that. No, she wore sandals with thick soles and woven leather. As far as he could remember, she had not possessed anything half as fine when she first joined the expedition.

"You love Cortés, don't you?" Vitale asked.

Doña Marina tapped the pestle against the rim of the mortar and inspected her work. "Only the free can love," Doña Marina said. "The rest of us… well, we can hope."

Vitale scratched his head, confused by the dejection in her voice. When Doña Marina joined the expedition, she was nothing more than a slave girl, a mere bedside comfort. She had yet to gain her freedom, that would come after the war ended, but she was no longer a disposable servant.

Not only did she have her own guards, she had the respect of the rank and file. A great deal of that had come about because of Cortés—surely she owed him some affection. Vitale rubbed a hand through his hair. Did he also owe Cortés the same? Cortés had forgiven him for mutiny, a capital crime, and let him off with nothing more than a mild reproach.

"Why you helpin' him if you don't love him?" Vitale asked.

Doña Marina emptied the mortar into a small cup and picked small bits off of the pestle. "I help because I want better life. As you say, he offers more."

Vitale grunted. He was no longer interested in what Cortés offered. Come what may, he intended to throw his lot in with a different crowd. "Maybe there are other ways of getting that same thing."

Doña Marina cast a darting glance toward the entrance. If the guard outside the room was following their conservation, he gave no indication of it. "What do you mean?"

"Nothing really," Vitale said. "Just curious—"

"About my loyalty?" Doña Marina asked.

Vitale frowned. Doña Marina's suspicions were as unwarranted as they were surprising. He sensed that he had made a mistake by making conversation with her and wished Olea would return.

Doña Marina put down the pestle. "Did Pedro send you here?"

Vitale started. Pedro de Alvarado was acting captain-general until Cortés woke up, but Vitale had few, if any, interactions with him. "What?"

"Did Pedro send you here?" Doña Marina asked, enunciating every word with such emphasis it chilled him.

"No. Is there a reason he might?"

"Pedro says I must serve the expedition no matter what happens to Cortés." Anger flashed across Doña Marina's face. "He says he will force my loyalty if he needs to."

Vitale blinked. Pedro had to be desperate to contemplate such drastic action, but he was not without cause. The army was riven by factions and many were loath to see him take over. Had it not been for his cruelty, the company might have been able to preserve good relations with the Mexica. At least, that's what many claimed. Vitale had his doubts. The company had done little to earn the love of the Mexica and much to earn their enmity. Rot could bring down a tree as sure as an ax.

"I hope Pedro doesn't do that," Vitale said.

Doña Marina laughed drily. "So nice of you to say. But you not care much, I think." Doña Marina cocked her head to the side. "Why you not care? If Pedro is captain-general from now on, it affect you also."

Unable to hold her gaze, Vitale turned away. He flicked a bug off his hand and tried to think of something smart to say.

"You going to desert?" Doña Marina asked.

Vitale's eyes widened. For a second, his heart stopped. *Thank God Cortés is still out of his wits.* Vitale took a deep breath to calm himself. The conversation had gone too far. The guard outside understood Basque better than Spanish, but he was in no mood to try his luck. "I'm thirsty," he said in a terse tone. "I must leave to fetch some water."

He stood and made his way toward the door.

"Tell me your plan, or I will talk."

Vitale froze. Would Doña Marina make a hollow threat? He closed his eyes and exhaled. It had been stupid to make conversation with her, and he had to face the consequences now. He opened his eyes and turned toward her.

She was beautiful, none could deny that. She had hair as luminous as silk and eyes that could peer deep into a man's soul. He had not expected her to be so perceptive, though. Solomon would have liked her. He swallowed a lump in his throat. It had been over a week since he last saw Solomon, and he now accepted that he would never see him again. He wondered if any other crew members would mourn him. Probably not. Solomon was just a pesky Moor to the Old Christians.

Vitale cleared his throat and said, "Company will need to send for supplies from Cuba at some point, and we got the ships to make the journey, thanks to Narváez. I mean to be on the ship that departs first."

"Will you return?"

"Would need a good reason. Not likely anybody will miss me." He held up his injured forearm for her. His forearm had swollen like a pregnant sow and would need to be drained of ill humors soon. "With an arm this busted, I got about as much use as a lame mule."

Doña Marina's face softened. "It must be nice."

Vitale snorted. "Being injured? Or knowing nobody will miss me?"

Doña Marina turned toward Cortés and laid a hand on his chest. "Knowing you can leave."

~ ~ ~

Cuauhtemoc rubbed his aching back. Attendants had carried him to Tlaxcala in a hammock to make good time, and he did not look forward to the journey back to Tenochtitlan. Despite having had ample time to stand and stretch, his insides felt jostled and unsettled. How he wished he could have traveled to Tlaxcala by foot. But a journey like that would have taken much longer and time was too precious to waste these days.

According to some reports, only four hundred *teteo* had made it back to Tlaxcala. If the Tlaxcalteca could be persuaded to revoke sanctuary, Cortés' army could be destroyed once and for all. The very thought of it made his heart turn white.

The *teteo* were not the only ones who were vulnerable, however. Cuauhtemoc had taken a great risk by entering Tlaxcala. The Tlaxcalteca hated all things Mexica, and Cuauhtemoc had brought only twenty guards. If the Tlaxcalteca attacked with a large force, they would be defenseless.

He took in a deep breath. It was a risk worth taking. If the Tlaxcalteca and the Mexica made common cause, the *teteo* could be defeated by month's end.

Cuauhtemoc scanned the pine trees for enemy archers. The branches were too thick and the leaves too many to make out much. He ground his teeth. He hated being so exposed. Perhaps it was foolish to put so much trust by the Tlaxcalteca. They had never professed any great love for Mexica people.

Cuauhtemoc glanced at his guards. They were even wearier than him, having run through the night to make good time to Tlaxcala. Ollin hid his exhaustion the best, but even he could not keep his shoulders from drooping.

If the Tlaxcalteca were to attack now, they could kill all of us. Cuauhtemoc squeezed the hilt of his *macuahuitl* and stared at the Tlaxcalteca guides. If they had sinister intentions, they hid them well.

He cracked his wrists and gazed up at the trees. Was something moving amongst the branches? He narrowed his eyes. Impossible to tell. It could be the wind for all he knew.

Why the Tlaxcalteca were so proud of their forests, he did not know. Forest provided for game and timber, but they did not provide corn or beans or cocoa the same way a *chinampa* could. Life next to the lake offered more than Tlaxcala ever could, and he wished he had brought more trade goods with him. If the Tlaxcalteca knew what his people could offer them, there would always be peace between their nations.

The loud blaring of a conch made him turn. A litter-bearing party had entered the clearing from the other side.

Cuauhtemoc shaded his eyes and scanned the group for familiar faces.

It did not take him long to pick out Xicotencatl. Not so long ago, the man had been his mortal enemy, but they had reached an understanding of sorts during the Battle at Otampan. Cuauhtemoc did not look upon him as a friend, but he trusted that Xicotencatl would try to make the parley a success.

Cuauhtemoc dropped to a knee as Xicotencatl approached. Ollin stared at him in shock but Cuauhtemoc shot him an expectant glance, and he did likewise. In a matter of moments, all of Cuauhtemoc's guards were kneeling in the dirt. Cuauhtemoc rubbed two fingers in the damp earth and pressed them to his lips.

The Tlaxcalteca attendants lowered the litter to the ground a few paces from Cuauhtemoc and brushed back the curtain. Sitting inside was a man with more wrinkles than an avocado. Judging by the rheumy gloss that covered both his eyes, he was blind as well as old. Cuauhtemoc prayed age would be kinder to him.

"Greetings, distinguished emissaries," Xicotencatl said, bending his knee only a fraction. "Welcome to Tlaxcala." Xicotencatl gestured to the wide expanse of ancient pine trees and tangled undergrowth. "Beautiful, is it not?"

Cuauhtemoc rose to his feet. "Indeed it is. The forests of Tlaxcala have no equal, and I am stunned by their beauty. Would not the capital of Tlaxcala have been a better place to meet, though?"

"We are hosting the *teteo* in our capital. Entertaining a Mexica delegation in full view of our… guests would have been impolitic." A dark look flitted over Xicotencatl's face. He cleared his throat and added, "Please allow me to introduce my father. We bear the same name so you may refer to him as Elder. He has a much greater talent for diplomacy than me, and we rely on his wisdom today and always."

Cuauhtemoc nodded and turned toward Elder. "I am honored to meet you."

Elder absorbed his words in silence. Was Elder hard of hearing? Cuauhtemoc glanced at Xicotencatl for explanation. He colored and looked away.

"How fare your *teteo* guests?" Cuauhtemoc asked, his voice louder this time.

Again, Elder said nothing. Off in the distance, a great-tailed grackle shrieked, and Elder craned his head in that direction. Cuauhtemoc thinned his lips. Elder had less tact than a child.

"One could not ask for better guests," Xicotencatl said. "They ask for little in the way of food and have few needs when it comes to accommodations."

Cuauhtemoc scratched his chin. Unless something had changed since the Battle at Otampan, Xicotencatl had little reason to speak fondly of the *teteo*. Perhaps... Cuauhtemoc smiled.

With just a few words, Xicotencatl had confirmed the reports regarding the sorry state of the *teteo*. If they were not asking much in the way of food, it was because they were still convalescing. And if they had few needs when it came to accommodations, it was because they were few in number.

Cuauhtemoc donned a serious expression once more. "That is most interesting to hear. I do hope your guests appreciate the generosity and the kindness your people have extended them. Tlaxcala is a bountiful land and has much to offer. I wish I could say the same of our lands, but we are a poor people and must make do with simple items. We hope you will find joy in the meager presents we offer, however."

Cuauhtemoc gestured to his attendants and they brought forward a bevy of priceless goods. Jade as green as jungle canopy, Quetzal feathers so luxuriant they could buy a house, and jaguar skins of the darkest hue were laid out for the Tlaxcalteca delegation.

An attendant whispered in Elder's ear as the presents were laid out. Cuauhtemoc brushed dirt off his knee and waited for him to finish.

"Yes, your country must be poor indeed if you cannot offer more than this," Elder said. "We will accept the presents, though they are worthless."

Cuauhtemoc bristled and forced down his anger. "You do us a great honor. We would be even more honored to enter into an alliance with your people."

"What can the Mexica offer in terms of an alliance?"

Cuauhtemoc straightened. "We will lift all sanctions and grant Tlaxcala exemption from tribute payments. We will also ask our vassals to make tribute to Tlaxcala."

Elder frowned. "Your envoys made the same offer. Surely you can offer more."

"Do you find the terms disagreeable?"

"Yes," Elder replied, without a moment of hesitation.

Cuauhtemoc narrowed his eyes. "Why?"

"Tlaxcala has never given tribute to the Mexica. Granting us exemption from a tax we do not pay is no great favor."

Cuauhtemoc ran his tongue along his teeth. Elder was deluding himself if he thought Tlaxcala did not pay tribute to Tenochtitlan. Many Tlaxcalteca men had died fending off Mexica offensives, offensives launched solely because Tlaxcala refused to recognize Tenochtitlan's authority. Elder had to count the lives of his countrymen cheaply if that price mattered not to him.

"We are prepared to do other favors," Cuauhtemoc said, forcing lightness into his voice.

"Like lifting the sanctions?" Elder asked. "The sanctions should have never been imposed in the first place."

"And the Tlaxcalteca should have never allied with the *teteo*," Cuauhtemoc replied. "Many *pilli* were killed during the Toxcatl Massacre. Men, women, children, cut down in the flutter of an eyelid. Do the Tlaxcalteca take great pride in what they did that day?"

"Your people have done far worse to our people," Elder said. "You do have some cause for anger, though. The Mexica have suffered many setbacks of late. Tell me, how many of your warriors died at the Battle at Otampan?"

"I do not see why you pretend ignorance, Elder. Surely a warrior as brave as yourself took part in the battle and saw the carnage firsthand." Cuauhtemoc took a moment to calm himself. Elder was trying to get his ire up, and he would be a fool to play his game. "For the sake of peace, we can forgive these deaths. After all, the victory belongs to the *teteo* since they did most of the killing that day."

A Tlaxcalteca attendant scowled at him, but Elder betrayed no expression whatsoever. "Our quarrel is with the *teteo*," Cuauhtemoc added. "They have committed great wrongs against us, and we wish to see them gone from the One World."

Elder slowly moved his jaw back and forth as if he were grinding down a seed. "What do we gain by destroying Cortés' army? More *teteo* will come after him. Will you help us fight *teteo* who come four years from now, twenty years from now?"

"Of course," Cuauhtemoc said. "The *teteo* cannot be allowed so much as a toehold in the One World."

"Our lands are much closer to the shore than yours," Elder said. "It is far easier for the *teteo* to reach Tlaxcala than Tenochtitlan, and we take a great risk by making them our enemies. How can we trust that you will fight alongside us, that you will not invade Tlaxcala when the *teteo* no longer pose a threat?"

Cuauhtemoc puffed out his chest. "My presence is proof. I am kin to Great Speaker Cuitlahuac, and I would not be here if my countrymen did not desire peace."

Elder shook his head and offered a forlorn smile. "We need better proof than that. After all, peace is a very new desire on your part." One of the Tlaxcalteca delegates laughed, but a stern glance from Elder silenced him. "Give us the children of one hundred *pilli*, and we will trust the Mexica wish to have peace with us."

Cuauhtemoc clenched his teeth. The *pilli* were the most privileged people in all of Tenochtitlan; they would never willingly send their children to some far away land to be looked after by a despised people. Perhaps Great Speaker could force their cooperation, but Cuauhtemoc doubted he would do as much. Even if he did, what would stop the Tlaxcalteca from asking for more children the year after and the year after that? A Great Speaker who agreed to send away the children of *pilli* would not be Great Speaker long.

"There must be some other favor—"

"It is not a favor," Elder clarified. "It is a demand, and one we insist upon."

Then you are a fool. "I will have to discuss your proposal with the Great Speaker."

Elder's face darkened. "You are not empowered to make decisions on his behalf?"

"Great decisions must be made by Great Speakers," Cuauhtemoc replied.

Elder scoffed. "We have nothing more to discuss, then. Fly back to Tenochtitlan. Tell your master our demands."

Cuauhtemoc pursed his lips. Elder needed a good thrashing, but it would be folly to give in to anger. Even if he managed to kill Elder, he would not be able to escape Tlaxcala alive. Neither would his men be able to escape. No, they would all be captured and subjected to brutal torture and any chance of an alliance would be dashed for good.

"Farewell, Elder," Cuauhtemoc said. "It was an honor to speak with you today. Truly, you are a great statesman, and we have much to learn from the Tlaxcalteca when it comes to diplomacy."

Cuauhtemoc gave Elder his back and issued orders to his men. If they were to make good time to Tenochtitlan, they would have to leave soon. He knew Great Speaker Cuitlahuac would reject Elder's demand, but there was no reason to stay in Tlaxcala any longer. Elder had no interest in a pact, and nothing could be gained through further conversation.

"Farewell, Cuauhtemoc."

The sound of Xicotencatl's voice gave Cuauhtemoc pause. Xicotencatl was the reason that Cuauhtemoc thought Tlaxcala would be interested in a pact. Had Xicotencatl played him for a fool? *Perhaps he was never interested in a pact and just wanted to humiliate us.*

Cuauhtemoc glanced back at Xicotencatl. His downcast expression was impossible to mistake. Xicotencatl also wanted peace… but Xicotencatl was just a warrior, not an esteemed statesman like Elder.

Xicotencatl offered Cuauhtemoc a small smile and threw a drinking gourd at him. Cuauhtemoc caught it in mid-air and hugged it close.

"You will need water for your journey," Xicotencatl said. "Hurry back to your master. Tlaxcala will be a poorer place without your presence."

Cuauhtemoc looked down at the drinking gourd. Half a braid of hair had been tied around its neck. He stroked the braid with a reverential thumb. He had given it to Xicotencatl during the Battle at Otampan as a sign of good faith. At the time, Cuauhtemoc had been convinced Tlaxcala and Tenochtitlan could put aside their differences to form a pact. Now he had grave doubts he would ever set foot in Tlaxcala again.

He thanked the Tlaxcalteca delegation again and turned to his men. They had a long journey back to Tenochtitlan.

Chapter 3

Malintze clicked open the canteen to check the water level. Half-empty. She would have to refill it soon. These days, the rains came regularly and she trusted that water would not be hard to come by outside of camp. Dry shelter, however, would be a challenge.

Seated on her pallet, she took careful note of the tent's interior. The cramped space did not provide much in the way of comfort, and the flimsy canvas did little to protect against heat or cold. All the same, she liked the tent. It belonged to her and no one else. There had been a time in her life when she possessed nothing—neither her body nor her smarts—but the tent was a reminder things had changed, if only slightly.

But if Cortés did not wake, the tent would no longer mark her as a woman of importance. It would mark her as a target. Pedro had not tried to visit since Cortés had fallen ill with fever, but she knew it was fear that kept him at bay, not respect. Once Pedro knew he would not have to worry about retribution from Cortés, camp would no longer be safe for Malintze.

She brushed her hair back. If she stole a horse, it might be possible to take the tent with her. It would be easy, really. She could stuff the canvas and the stakes into some kind of bag ... Malintze shook her head. There was no point in lying, not to herself at least. Taking down her tent would attract too much attention, and she needed to slip away quietly if she was going to escape.

Stealing a horse would be both risky and complicated. The *teteo* valued the horses more than gold, and she had no experience riding on her own. *A fall could turn me into a cripple.*

She rubbed her hands together. Just the thought of clambering onto a horse made her heart quicken. Every time she had ridden one in the past, she had others for company, experienced riders who could offer assistance. To ride through unfamiliar territory, without a single person for company, would be nerve-racking at best and dangerous at worst. In the past, she never would have contemplated doing something so dramatic.

But if Cortés did not wake and Pedro continued as captain-general, staying in the *teteo* camp would be folly. When Cortés first came down with fever, she had been confident he would recover. But he had spent almost a week flat on his back, and it seemed unlikely he would soon regain his strength. Yes, it was still possible. But she saw no reason to bet her future on such an uncertain outcome, not when she had already risked so much by staying in camp. The time had come to make a different gambit. If she was going to escape, she was going to have to do it before Pedro consolidated command. Otherwise, he would force her loyalty.

Malintze reached under her pillow and grabbed her knife. It was carved from obsidian and thrice as heavy as a steel blade, but she liked that. Heft made a weapon feel more substantial, more reliable. She ran her finger along the flat of the blade. The knife was sharp, perhaps too sharp. She needed to wrap the blade in something, or it would cut through her netbag.

"Malintze, may I come inside your tent?"

Malintze stiffened. Why would Doña Luisa seek her out? Her stomach dropped. Pedro must have sent her. She was married to him after all.

"Is anyone with you?" Malintze asked in Nahuatl.

"No, I'm alone."

Malintze hid the knife under her pillow. Something about Doña Luisa's tone seemed wrong, but a flimsy tent flap couldn't keep a determined intruder out. Malintze placed her hand next to the pillow and took a deep breath. "Come in."

Doña Luisa brushed aside the tent flap and seated herself on a stool next to Malintze's bed. The daughter of Xicotencatl and a proud Tlaxcalteca woman, Doña Luisa always projected an air of self-assurance and noble grace. Not today, however. Today she seemed dejected and defeated.

"What vexes you?" Malintze asked.

Doña Luisa sighed and looked up at her. Her face was warm and amiable as ever, but a profound sadness lurked behind her eyes. "It has been awhile since we had Spanish lessons. How come you do not visit me anymore?"

Because of your husband. Malintze pressed a hand to her heart. "Please forgive me. So much has happened since we left Tenochtitlan, but that is no excuse. Friends must look after each other."

Doña Luisa smiled and stared deep into her eyes. "Do you think Pedro would make a good captain-general?"

Malintze started and looked away. She pushed her hand a little closer to the pillow. She did not want to lie to Doña Luisa, but she did not know if she could be honest with her, either. "A good captain-general should not be quick to violence."

Doña Luisa nodded. "Pedro has such a temper. I think he's getting better, though. I try my best to calm him." She brushed dirt off her tunic. Cotton was a cherished commodity in Tlaxcala, even when frayed and dirty, and Doña Luisa loved the dress dearly. So few of her other items had survived the Sad Night. "Pedro's not a bad husband, he's not like he used to be."

Malintze stared at her skeptically. "I mean it," Doña Luisa added. "Some Mexica warriors tried to grab me during the Sad Night. He killed three men to save me. I never expected him to do something like that for me. For anyone really."

"I'm glad he helped you," Malintze said. "We lost so many during the Sad Night, and it would have grieved me to lose you also."

Doña Luisa nodded. After a long pause, she said, "He won't put me aside for a Spanish lady, I know that."

Malintze pursed her lips. She did not have nearly as much faith in Pedro as her friend. Doña Luisa was not Pedro's first wife, nor would she be his last. Certain men always wanted more. They needed to have something to conquer, something to call their own. The most Doña Luisa could hope for would be a special place in Pedro's heart. If he had one.

"He likes having me around," Doña Luisa continued. "Tlaxcalteca give him more respect when they know his connection to me. I take care of him when he's hurt, I'm important to him. And…" Doña Luisa cleared her throat and sucked in a deep breath. "Pedro talks about home, but he never talks about going back. He doesn't miss it, not like he used to. I think he means to stay in the One World. He wants to make something of himself here."

Malintze frowned. Cortés had great ambitions when it came to the One World, but victory did not matter half as much to him as recognition. He needed to have others hail his genius, the people he had grown up with, the people who had undercut him at every turn. He would sail all the way back to Spain to bask in their praise and hector them for their lack of faith, she was sure of it. She assumed Pedro was no different in that regard, but she did not care much either way. They belonged to the same garment, even if they were cut from different cloth.

"What makes you say this?" Malintze asked.

Doña Luisa opened her mouth to answer and stopped herself. She let out a heavy sigh and asked, "Do you think Pedro will be punished now that Cortés is awake?"

Malintze's eyes widened. Her breath caught in her throat. "Cortés is awake?"

Doña Luisa stroked the canteen gently, lost in her own world. "He woke up almost an hour ago."

Malintze's chest tightened. To think she had almost run away. "Did he seem weak?"

"He cannot walk yet, but the healers say he will get better," Doña Luisa said, her voice colored with worry. Her hand shook a little, *spilli*ng water out of the canteen.

Malintze knelt in front of her friend and closed the canteen's cap. "Doña Luisa, you need not fret so much. Whatever happens to Pedro, you will be provided for. Besides, there's no reason to think any harm will befall Pedro."

Doña Luisa blinked. "You don't think Cortés will punish Pedro?"

"No, why would he?"

Doña Luisa shifted in her seat. "He might blame him for the Sad Night. So many of the *teteo* keep saying the Mexica would not have attacked if it weren't for the Toxcatl Festival—"

Malintze waved her hand dismissively. "Pedro should not have attacked the Mexica during the Toxcatl Festival, but he did not betray Cortés by doing so. Cortés is disappointed in him, but he will not punish him."

"Are you sure?"

Malintze placed her hand on Doña Luisa's shoulder. "Trust me, nothing matters to Cortés as much as loyalty. Pedro has always been loyal to him. Cortés will remember that."

Doña Luisa let out a deep breath and thanked Malintze. She tried to hand Malintze her canteen, but

Malintze insisted she keep it. She had no need for it and could procure a new one easily enough.

Doña Luisa gave her a quick hug and stepped out, leaving Malintze alone with her thoughts. Pedro would have chased after Malintze if she had run away, but he would not have put much effort into a search. After a day or two, he would have given up.

Cortés, however, would never abide such a betrayal. He would raid every *altepetl* in Mexico to find her, would chase her to the ends of the One World and beyond. She was too central to his ambitions for him to let her go; others could translate but he would never need them the same way he needed her. Malintze sighed. It would be folly to try and escape now that Cortés was on the mend. She pulled out her knife and stared at her dark reflection.

Her visage was not as pleasing as it once was. A thin scar marred her forehead, courtesy of a Mexica arrow. Her lips, so plump and so full in the past, were now cracked and peeling. The campaign had given her much, but it had taken away a great deal also. Her menses no longer came at predictable intervals and severe headaches afflicted her late at night. Terrible memories haunted her sleep and complete strangers prayed for her death. She tucked the knife away again. Come what may, her place was in the *teteo* camp. With Cortés.

~ ~ ~

Cortés pushed himself up to a sitting position. His stomach was sore and his arms were weak; he did not trust himself to stand. He splayed his legs across the bed and leaned against the stone wall. The chilly surface made him shiver, and he looked for something he could put between his back and the wall.

He spotted a stack of blankets on the other side of the room. It might as well have been a league away. He hissed in frustration. Olea, his guard, turned toward him, an unspoken question on his face.

Cortés averted his gaze. Olea was a hard man, born and raised in the north of Spain. Winters there were long and brutal and claimed the lives of many. To ask Olea for a blanket would be an admission of weakness he could not bear to make right now. The fever had already robbed him of his strength. He would not let it rob him of his pride also.

His gaze settled on Doña Marina's stool. It was a small and uncomfortable thing, but she sat on it every time she tended to him. A warm feeling blossomed in his chest. Doña Marina, his loyal caretaker. The fever had robbed him of his strength, but not his senses. At least, not completely.

He remembered Doña Marina tending to him, shooing away physicians who wanted to bleed him with their sharp knives, singing under her breath as she laid cold compresses on his feverish skin. He assumed she never cared for verse, so many of his honeyed compliments did not seem to register with her, but he had been wrong. He did not deserve her love, but he was grateful for it anyway.

A niggling of doubt formed in the pit of his stomach. He worried sometimes that Doña Marina did not love him, that she simply tolerated him. A ridiculous thought, of course, but a persistent one. So rarely did she spare him a smile, so rarely did she gaze at him with longing eyes. He shook his head. Outward appearances of affection mattered not. Only love could compel a person to sit on an uncomfortable stool for days on end, nothing else.

The sound of heavy footsteps reached Cortés' ears. He smiled. That could only be Sandóval. He marched more than he walked, charging through hallways and fields much the same way he went through life: with great determination and no thought for the opinion of others.

Sandóval gave a perfunctory bow as he entered the sick room. "You summoned me?"

Cortés grunted. Of course, Sandóval would not bother with pleasantries. He always had his mind on important strategies and could not be bothered with greetings or warm wishes. Pedro was a much better conversationalist, but Cortés was not ready to send for him yet. Not only had he poisoned relations with the Mexica with his stupidity at the Toxcatl Festival, he had the audacity to declare himself acting captain-general in Cortés' stead.

He had granted Pedro too many favors and needed to rein him in. Not yet, though. First, he needed to speak with Sandóval and learn what had happened while he had been indisposed with fever.

"Yes, I summoned you," Cortés said, surprised by how weak his voice sounded. Cortés gestured to the stool Doña Marina used whenever she tended to him. "Please take a seat."

Sandóval trudged forward and plopped himself down on the stool with little grace or dignity.

"How fares the army?" Cortés asked.

"Not well," Sandóval said. "Almost three quarters of the men we marched into Tenochtitlan with are dead or wounded."

Cortés winced. Sandóval could be as blunt as an anvil. "It is my hope that our victory at Otampan has improved morale."

"Hope cannot raise men from the dead."

Cortés reached for his water skin. He took a small swig and swished the water between his teeth. His mouth felt dry as cotton, but he did not dare drink more. He had already ejected the contents of his stomach twice today and had no interest in doing so again.

"Have reinforcements arrived?" Cortés asked.

Sandóval shook his head. Cortés cursed inwardly. Reinforcements should have arrived by now. He had sent for supplies from Cuba only a short time after the battle at Otampan and called upon Spain for aid before he even marched for Tenochtitlan. He sucked in a deep breath. Supplies would arrive soon, he had to trust in God. He smiled wanly and focused his attention on Sandóval once more. "Have there been any mutinies?"

"None amongst the Christians."

Cortés thinned his lips. "How fare relations with our Tlaxcalteca hosts?"

"They have not turned on us yet."

Cortés' face curdled. "Yet?"

"The Tlaxcalteca no longer wish to honor the pact we made with them last year," Sandóval said. "They insist upon a new agreement with new conditions."

Cortés' stomach clenched. If the Tlaxcalteca were to withdraw their support, the campaign was doomed. They had fought the Tlaxcalteca before, and won, but victory had come at a dear price, one too high for an army already devastated by a calamitous retreat. "What are their conditions?"

"Neighboring nations do not recognize the authority of Tlaxcala. They wish to make war on those neighbors and desire our assistance."

Cortés relaxed. "That doesn't sound so disagreeable. It would be folly not to march on Tenochtitlan again. We will never recover the gold if we do not take the city—"

"They do not wish to take Tenochtitlan at this time," Sandóval said.

Cortés blinked. That couldn't be right. He must have heard wrong. He stared at Sandóval. His hard-set expression did not slip, and Cortés had to look away. Before the fever, he would have never debased himself so, but he had precious little energy these days and could not waste it on somebody as obstinate as Sandóval.

"You must be mistaken," Cortés whispered. "Tenochtitlan is the richest *altepetl* in all the One World. It does not make sense to make war on other settlements."

Sandóval shook his head, his mien as placid and impassive as ever. "They mean to make war on neighbors closer to home, beginning with Tepeaca. They want to launch an offensive twenty days from now."

Cortés rubbed his ear lobe. Twenty days would allow his men ample time to recover, but he did not see much benefit in attacking Tepeaca. It offered little in the way of riches or honor. "They are at peace with Tepeaca, and the *altepetl* is very poor. Why would they wish to make war against them?"

"Tepeaca is not poor," Sandóval said in a level voice.

His utter certainty gave Cortés pause. *Has fever rattled my memory?* Cortés rubbed his head against the wall, and the rough stone chafed against his thinning hair. When he was in the worst throes of fever, he could hardly feel anything. Not since he lived in Medellin had he ever experienced such a debilitating brush with sickness.

Cortés shivered. He did not like thinking about that chapter of his life. The New World had its dangers, but at least it had gold. Medellin had nothing. Here he could make something of life, there never. "Is there much gold in Tepeaca?"

"No. But the Tlaxcalteca are interested in a different kind of treasure."

Cortés grunted. No other treasure meant half as much as gold. One day the Indians would recognize as much, once they stopped fawning over green jade and Quetzal feathers. He had landed in the New World sixteen months prior, but the local customs still mystified him. What kind of people would use fruit seeds as currency? Even the Moors would not do something so perverse, so backward.

A great weariness came over him. It did not matter what he thought of customs here. Without the aid of locals, his company would never win any meaningful victories in the New World. Cortés exhaled loudly. "What great treasure can Tepeaca provide us?"

Sandóval stared at him as if the answer were the simplest thing in the world. "Slaves."

Chapter 4

Pozon jabbed his finger into the maguey fibers to test the strength of his throwing sling. His fingers were small, he had only nine years to his name, but he could not fit his finger between any of the knots. He smiled and looked at his sister, Yaotl. She was only two years older than him, but she always beat him in throwing contests. Not today, though. Today, he would hit all the targets, and Yaotl would feel silly for even trying to win.

Pozon stretched the throwing sling taut. He had made five total and was proud of each one. Nahtli said none of the boys in the village could make one as well as him, and Nahtli was never wrong. Tahtli liked his slings so much he took them with him every time he went to market at Tepeaca. Pozon lowered his sling and stared up at the thirteen skies.

Yesterday's gray clouds were gone, and he hoped they stayed away. If Tlaloc sent the dark clouds, big drops of water would come down, and the field would become muddy and runny. Nahtli would get upset if they stayed out in the rain, and they would be forced to hurry back to the house.

"Pozon, put your head down!" Yaotl shouted. "You look like a big turkey with your head tilted back."

Pozon stuck his tongue out at Yaotl. She could be so mean. Why did she have to make him feel so silly? Last month, a boy gave Pozon a black eye during a wrestling match. Once Yaotl found out, she gave the boy two black eyes. None of the boys wrestled with Pozon now.

Yaotl was always making trouble for him that way, and he wished she could be more like other girls. Then his friends wouldn't make fun of him for having a Yaotl who kicked and punched like a boy. She even threw a sling like a boy!

Pozon checked his sling once more. It didn't matter how well she threw. He had the better sling. He would win today's throwing contest, and she would learn not to embarrass him.

"You couldn't hit a dead turkey from five paces," Pozon shouted.

Yaotl narrowed her eyes. "You're just jealous you can't throw as good as me."

"Liar," Pozon said. "I bet you can't hit that tree."

Pozon pointed to a sapling thirty paces away.

"Which tree?" Yaotl asked.

Pozon pointed again. Yaotl shot him another confused glance. He flared his nostrils and ran toward the tree. Was Yaotl losing her vision? There were only a few trees in the field, and she should have known which tree he was talking about. He patted the trunk of the sapling, and then ran back.

He had run too fast. His lungs hurt now. He bent over to take in breath. When he looked up, Yaotl flashed him a victorious smile. "I knew which tree you meant. I just wanted to tire you out. You don't throw as well when you are tired."

Pozon checked his anger and squared his shoulders. Yaotl was constantly playing tricks on him. "You go first."

Yaotl shrugged. She tucked a rock into the cradle of her throwing sling, tilted her wrist, and spun the rock above her head. She released it with a quick snap of her wrist, and the sling went flying toward the defenseless sapling. The trunk was so skinny Pozon could almost wrap his fingers around it, and he wished he had picked a bigger target. Yaotl did not seem to mind. Her sling wrapped around the trunk like a piece of twine and slammed into the bark with so much force that chips of bark flew in every direction. A startled crow took to the air, cawing and shrieking in alarm.

"See if you can do better than that," Yaotl said, her voice full of challenge.

"Of course, I can! You're just a withered ear of corn—I am going to hit that tree so good you'll be embarrassed forever."

Pozon wiped his brow with the back of his hand. It was still early morning so the heat was fairly mild. Nonetheless, a few beads of sweat had already formed on his forehead. He reached for his sling and focused on the tree. If he hit the same spot as Yaotl, she would be really impressed.

He spun his wrist as far as he could and prayed to the gods for strength. Pozon released the sling, confident that it would wrap itself around the trunk of the tree just like Yaotl's sling. Instead, the sling grazed the side of the tree and landed in the wild grass.

Yaotl huffed triumphantly. "I knew you would miss."

"I meant to do that," Pozon grumbled. "Wrapping the sling around the tree is easy. Just grazing it is harder."

Yaotl shaded her eyes and pointed to a tree forty paces away. "Hit that one if you are so good."

Pozon snorted and reached for a new sling. He made a careful evaluation of each knot. His throwing technique had been perfect, so what had gone wrong with the last one? A breeze must have thrown off his aim. He'd be more mindful of that with his next throw.

He stared at the tree Yaotl had pointed to. This one was much taller and thicker than the sapling so it would be impossible to wrap his sling around the trunk. As long as he could hit the tree, he would be pleased with himself.

He picked up some dirt and crumbled it between his fingers. Tahtli always did that before he threw something far, not that Pozon understood why. He picked up a sling and brought it to a slow whir. He peered at the leaves of the tree, tried to see if they were moving. They looked still to him.

He released the sling and threw it toward the tree with all his energy. It landed five paces short of the tree, disappearing into the wild grass.

He risked a glance at Yaotl. She flashed a mischievous grin, and he averted his gaze.

"The breeze threw off my aim."

Yaotl laughed. "It won't throw off my aim."

She picked up another sling and twirled it with dizzying speed. Pozon wanted to push her to throw off her aim, but she would push him back. He didn't have the energy to fight her off today. Besides, Yaotl always won their wrestling matches.

He straightened. Maybe she threw better than him because she had better posture. Yaotl turned toward him, and he quickly looked away. Yaotl could not know he was trying to learn from her. If she found out, she would tease him without mercy.

"I am going to graze the tree, just like you did."

She tossed her long hair back and released her sling. It flew fast as a sparrow but missed the trunk by a half pace.

"Ha!" Pozon shouted. "I knew you wouldn't be able to do it. You throw like a Tlaxcalteca."

Yaotl scowled at him. "Don't say that."

Pozon smiled. Yaotl never seemed bothered by his teasing, but he had finally found something that upset her. Pozon jumped in front of Yaotl and circled around her as he did a silly dance. "You throw like a Tlaxcalteca—"

The air rushed from his lungs as Yaotl tackled him with all the force of an enraged bear. She quickly pinned him to the ground and dug her knee into his back so that he couldn't move.

"Take it back," she said. "Take it back, or I'll tickle you until you scream."

Pozon tried to wriggle out from underneath her. The damp dirt would stain his loincloth, and Nahtli would be sure to give him harsh words. To simply give in to Yaotl's demand was unthinkable, though. "You throw like a Tlaxcalteca girl!"

A sudden spasm seized Pozon, and he wriggled like an eel as Yaotl dug her fingers into his ribs. He howled like a coyote, but still Yaotl did not relent. She was as deft as a cotton weaver with her fingers, and there was only one way to make this terrible torture stop.

"I take it back," Pozon shouted. "I take it back."

Yaotl took her knee off his back and sat down next to him. Pozon pushed himself up and took a deep breath. Yaotl was too good at finding his tickle spots. Her fingers knew exactly where to go, and he had no defense against such a determined attack.

He brushed dirt off his shoulder and scowled at her. "You didn't have to do that. I would have stopped if you had asked me to." Yaotl scoffed but didn't say anything. She seemed deep in thought, and her quietness unnerved him. "Yaotl, what's wrong?"

"Have you heard about what's happening in Tlaxcala?"

Pozon shook his head.

"Tahtli and Nahtli said the *teteo* received reinforcements from the coast a few days ago," Yaotl said in a low voice. Pozon shivered. He did not know what reinforcements meant, but Yaotl seemed very worried about it so reinforcements had to be something bad. "Nahtli worries the *teteo* are going to join the Tlaxcalteca for another march."

Pozon scratched his head. Why would Nahtli worry about that? The Tlaxcalteca were always fighting somebody. In the past year, they had fought the *teteo*, the

Choluteca, and the Mexica. These days, they fought on the same side as the *teteo* but nobody expected their pact to last. Neither people seemed inclined toward peace, and neither had gained much through friendship. At least, that's what Tahtli said.

"Why is she worried about that?" Pozon asked. "We are not their enemies. That is something for Tenochtitlan to worry about."

"Nahtli is worried that war will reach Tepeaca," Yaotl said. Pozon furrowed his brow. If war were to reach Tepeaca, it would be sure to reach the village. Yaotl had to be mistaken, though. Tepeaca had no quarrel with any of the neighboring people.

The warriors complained bitterly every time Tenochtitlan sent tribute collectors, but none dared to interfere with payment. Villages that refused to pay tribute risked open conflict with Tenochtitlan, and nobody wanted that. Except for the Tlaxcalteca.

Nahtli said the Tlaxcalteca were a strange people who could subsist on pride when everyone else had to make do with corn. He always laughed when she said that joke. Not because he understood it; few of Nahtli's jokes made sense to him. Nonetheless, he always laughed at them. Grown-ups liked that type of thing.

"Tahtli is also worried," Yaotl added. "He says we should go south and stay with Uncle."

Pozon frowned. That did not sound like a good idea at all. Uncle never sired any children and was very quick-tempered. Yaotl knew that better than anyone. Her nose was still crooked from the time Uncle hit her for being too loud. Pozon hated Uncle for doing that, not that he would ever admit as much.

He stared into Yaotl's face. How had such a good day become so serious? He wanted to go back to playing and laughing, but it was impossible to do that now. He had spent almost all his life in the village and had no friends outside of it. "I don't want to go south."

"Neither do I," Yaotl said. Her voice sounded sadder than his. "We may leave at the end of the month, if they are still worried."

Pozon's eyes widened. The end of the month was only a few days away. Tears brimmed in his eyes.

Uncle was so far away from everything. Uncle probably wouldn't even let him make slings. Uncle would just make him do chores all day and criticize him for every little thing.

Yaotl squeezed his hand. "We have to trust Nahtli and Tahtli."

Pozon nodded glumly and sniffled. Yaotl brushed dirt off his face and stood. "I will go get the slings. You stay here."

Pozon pulled up a grass shoot and threaded it between his teeth. His stomach grumbled. He was hungry, and he regretted not eating more earlier in the day. He wanted to go back to the house, but he was not going to leave Yaotl in the field by herself. Besides, the walk back home was half a long-run. Who would want to walk that far by themselves?

He glanced at Yaotl. She had already picked up the two slings and was now making her way toward the big tree. He stood. He should run up and scare her. Otherwise, she would think he had forgiven her for tickling him and making him look silly again.

He adjusted his loincloth and was about to take off running when he noticed a distant glittering. Pozon shaded his eyes. Something bright and large was heading his way. Yaotl froze and glanced in the direction of the strange thing. She was even closer to it than him.

"What's that noise?" Yaotl asked.

Pozon strained his ears. Off in the distance, he could hear a soft tinkling and a heavy stomping. What kind of animal would make a sound like that?

He stepped forward. He still couldn't see much, but his sense of unease was growing. Something about the animal didn't seem right. The thing was getting closer and he could make out more details now. It wasn't so much one thing as many things—a large herd of giant, hornless stags were racing toward Yaotl and him! Perhaps most frightening of all were the strange people riding on top of the stags. They wore shiny clothing that glinted whenever it caught the light and shouted things that made no sense.

Pozon gulped. The *teteo* were supposed to ride animals just like that. He had heard the stories but never believed them. Not until now.

"Run, Pozon!" Yaotl shouted.

Pozon tried to do as Yaotl urged, but his legs would not obey. Yaotl was too close to the herd. They were only sixty paces away from her. Yaotl was the one who needed to run, not him. But instead of running, Yaotl readied a sling.

More than twelve hornless stags were bearing down on her, but she did not retreat even one pace. Instead, she pushed a rock into her throwing sling and started spinning it above her head. With a simple flick of her wrist, she sent the sling whirring toward the enemy. A loud smack let him know the sling had hit the shiny material that covered the stag's shoulder, but the stag charged forward undaunted.

Yaotl readied her next sling. Yaotl was smart. She wasn't going to aim for a shoulder again. Just by looking at her, Pozon could tell that she was going to aim for something smaller. Yaotl would stop the *teteo* beasts. He was sure of it. He could tell from the way that she puffed out her chest that she knew it, too.

Yaotl released the next sling and it went flying toward a raised hoof. Her aim was perfect, but a dark-haired *teotl* leaned over the side of the stag and slashed downward with a glittering stick, slicing the sling in two.

Pozon rubbed his eyes. What he was seeing was not possible. Yaotl glanced back at him, and the look of terror on her face was so stark, so unmistakable it made his breath catch. She reached for another sling as the dark-haired *teotl* neared and shouted something over her shoulder. A flash of silver cut Yaotl off mid-speech, and he watched dumbstruck as a *teotl* weapon sliced through Yaotl's wrist and severed hand from arm.

All of a sudden, his legs were moving of their own accord, and he was sprinting back to the house, back to the only place that might be safe. A stitch quickly formed in his side, but he couldn't think about it. All he could think about was the sickening expression on Yaotl's face when she turned to look back at him, the way the *teotl* weapon cut through flesh and bone like soft tallow.

He pushed himself to run faster, but his legs were heavy and his breath short. The rumbling behind him was growing louder and louder, but his steps were getting slower and slower, and the stitch in his side was growing larger and larger.

Something crashed into him, and he flew forward. His head smashed into a rock, and the pain made him go dizzy. He clenched his eyes closed and lay still. His sense of time and place faded, and he drifted in and out of consciousness.

By the time he came to his senses, Tonatiuh was directly overhead and his back felt itchy. He pushed himself up, held a hand to his throbbing temple. The sudden jolt of pain made him wince, but it sharpened his senses also.

The smell of offal wafted toward his nose, and his gorge rose up without warning. He turned his head to the side and emptied his stomach of all that it had ever contained. The sour taste of bile filled his mouth, and he wiped his mouth with the back of his hand.

He heard laughing nearby and felt somebody grab him. He was too weak to fight and let them drag him away. He caught a glimpse of sandals, heard a few snatches of Nahuatl. Couldn't make sense of it, not with his head pounding so hard.

Pozon looked up. A chill passed through him. *Teteo* were raiding his village! Not just *teteo*, though. Tlaxcalteca warriors were helping them. Guilt seized him. He should have run faster. It was too late to help anybody now.

His captors dragged him toward a small group of rope-bound villagers and dumped him to the ground. He looked for Nahtli and Tahtli in the group. He didn't see them anywhere, didn't see Yaotl either. His stomach twisted. He should have helped Yaotl. He should have helped her throw slings. He should have been brave. Instead, he let himself get captured.

A *teotl* stopped in front of him. He froze. The dark boots looked familiar. So, too, did the *teotl's* weapon. It was long and silver, just like the weapon that had been used against Yaotl. Pozon stared into the *teotl's* face.

All the *teteo* were supposed to be hairy and big, but this one was small and smooth-faced. The *teotl* had features more like a woman than a man, but that didn't seem right. Men waged battle, not women. Pozon had never heard of a female warrior, and he wondered if he might be dreaming. So many of the day's events did not seem real.

Somebody started tying his hands back behind his back. The rope dug painfully into his skin, and he grimaced. He had many bad dreams before, but he woke up whenever he became really afraid. Why wasn't that happening now?

Because I am not dreaming. He tried to dismiss the treacherous thought, but he was too exhausted for denial. His shoulder slumped, and he gave in to despair. The *teotl* knelt in front of him and lifted his chin.

She had skin white as an eggshell and eyes dark as obsidian. He had witnessed her cruelty firsthand, but her kind face gave no sign of malice or ill-intent. She was a woman of opposites, and he wished she would go away. Perhaps sensing his inner turmoil, she smiled at him and said in surprisingly good Nahuatl, "My name is Maria de Estrada, and you belong to me now."

Chapter 5

Juan Garrido leaned against a tree and rubbed his injured thigh. He received the injury during the Battle at Otampan, more than a month prior, and his leg still pained him whenever he put too much weight on it. Everybody told him he was lucky—the Indian slings could cripple and kill—but gratitude did not come easy when he could not walk half a league without assistance.

His injury had prevented him taking part in the Tepeaca campaign but that bothered him none. The campaign was a glorified slave raid, and he had no wish to partake in that type of enterprise.

Few shared his misgivings. As far as the others were concerned, the slave raids were just desert for a campaign that had yielded little in the way of material wealth. He could not fault their logic. All the gold that had been gained had been lost during the retreat from Tenochtitlan, or sent across the ocean at Cortés' behest.

All the same, Garrido did not care overmuch that he had been unable to take part in the slave raids. A man could gain much by owning a slave or two, but Garrido preferred gold to any other form of wealth. Captured people could run away and die, yet gold would do neither. Gold was more loyal than the best-trained hound and could confer prestige on the most miserable wretch. It could even be used to build monuments to God.

Garrido stared at his fellow Christians. Behind and in front of him, they milled about, happy and content. Tepeaca had put up only a feeble defense, and the company had gained hundreds of slaves in the course of a few days. Some of the soldiers grumbled the best-looking women had gone to the officers, but most seemed content with their lot.

Off to his right, a group of men laid out a ragged mat and sat down to play cards. Garrido was tempted to join, but he wanted to rest his leg a little longer. If he ever made it back to Kongo, he would bring a deck of cards with him. Of all the pastimes he had been introduced to by the Old Christians, that was the one he enjoyed the most. He knew cards often went hand-in-hand with vice, but his people loved Jesus. They would not succumb to sin as easily as the Iberians.

Garrido lowered himself to the ground and pressed his back against the tree. The bark dug deep into his skin, but he was too tired to find a more suitable backrest. Besides, the man on his left had been resting against the tree for nearly half an hour and seemed content with his lot. Whereas others might have spent that time grousing about the weather or their aches, the man busied himself by whittling away at a small block of wood with singular dedication.

The whittler went by the name Martin López, if Garrido remembered correctly. Appearance wise, López was not all that striking. He had the olive skin so typical of men from the south of Spain and had a pointy beard. If there was any aspect of his appearance that was notable, it had to be his hands. His nails practically gleamed, and his palms were as clean as a nun's frock. His personal hygiene, however, did not extend beyond his hands. His face was lined with dirt, and his stained tunic was frayed and torn.

"How much longer you gonna stare at my carving?" López asked.

Garrido started as if he had been stricken. "Beg pardon. I did not mean to offend."

López grunted and blew on his whittling knife. He wiped the blade with his sleeve and dug it into the wood once more. Garrido cocked his head to the side and tried to guess what López was carving. The more he stared, the more convinced he became that a tangible shape had yet to emerge.

"What are you carving?" Garrido asked.

López puckered his lips and glared at Garrido. "What gall you have! Are my skills so poor you must ask to know?"

Garrido flushed and looked away, wishing he had gone to play cards instead of making conversation with this strange man. López laughed as if he had read his thoughts and clapped him on the shoulder with the wood block.

"No need to beg pardon, Garrido. I've hardly yet begun, and there's no harm in asking what I've put my skills to." López held up the block of wood for him. "I mean to carve a ship. By the time I'm done, it'll be the most beautiful thing you've ever seen."

Garrido stared at the block of fine-grained wood. He did not see a ship in the making, nor anything of the sort. All he saw was a cut of timber that was neither exceptional nor beautiful.

"How do you know where to cut and whittle?" Garrido asked.

"Easy," López said. He pointed to his ear. "I listen."

Garrido laughed. "The wood speaks to you?"

"Of course it does. A good carver is a good listener." López held up the block of wood for a closer inspection.

Garrido frowned. He had assumed that López was making another jape, but he wasn't so sure now. "What does the wood say to you?"

"Oh, same thing as always."

Garrido waited for López to say more, but he stayed quiet as a mute.

"And what's that?" Garrido asked.

"Don't cut me." López scraped his knife along the block of wood and sawed off a small chunk.

Garrido shifted in his seat. "I thought you said a good carver is a good listener."

"I did," López said. "Never said I was only listening to the wood, though. A knife can speak just as much as a block of wood. Listen carefully, and you can hear steel whisper. Sometimes she tells you to cut, other times to hurt, and every now and then she tells you to kill."

Garrido pursed his lips. He liked to think his hand was guided by God, but López was suggesting something much different. Something almost blasphemous. "Why would a knife tell you to carve a ship? Why not something beautiful, like a cross or the Virgin Mary?"

"Those are things for holy men to carve," López said. "I'm just a soldier, and I carve what I know."

Garrido nodded apprehensively. "How'd you come to know ships so well?"

"Spent my early years in Seville." López set the block of wood down on his lap and stared into his face. "How about you? Just what part of the world do you hail from?"

"I call Kongo home."

López cleaned the knife on his sleeve. "That near Fez?"

Garrido smiled. It never ceased to amaze him how ignorant some of the Christians could be of his homeland considering how eager they were to Christianize it. "Kongo is much farther south. In Kongo, when you look up at the sky, the stars you see are very different. There is no summer or winter there. Only dry season and wet season."

López rubbed his thumb along his block of wood. "Mexico is the same, when it comes to seasons at least. How'd you get from Kongo to here?"

Garrido reflected on his journey from Kongo to Europe. It had taken weeks of sailing to reach final port, and he had nobody for company other than the Black Robes. It was a lonely and trying experience, made all the worse by the knowledge he would never see family or friends again. That his own Father had disowned him. "I sailed."

"I imagine it was a long journey. Do you think you could have walked here from Kongo?"

"Of course not," Garrido said.

"Then you should know how beautiful ships can be." López picked up the block of wood and resumed his whittling. "Ships are the most beautiful thing man has ever created. It was a ship that brought you here, and it was a ship that brought me here. Ships are how we receive supplies from Cuba and Spain, ships are how we let Christendom know of our victories. A nation that lacks for ships can never be great."

Garrido bristled. "Ships don't make a nation great. Only love of Jesus can do that."

López shook his head. "Word of God does not spread without ships. Tell me, did word of Jesus reach Kongo before the Portuguese ships?"

Garrido scratched his head as he tried to remember. Portuguese ships had arrived in Kongo before he was even born, so he could not say with much confidence. A profound sadness took hold of him. If he were still home, he could ask the elders, but their knowledge was forever lost to him.

"Think on the matter as long as you need to," López added. "Won't change the truth either way. Believe me, were it not for ships, word of God would never spread to barbarous lands."

Garrido thought on some of the stories he had heard about the West Indies. Prior to the coming of the Christians, people pranced about in their natural state, worshipped multiple gods… He shuddered. A blessing those days were over. "There may be some truth to what you say," Garrido said carefully. "Will ships help us conquer Tenochtitlan you think?"

"Of course they will," López said, his voice brimming with confidence. "Captain-general knows it too. He says when we get to Lake Tetzcoco, we will encamp near the shore. I will be given everything I need to build a fleet so we can take Tenochtitlan once and for all."

Garrido blinked. López did not seem daunted in the slightest by his task. If anything, he seemed to relish the challenge involved. "The Mexica will probably try to attack our camp. A single attack could undo months of work. Are you confident you can build a fleet in those circumstances?"

López shrugged. "I have no choice but to try. We cannot take Tenochtitlan without ships." López balanced the block of wood on his knee and ran a whetstone along the length of his knife. "I am touched you are so concerned with the fate of my fleet. Would you care to volunteer for guard duty once we begin construction?"

Garrido stared at López's knife. He hoped López was not the type to take offense easily. "I think we should build the ships in Tlaxcala," Garrido said. López narrowed his eyes, and Garrido quickly added, "While we are here, we can gather timber in safety and easily send for supplies from the coast. Once we reach Lake Tetzcoco, it will be harder to gather supplies and much easier for the Mexica to disrupt our building efforts."

López snorted. "And how are we supposed to transport the ships to Tenochtitlan if we do that? There is no river we can sail to reach Tenochtitlan. Are we supposed to carry a fleet over a tract of land as mountainous as Basque country? Hercules would not be equal to the task."

"Perhaps not, but an army might be equal to the task," Garrido replied.

López ran a hand through his unruly beard. "What are you suggesting?"

Garrido mulled his reply. He was no shipmaster, but he knew a fleet could not be constructed in the course of a day. Chances are it would take months, and the Mexica would do everything they could to sabotage building efforts. "We could build the ships here, where it's safe. Once the ships have been sounded, we could disassemble them and carry them over the mountains. Carry them all the way to Lake Tetzcoco if need be."

López tilted his head backward and gazed up at the heavens. "That would be most time-consuming.... but it could work." López turned toward him. "What's your name again?"

Garrido extended his hand. "Call me Juan Garrido."

López stared at his hand as if it were an unfamiliar cut of meat. After a trice, he clasped hands with him. Garrido could not help but notice how much their skin tones differed. He hoped that would not be an issue with López. Some Christians did take exception to his coloring, but only because they assumed he was ignorant of the Holy Trinity. Once they learned of his deep love for Jesus, they could be most friendly with him. Sometimes.

"Glad to make your acquaintance," López said. "Cortés is allowing me to pick the men who will help with construction efforts. Would you like to help me build something beautiful?"

~ ~ ~

Cuauhtemoc strode through the halls of Motecuhzoma's palace with a small group of guards. Ollin walked beside him, an honored warrior in his own right. Ollin had a bright future ahead of him, Cuauhtemoc was sure of it. Once the war was over, Ollin would be granted many honors and privileges.

Thus far, the war was not off to a good start. The barbarians had drawn first blood during the Toxcatl

Massacre, but the Mexica destroyed more than half their forces when they fled the city for Tlaxcala. The Battle at Otampan had prevented the Mexica from achieving total victory, and there had been no major battles since then. At least, none between the barbarians and the Mexica.

The barbarians had laid waste to Tepeaca and forced all the survivors into slavery. Perhaps most shocking of all, they burned their victims with ugly symbols to mark them as slaves for life. Nothing like it had ever happened in the history of the One World, and it was a tragedy as much as it was an opportunity. Men who lacked the courage to take up arms against the Mexica could no longer claim that the barbarians valued peace. Even the most softheaded people had to now see the *teteo* would bring nothing to the One World besides death and destruction.

Cuauhtemoc strode through a doorway and entered a high-ceilinged room illuminated with blazing braziers. He spotted Great Speaker Cuitlahuac—along with Milintica and some sons of Motecuhzoma—on the other side of the room and made his way toward them.

Motecuhzoma's sons clustered together, whispering to each other every now and then. Milintica stood apart from them and offered a small smile as Cuauhtemoc approached. He returned the smile without much affection. Men like Milintica existed in every government, men who stood tall in times of peace but bent whichever direction the wind blew, and Cuauhtemoc did not feel any great need to feign friendship.

He dropped to a knee in front of Great Speaker and Ollin did the same. Great Speaker raised them to their feet with a small motion of his hand and said in a level voice, "Dismiss your guards, Cuauhtemoc."

Cuauhtemoc furrowed his brow. The order was as unusual as it was curt. Despite his reservations, he did as commanded.

Ollin joined the guards as they departed but took only a few steps before Great Speaker said, "You will stay, Ollin."

Ollin shot Cuauhtemoc a confused look but did as instructed. Only a fool would disobey a Great Speaker's direct order.

The guards filed out of the room, and Cuauhtemoc waited for Great Speaker to say more. To his surprise, Great Speaker remained quiet. It was not typical of him to brood; he was generous with his thoughts and outspoken by nature. *So why is he so pensive of a sudden?* Cuauhtemoc looked to the others for explanation, but they were as confused as him.

"Great Speaker, why have we been summoned?" Milintica asked.

"Michoacan has rejected our offer of an alliance," Great Speaker said, his voice laced with dejection.

Cuauhtemoc's mouth went dry. Michoacan and Tenochtitlan had never been on friendly terms, but he assumed the news from Tepeaca would make them understand the need to ally against the *teteo*. The Tlaxcalteca had made it clear they would not be withdrawing their support for the *teteo*, and the Mexica needed allies like Michoacan to prevail against the combined forces of the barbarians.

"Why did Michoacan refuse our offer?" Ollin asked.

"They say they have no quarrel with the *teteo* and do not wish to antagonize them," Great Speaker said. "They will not march against us as we fight the *teteo*, but they will not march to our aid either."

Cuauhtemoc shook his head and cursed under his breath. If Michoacan would not ally with them, it was hard to imagine what powerful nation would. "If other nations will not lend us their aid, we cannot march against the barbarians. Sending our warriors over the mountains to make battle in some far-off place will lead to another

Otampan, and that must be avoided at all costs. We ought to prepare our defenses and make ready for a battle closer to home."

Milintica nodded. "I agree we must keep most of our warriors close. If we send them away from the capital, we leave ourselves vulnerable to attack. Fortunately, we should be able to kill the *teteo* with only a small force of Mexica warriors."

A ripple of confusion spread through the room.

"And how would we do that?" Ollin asked.

"By allying with the Tlaxcalteca," Milintica said simply.

Cuauhtemoc fought the urge to roll his eyes. "They rejected our offer of an alliance."

"Only because we rejected their conditions," Milintica corrected.

Cuauhtemoc stiffened. Milintica was right, much as he hated to admit it. The Tlaxcalteca demands had been outrageous, though. Great Speaker had promised to lift all sanctions on Tlaxcala and share tribute with them, but the Tlaxcalteca were greedy and insisted upon more. During the parley in Tlaxcala, they had demanded the Mexica surrender one hundred children as a guarantor of faith. Great Speaker had flown into a rage when he heard their demands and cut off all communications with them.

"The Tlaxcalteca are not interested in an alliance with us anymore," Ollin said. If he was trying to hide his exasperation, he was doing a poor job of it. Ollin had the careworn expression of a parent who was tired of having to explain simple matters, and Cuauhtemoc hoped he would not let his frustration get the best of him. "They made that very clear with their attack on Tepeaca."

"Then we must offer them more. Otherwise, we cannot hope to recapture their interest," Milintica replied.

"How much more can we offer than a hundred children?" Cuauhtemoc asked. "If we send them one hundred and twenty children, would that be enough?"

"Probably not," Milintica replied. "We may have to send them all the green jade we possess, along with all our Quetzal feathers. If that is not enough to gain their trust, then we send our children also. If we need to send them the children of a thousand *pilli* to gain their hand in friendship, then we ought to do it. Defeating the *teteo* must come before all else."

Cuauhtemoc's eyes went wide as a Choluteca platter. Never in all his life would he have expected Milintica to make such an outrageous proposal. Milintica had no children of his own, but few men in Tenochtitlan worshipped green jade like him.

"We must not forget the Tlaxcalteca have much to lose by betraying the *teteo*," Milintica added. "Many weeks have passed since we won our last victory against the *teteo*. Most of their people must have recovered by now, and new ones have arrived on the coast. They are much stronger than they were just a month ago, and the Tlaxcalteca will lose many warriors if they make battle against them. With our aid, they can prevail against the *teteo*, but we cannot expect them to take a great risk without offering a great guarantor of faith."

Ollin snorted. "I am confident you would feel different if you had children of your own."

"You are mistaken, Ollin. My answer would be the same. If need be, I will sire children solely to hand them off to the Tlaxcalteca. Our confederacy means more to me than anything. There is nothing I would not sacrifice to protect it. Can you say the same?"

Ollin scowled and looked away, his face contorted by shame and anger. Cuauhtemoc assumed Motecuhzoma's sons would say something, but they stayed silent, perhaps thinking about who they would be willing to send away.

Their discomfort was manifest, and they turned to Great Speaker for guidance.

Great Speaker looked as if he had swallowed a bitter draught and stared at the stone floor. After a moment, he unclenched his fist and turned toward his subjects.

"Our children are the future of our nation, and I would never entrust them to the Tlaxcalteca," Great Speaker said, his voice dripping with disdain. "Let us not forget what they did to the children of Tepeaca, an *altepetl* they had no quarrel with only a short time ago. They have long hated us and would be most tempted to mistreat any hostages we give them. Our children will stay here with us in Tenochtitlan, where they belong. The gods have always guided us to victory, and we will smite the barbarians the same as we have done with all our enemies. If no other nation will come to our aid, we will fight the barbarians alone. When we are victorious, we will teach those nations the cost of their folly."

Milintica made no objection. An uncomfortable silence settled over the room. Cuauhtemoc wanted to believe Great Speaker, wanted to believe him with all his heart, but bluster would not be enough to save Tenochtitlan. Only a strong army could. Or an unconscionable deal.

Chapter 6

Garrido tied his horse next to López's mount. López rode a dappled mare, a magnificent mount that stood fifteen hands high, but Garrido had to make do with a sway-backed packhorse more fit for a squire than a soldier. He could not claim the packhorse as his own, but that bothered Garrido little. The mere fact that he had been lent a horse was another reminder that his standing had improved considerably in recent weeks. When he served with Narváez, he might have been allowed to groom the horses, but he never would have been allowed to ride one. Even in Kongo he had never been allowed to ride a horse on his own; Father banished him before he reached riding age.

Garrido glanced at López. They spent more time together of late, and he had come to learn a great deal about the unflappable Sevillo. López, like all of the men who sailed for the New World, had outsize ambitions. But unlike so many of the men, he needed more than slaves and gold.

López needed to have his talents applied to something grand, something spectacular. He did not seem to care overmuch, however, whether his talents were used for war or peace. Cortés had tasked López with building a fleet of brigantines, but López seemed convinced he was building the Cathedral of Saint Mary.

The Cempoalteca also seemed to understand that López was an important man. Every now and then, they shot him furtive glances. Despite their obvious curiosity, they kept their distance. Garrido frowned. He had not spent much time in Cempoala, but the locals had been much friendlier when he first met them. Now they were cool and reserved, and he could not fathom what had brought about the change.

Garrido knew the Christians had mistreated some of the Cempoalteca in the past, but they had made amends with gifts and apologies. He supposed it was possible the Cempoalteca still held a grudge, but he espied no hatred in their features.

Garrido turned toward his traveling companions. Most of them were busy taking food or making water, but Guy Ronzales busied himself by brushing down a horse.

"Ronzales, do the Cempoalteca seem a bit odd to you?"

"Of course they seem odd. They're Indian."

"What does it matter that they are Indian? Many of the Cempoalteca have converted—"

"False converts, all of them," Ronzales said dismissively. "To be a true Christian, you must be born into the faith. A tree reared in the shadows is stunted, and the same is true of man."

Garrido pursed his lips. He did not find Ronzales' line of thinking convincing, but he knew better than to say as much out loud. He took a moment to take stock of his surroundings.

Cempoala was not nearly as majestic an *altepetl* as Tenochtitlan, but it was not without charm. While the pyramids of Cempoala did not reach stunning heights, they were painted in brilliant hues and were connected by well-manicured roads. On most days, the walking areas were crowded and bustling.

Today, they were empty and barren. Garrido shaded his eyes and stared up at the heavens. Not a rain cloud in sight. It was a beautiful day, the likes of which he had not seen for weeks, but there was hardly a soul in sight.

A frisson of dread crept up his spine. *Perhaps we made a mistake in coming here.* Reinforcements had arrived at Fort Veracruz a few days ago, they seemed to arrive every week now, and López had been so keen to discover what they had brought that he insisted upon a journey to the coast. Cempoala was a logical place to stop for food and water, but Garrido wondered now if they might have been better off making straight for Fort Veracruz.

He let his gaze drop and focused on sights closer at hand. On the other side of the street, only ten paces away, a malnourished boy flapped his blanket at the occasional passer-by. Something about his vacant expression made Garrido uneasy, and he turned away. After a minute or so, he stole another glance at the boy. The boy's vacant expression had not changed in the slightest.

Garrido sighed and made his way toward the boy. He stopped in front of him, unsure how to greet him. He had only been in the New World half a year and had picked up just a few Nahuatl phrases during that time.

"Know Spanish?" Garrido asked.

The boy nodded. "I fluent. Move to Cempoala little ago, learn so much."

Garrido smiled weakly. "That is most impressive. How much are you selling your blankets for?"

"Five cocoa beans. Take gold also, though. Quarter finger of gold."

Garrido's eyes widened. The boy had to be mad if he thought he was going to spend that much gold on a blanket. Garrido cocked his head to the side and studied the cotton blankets with a careful eye. They were well-woven, he could not deny that. The color patterning seemed peculiar, though. For the most part, it was bright and vivid, but a smattering of dark patches ruined the color scheme. "What happened to these blankets?"

"Sick person used this blanket. I cleaned it, though. It's very clean, no bad smell at all. If stains bother, I give you a small price."

Garrido rubbed his forefinger against his thumb. "It's a very nice blanket. Why sell it?"

The boy looked down, shame-faced. "The weaver died," he said in a small voice. "They no need it now."

Garrido retreated a half-pace. Had the boy stolen the blanket? He would not lose the last of his gold to a cutpurse, not when he had lost so much already. "Did you know the blanket weaver?"

The boy sniffled and wiped his nose. "She was Nahtli. She weave better than me. I need sell blankets to eat. Do you want blanket? I can give you small price."

Garrido stared at the boy's left hand. Two of his fingers were conjoined at the knuckle. With a disability like that, weaving would be most difficult. "Where's your Tahtli? He should be helping you."

"Tahtli dead," he said simply. "He also got sick."

Garrido's face softened. Few had a tougher lot in life than a young orphan. "Isn't there someone who can help…"

He shook his head. "All sick. Great Rash kill them."

Garrido scratched his chin. Rashes did not kill people. Leastways, none of this world. Was God punishing these people the same way he punished the ancient Egyptians with the plague of boils? "Can you tell me more about this rash?"

The boy rubbed his shoulder. "When you get the rash, you develop big sores all over your body. They become so big they burst and make everything smelly."

Garrido nodded. "Sounds like they came down with smallpox."

The boy quirked an eyebrow. "Smallpox?"

"It's a pestilence feared like few others. I was struck with the pox when I was little older than you. It is a most terrible affliction. Were it not the grace of God, I surely would have perished. He put me through a great trial, but

I am stronger for it." The boy stared at him with a blank expression. "You are not familiar with smallpox?"

The boy shook his head again. Garrido found his ignorance difficult to comprehend. Spain was full of boys who had no use for schooling, but even the poorest street urchins knew of smallpox. People in Kongo were not as familiar with disease as the people of Spain and Portugal, but they at least knew of it.

"It's a terrible malady," Garrido added. "Count yourself lucky that you didn't…" Garrido trailed off.

Tears welled in the boy's eyes. "Please, I hungry. Buy one of my blankets. So many in Cempoala have Great Rash and don't help me."

Garrido took a deep breath and reached for his purse. He managed to escape Tenochtitlan with only three bars of gold and had been forced to trade most of it away for food and armor. Of his three gold bars, he now had only two small nuggets worth no more than a maravedi or two. He had no wish to part with the last of his gold, but he had a duty as a Christian to help those in need. He handed over both.

The boy's face brightened, but only for a moment. "Do you have more?"

Garrido sighed. "I'm sorry, I do not. God has chosen you for a great trial—"

The boy grabbed his hand. "I will let you do things with me, if you have more."

Garrido's eyes widened. A mixture of pity and disgust seized him. Surely the boy was not so desperate that he would sell his body for gold. He wanted to believe he had misunderstood the boy, but there was no mistaking the desperation in his eyes. Garrido pulled his hand out of the boy's grip. He wiped his hand against his tunic and said, "Sodomy is a sin. I pray your fortunes soon improve and that you reject sin so you can accept the love of Jesus into your heart."

Still struggling with his revulsion, Garrido made his way back to López and the others.

"What troubles you?" López asked as Garrido neared.

Garrido forced a smile. López had a unique ability to read him, and Garrido could rarely keep something secret from him. He did not wish to tell him of the boy's sordid offer, though. The boy already had cause enough for shame already. "The angels of God have poured out a bowl of wrath on these lands."

López looked at him quizzically. "What mean you?"

"The villagers have been afflicted with smallpox."

"We shall not stay long then," López said and crossed himself. He relayed the news to the others, and a hushed silence fell over the group. Almost all of them had contracted the accursed pestilence at some point in their lives, and many of them had lost loved ones to it.

Garrido glanced at a row of nearby houses. It was mid-day, but he spotted only a few cooking fires. Garrido curled his nose as a terrible smell came wafting his way on the breeze. Death had a distinctive smell, and it hung over the city like the specter of God's wrath. Garrido shivered. An outbreak of smallpox could cripple even the most vibrant community, and he prayed God would take mercy on the poor *altepetl* of Cempoala.

~ ~ ~

Cuauhtemoc waded through the Sacred Precinct's crowded courtyard in search of familiar faces. Great Speaker had celebrated his coronation months prior, and today's celebration would mark his formal confirmation. Ordinarily, a coronation war would precede the confirmation, but Tenochtitlan could not afford such a luxury at this time. Not when the *teteo* and the Tlaxcalteca were growing stronger by the day. No, the Mexica had to focus on improving the defenses of Tenochtitlan, not making war on some weak *altepetl* in some distant remove.

Cuauhtemoc stopped in front of Ollin. His dear friend dropped to a knee in a show of deference. Ollin rubbed two of his fingers on the ground, but Cuauhtemoc stopped him before he could make full obeisance.

"Enough of that," Cuauhtemoc said. "You are a brother to me, and I will not have you grovel before me as if you were some humbled vassal."

Ollin laughed and brushed dirt off of his knee. "Nobody has ever accused me of being humble."

Cuauhtemoc squeezed Ollin's shoulder and grabbed his forearm. "I am glad you can still find cause for joy these days. Despair tempts me greatly whenever I think about the news from outside the valley."

Ollin sobered like a man doused with cold water. "Yes, the events of recent weeks do not give much cause for joy. Ever since the battle at Otampan, little has gone our way."

Cuauhtemoc winced. The memory of Otampan was still fresh, and he did not wish to be reminded of it on a day like this. "Do you think Great Speaker will arrive soon?"

"I suspect not," Ollin said. "The dancing has yet to begin, so Great Speaker will probably wait until mid-day to make an entrance."

Cuauhtemoc groaned. Ollin was probably right, but he hoped Great Speaker would break with tradition and arrive earlier than expected. He lacked the energy to feign joy all day and wanted to dedicate himself to more important tasks. Eventually, the barbarians would march for Tenochtitlan again, and the *altepetl* needed to be made ready for battle. Canals had to be widened, long spears had to be made, and buildings had to be reconstructed.

"I only arrived a short time ago," Ollin added. "Are a great many representatives in attendance?"

Cuauhtemoc laughed. "You need not have a polished eye to know the courtyard is full, Ollin. Look around you!

Hundreds upon hundreds have come to pay their respects to Great Speaker. This confirmation ceremony will not be soon forgotten."

Ollin nodded and stepped back so a *pilli* with a rotund belly could pass. "Yes, the courtyard is most crowded, anyone can see that," Ollin said, his eyes still affixed to the *pilli* who had passed by him. "But I prefer a small jar with ripe kernels to a large jar with rotting kernels."

"A good thing that a large jar can hold ripe kernels, then! Chalco, Xochimilco, Iztapalapa, Xaltocan, and Tetzcoco have all sent representatives."

Ollin's face darkened. "Those are all lakeshore settlements. Did any *altepetl* outside our valley see fit to send representatives?"

Cuauhtemoc tucked his tongue in his cheek. Sometimes Ollin could be too observant for his own good. "I recognize the representatives from the lakeshore settlements much better than I would recognize the representatives from elsewhere."

Ollin smiled weakly. "Perhaps, but you would still recognize them. Try to twist something all you want, but you do not fool me. You know the family history of every Speaker from Tula to Huitzlan. Great Speaker can learn much from you, and he would be wise to heed your counsel."

Cuauhtemoc rubbed the nape of his neck. He did not like the direction of the conversation. Great Speaker deserved the plaudits, not him. "The day is early yet. More representatives may soon arrive."

The words had barely left Cuauhtemoc's mouth before a loud cheering erupted on the other side of the courtyard. Cuauhtemoc turned. The delegation from Tlacopan had finally arrived, attendants and all.

"The people of Tlacopan must not have any capacity for shame," Ollin grumbled. "Otherwise, they would beg our forgiveness for letting the barbarians escape the night of the Night of Glory.”

Cuauhtemoc frowned. He had been unaware that Ollin harbored such animosity toward Tlacopan. “The *altepetl* could have done more to help, but we ought not forget—”

“Could have done more?” Ollin sputtered. “The barbarians would not even be alive if the people of Tlacopan had done their duty! Had Tlacopan given us true assistance during the Night of Glory, we could have wiped out their entire force that night. Instead, they let the barbarians slip through their territory like water through their fingers.”

“Ollin, I am sure you remember that conditions were very poor that night. Had we requested assistance from Tlacopan during the Night of Glory, I am sure they would have come to our aid. But we did not do so until it was much too late, just as we did not pursue the barbarians until it was much too late.”

Ollin’s face fell. After a long pause, he sucked in a deep breath. “Cuauhtemoc, can I speak plainly with you?”

“Of course.”

“When we were returning from Chalco, you told me we should hope the peoples of the One World see us as their allies rather than masters. I was not inclined to agree with you at the time, but I have been thinking on what you said. I think there may be some truth in it.”

Ollin could be as stubborn as stone, and Cuauhtemoc was genuinely surprised to hear him admit to a change in thinking.

“I fear we may not have true allies, warriors we can count on in times of need,” Ollin added. “Before Otampan, I think some nations might have rallied to our standard out of fear, but I do not know if we can always count on that in the future. We are not as strong as we once were, and I worry for the future. Were it not for the Great Rash, despair would be most tempting."

Cuauhtemoc furrowed his brow. The Great Rash was a terrible plague, and he could not fathom why Ollin might consider it fortuitous. "Do you think the Great Rash is cause for hope?"

Ollin smiled. "Cuauhtemoc, surely you have heard the stories from Cempoala. The Cempoalteca have lost so many to the Great Rash that harvests will go uncollected. Their healers are powerless to help the afflicted, and there is talk that Cempoala may lose a third of its population to the Great Rash. The gods are punishing Cempoala for giving succor to the barbarians, and they are sure to punish Tlaxcala also. If the gods are kind, they will smite every nation that thinks of making common cause with the barbarians."

Cuauhtemoc scratched his cheek. The gods were not opposed to meddling in the affairs of mortals, but Cuauhtemoc doubted the Great Rash was their doing. And even if it was, that was no guarantee of good tidings. The gods could be incredibly magnanimous, but they were just as capable of shocking cruelty. Or indifference. "If the Great Rash was sent to punish those who make common cause with the barbarians, why are the Maya also suffering?"

Ollin blinked. "What do you mean?"

"The Great Rash, or something very similar, has reached the Far South, and it has proven most deadly. Entire villages have been wiped out, and the very fabric of society has come undone. Dogs and vultures are fat with carrion, and the stench of death hangs over all the land. Once the Great Rash comes to a place, it spreads quickly and spares few. I shudder to think of what would happen if it reached Tenochtitlan."

Ollin squared his shoulders. "Maya lands are very far from here, and Cempoala is not that near either. I do not think the Great Rash will come to Tenochtitlan. The gods will not allow it."

Cuauhtemoc sighed. He wished he had the same confidence as Ollin in the good will of the gods. But the battle at Otampan had shaken his faith, and the cruelty at Tepeaca had made a mockery of it. He did not want to believe the gods had forsaken the Mexica, but he would not begrudge somebody for thinking it so.

"It was not so long ago the barbarians were encamped near Cempoala," Cuauhtemoc said. "Many were sure they would not be able to summon the strength for an inland march and that distance would prevent them from reaching Tenochtitlan. Tell me, were you one of those people?"

Ollin quieted and stared at the ground. Cuauhtemoc took no pleasure in his hollow victory and turned away from his friend. His gaze drifted to a group of *pilli* half a stone's throw away. They had dressed themselves in their finest regalia—their headdresses were stuffed full of Quetzal feathers and their jade jewelry sparkled like nighttime stars—and gave no outward indication of worry or fear. On the contrary, they appeared remarkably untroubled, and he marveled at their composure.

Judging by their expressions, one would think they had no cause for angst, that none of them had heard the stories regarding the *teteo*. He wished he could take comfort in their blissful abandon, but he was more inclined toward pity. He had lived in Tenochtitlan long enough to know that calm waters did not last.

Chapter 7

Pozon stood in the corner of Cortés' tent as Master Estrada and Master Farfán crowded around the high table. They, and the other *teteo*, were looking at something they called a map. Why they thought it was so important, he did not know. He knew better than to ask, though.

Neither of his masters—not Maria de Estrada or her husband, Pedro Sánchez Farfán—liked it when he asked questions. He found it hard to please them and did not understand why they beat him so often. Tahtli and Nahtli never beat him, and he wished he could go back to the village with them. But Tahtli was dead, and Nahtli was a slave in some place called Veracruz. There was no village to return to anyway. The *teteo* and the Tlaxcalteca had burnt it to the ground the same day they captured him.

Pozon prodded the burn mark under his eye. The *teteo* had branded him the same day they took him captive, and the wound still needed time to heal. When it did, he would have an ugly symbol on his cheek, like all the other captured slaves. Did Yaotl get branded as well? He hoped not but had no idea. He had not seen her since he was captured, did not even know if she was alive.

He ceased his prodding and put aside his dark thoughts. Thinking about everything that had happened to his family made him sad, and he could not be sad right now. The Masters did not like it when he cried in front of others.

Pozon puffed out his chest and hugged the wine skin close. A few months ago, he had never even heard of wine, but the Masters liked it a lot, so he always made sure to have some at hand. Or at least, he tried to. Like so many of the things that came from beyond the mists, it was always asked after but rarely available.

Some of the other slaves said wine helped make a person less sad. He was tempted to steal a sip to see if it was true. But only bad slaves stole, and he didn't want to be a bad slave. Bad slaves were whipped and chopped. Sometimes they were even set upon by mastiffs.

A woman said something in Nahuatl. Pozon snapped his head toward Estrada, ready to do as she commanded. A wave of relief washed over him as he realized it was Malintze, not Estrada who had spoken. Owing to her accent, he could understand little of what she said other than something about reinforcements from Veracruz. Sister had taught him the word reinforcements during their last day together... A lump formed in his throat. He did not like thinking about that day.

A pair of Tlaxcalteca warriors, so close he could almost touch them, started talking about the Great Rash. Pozon suppressed a shiver. The Great Rash had come to camp recently and few were safe from it, save the *teteo*. Pozon had been pleased to see many of his Tlaxcalteca tormentors succumb to the Great Rash, but the joy curdled once he learned slaves could also succumb to it. He had been spared for some reason, but it was hard to know whether his luck would hold. It seemed a new slave fell ill every day.

Estrada bade him over with a wave of her hand, and he ran toward her. "Bring me some zapote."

Pozon waited for her to say more, but she had focused all her attention on the map and did not spare him a single glance. What was a zapote? He wanted so desperately to ask her, but no good could come of that so he slipped out of Cortés' tent without another word.

The light provided by Tonatiuh was dwindling, and he hurried to Estrada's tent. Camp could be a scary place after dark. He paused outside Estrada's tent. It felt odd to enter the tent without anyone else around, but he knew better than to keep Estrada waiting. He took a deep breath and stepped inside.

A bug flew past him, and he tied the tent flap closed to keep others from entering. The glint of a knife caught his eye as he surveyed the tent interior. He dropped into a squat to better examine the weapon. *Teteo* knives were made from a strange material called steel and weighed no more than an avocado. He knew from firsthand experience how deadly they could be and hoped the *teteo* might gift him one. Perhaps if he asked Estrada....

He dismissed the thought. She would never allow him a knife, and he would not dare to steal one. Every now and then, he pilfered food to keep from starving, but he could not hide a knife in his loincloth the same way he could bread morsels or bacon crumbs.

Pozon stole toward a row of lidded jars tucked in the corner of the tent. Carved from clay and two hands high, each jar had been stuffed full of victuals. He peeked inside the first one. Hard tack. The *teteo* had brought lots of hard tack from beyond the mists, but Pozon would never understand their fondness for it. Taste wise, it was about as pleasing as bark.

He opened a different jar. *Pitahaya* had been stuffed inside and ants were crawling along the skin's thick fruit. The Masters hated bugs—whether they were on their food, in the air, or simply around—and Pozon knew better than to simply let the bugs be. He crushed them with his thumb and did not stop until he killed all of them.

His stomach rumbled, and he breathed in the *pitahaya's* faint aroma. The Masters would know if he ate even one. He glanced at his thumb. Ants were a delicacy in many parts of the One World, but they were seldom eaten raw. His stomach grumbled again, and he nibbled on the edge of his thumb.

The ants had a sour aftertaste and were not all that filling, but he was grateful for the sustenance. He packed the *pitahaya* away, confident that the *teteo* never used the word *zapote* for *pitahaya*. As far as he knew, the *teteo* did not have their own word for *pitahaya*. Unsure what do next, he opened the last jar.

It was brimming with *tzapotl*, and his stomach rumbled with a newfound vengeance. He did his best to ignore his hunger pangs and tried to recall all the *teteo* words he had learned. No matter how hard he tried, he could not remember their word for *tzapotl*, could not even remember if they had their own word for it. He made another cursory search of the tent. There were no other jars to check. Perhaps zapote was just another word for *tzapotl*.

He grabbed a handful and then stopped. Estrada had not specified how much she wanted. If she only wanted a few, a handful would be fine but what if she wanted more? Best to bring the entire jar, just to be safe.

Clutching the jar to his chest, he stepped out of Estrada's tent and hurried back to Cortés' redoubt. Off to his left, *teteo* started shouting. He froze in place. If they were shouting for him, it could only be bad for reasons.

Pozon squeezed his eyes shut and forced himself to stand upright. A loud commotion made him open his eyes, and he watched as a group of *teteo* rushed past, dragging a semi-conscious captive behind them. They muttered something about runaway Indian, and Pozon broke into a sprint. He did not know the captive well, but he knew runaways were subjected to terrible punishments.

He made it inside Cortés' tent just as the whipping began. Many of the outside sounds were muffled by the tent's thick fabric, and he gave thanks for that. Bad sounds always found their way into his dreams, and he had enough trouble sleeping as is. He made his way toward Estrada, his stomach churning like a rain-swollen river. He opened the jar as he neared and waited for her to notice him.

Pozon stood on the tips of his toes to see more of the map. He could not read any of the words etched into the vellum parchment, but some of the symbols were vaguely familiar to him. He tried to decipher their meanings and was so consumed by the task that he started when Estrada reached into the *tzapotl* jar. His reaction earned him a withering glare, and she banished him to the corner with a few sharp words.

He quickly made himself scarce. The *teteo* mentioned the word allegiance. What did that mean? Perhaps it was related to pact, but he could only guess. One day, he would become fluent in their language. He knew only bits and pieces, but he worked every day to learn more. He'd be a translator one day, like Malintze, and *teteo* would give him respect then.

The *teotl* called Sandóval cleared his throat and let loose a long string of words. He repeated the words Ixtli and allegiance, over and over. Pozon rubbed the nape of his neck. Why would the *teteo* be interested in Ixtli, the War Chief from Tetzcoco?

Cortés pointed to the map and said something about a raid. Pozon's stomach dropped. He knew the term raid all too well. He realized with a jolt why the *teteo* were crowding around the map; they were deciding which places to attack next!

His knees went watery as he remembered the day the *teteo* attacked his village. He soiled himself when they pressed the hot brand against his cheek, writhed like an eel once they dropped him to the ground. It was the worst pain he had ever experienced, and he begged for death afterward. His pleas went unheeded, however, and infection never set in. The injury had yet to fully heal, and Pozon hoped it would fade with time.

The littlest of things reminded him of it—the smell of burning meat, the sight of glowing embers—but he didn't think about the scar nearly as much as he used to. But if the *teteo* and the Tlaxcalteca resumed their raiding, camp would be full of even more people with ugly burn marks. Day in and day out, he would be forced to confront the brutal realities of his new station in life. For the rest of his years, perhaps.

He muttered a prayer to the *teteo* God, and his own gods for good measure, but he knew it was pointless. So long as the *teteo* had the Tlaxcalteca for allies and the horses for weapons, there was no force powerful enough to stop the slave raids from beginning anew.

Part Two
October-May, 1521

Chapter 8

Anahuaca's body was wrapped in amatl paper, but it was not nearly thick enough to hide the hideous pustules that covered his torso. Dead *pilli* were always wrapped in amatl paper to help ensure they could travel safely through the nine Underworlds, and Cuauhtemoc hoped the staining would not imperil Anahuaca's journey.

Cuauhtemoc sighed quietly. His people were trying so very hard to hold on to tradition, but events of late made that difficult. Beyond the mountains, the barbarians were carrying out a campaign of unspeakable cruelty and now controlled the eastern valley and the highlands. It was as outrageous as it was shameful, but the Mexica could do nothing to stop the slave raids as they were dealing with a foe unlike any other: the Great Rash.

Despite the protestations of the Givers and the prayers of many, the Great Rash had made its way to Tenochtitlan. He had assumed the Mexica would be better prepared for it than the coastal people, but nothing could have prepared the *altepetl* for such wanton destruction. The sickness had swept through the city like a tidal wave, and families everywhere were suffering in the most terrible ways.

Anahuaca was the first in his family to succumb to the strange illness. In Cuauhtemoc's eyes, that made him lucky. Unlike so many other men, Anahuaca would not have to watch as his household sickened and died. Countless warriors had taken their own lives because they could not bear to watch their loved one's waste away.

A thin curtain of smoke wafted toward Cuauhtemoc. Tradition dictated that important persons were cremated when they died, but Anahuaca's fire still needed tending. *Pilli* had formed a small line in front of the growing flames, and many of Tenochtitlan's most distinguished citizens were in attendance. Curiously, Great Speaker was absent, but his chief advisor, Milintica, had come in his stead.

Most curious of all, Milintica made a point to stand next to him, even though Cuauhtemoc had made a point to stand by himself. Cuauhtemoc thought to ask him why but decided against it. He was too tired to initiate conversation and did not wish to speak with anyone, not unless he had to.

Cuauhtemoc stared at Anahuaca's death bundle. Anahuaca was never one much for conversation, either. He was ever a man of action and would make his journey through the Underworlds with all manner of green jade and fine feathers, as was only fitting for a distinguished warrior.

Cuauhtemoc gazed up at the thirteen skies. *How will I fare on my journey through the Underworlds?* If he allowed the barbarians to gain control of Tenochtitlan, he was not sure the gods would forgive him.

"Looking for rain clouds?" Milintica asked.

Cuauhtemoc managed a weak smile. "If Tlaloc is kind, he will not send rains until after the cremation."

"The gods have not been kind of late," Milintica muttered. He tilted his head toward Anahuaca.

"We must pray for better fortune," Cuauhtemoc said, his voice melancholy and his tone lifeless. He prayed every day, but the gods did not seem to pay his wishes much mind.

Milintica sighed. "Perhaps it is too late for deliverance. We are losing many of our best people to this accursed plague."

Cuauhtemoc kept quiet. Milintica cared more for the *pilli* than any other people in Tenochtitlan, but he was mistaken if he thought only the *pilli* were suffering. All of Tenochtitlan was suffering, from the poorest waifs to the richest lords.

"I am sure you have met many healers during your travels through the One World," Milintica said. "Do you know any who would be able to treat the Great Rash?"

Cuauhtemoc mulled his question. The healers had proven oddly susceptible to the Great Rash, so much so that many had given up the trade. He could not fault them for succumbing to fear anymore than he could fault them for succumbing to the Great Rash. Every traditional remedy had been tried—crushed black beetle, bitumen, even octli—but nothing worked. After a long pause, Cuauhtemoc said, "I cannot say."

"I pray we learn the answer soon. Otherwise, the fools in the marketplace will only become louder."

Cuauhtemoc chuckled drily. He knew exactly which fools Milintica was referring to. Certain people were convinced that the Great Rash was not of this world, that the gods were punishing the Mexica for a lack of faith. They insisted upon a new campaign against the *teteo* and the Tlaxcalteca and the Purepecha and the Huastecs and the Totonacs because only a military undertaking of gargantuan proportions would earn their protection.

"I hear that steam can help with the lesions," Cuauhtemoc said. "Ollin's cousin was stricken by the Great Rash, but he made a full recovery after visiting a bathhouse."

Milintica's face curdled. "Do not put any store by such foolish talk. If you wish to keep your health, you will stay away from the bath houses."

Cuauhtemoc frowned. Milintica often frequented the bath houses and his newfound animus was surprising. All the *pilli* frequented bath houses, and it was as much a part of Tenocha culture as fasting and praying. "Washing regularly is good for the health—"

"In ordinary times, yes. But I fear that is no longer so."

"What do you mean?"

Milintica's face softened. "You have not heard, have you?"

Cuauhtemoc's pulse quickened. "Heard what?"

"Cuitlahuac has been stricken with the Great Rash."

Cuauhtemoc's breath caught. He felt as if he had been kicked in the stomach and took a moment to collect himself. If Cuitlahuac were to succumb to the Great Rash, Tenochtitlan would once again be without a Great Speaker. Even in ordinary times, the death of a Great Speaker was enormously disruptive. In a time of plague and war, it could prove calamitous. "Is he likely to recover?"

Milintica shook his head. "His face and his neck are covered with pustules, and he spends his waking hours screaming and raving."

"We must not abandon hope. Not all who are struck by the Great Rash succumb to it."

"Of course. I will keep Great Speaker in my prayers, and I am sure others will do the same," Milintica said. "I will also pray you heed my advice regarding the bath houses."

Cuauhtemoc turned toward Milintica. "Are you suggesting that Cuitlahuac has been stricken with the Great Rash because he went to a bath house?"

Milintica sighed. "I cannot say for certain; I have never trained as a healer. But I know Cuitlahuac was at a bathhouse with a sick man only two weeks ago because I was there with him. Ten other men were there, and five of them have sickened. If I become sick, it will be six."

Cuauhtemoc frowned. "You are sure the sick man had the Great Rash?"

Milintica glanced toward the growing fire. "The sick man was Anahuaca." Cuauhtemoc's eyes widened. Only a fool would deny that Anahuaca died from anything other than the Great Rash. Some of his pustules were as big as drinking bowls. "When Anahuaca went to the bath house, I do not think he had any pustules," Milintica added. "Truth be told, he looked rather hale."

Cuauhtemoc stared at Anahuaca's death bundle. He wanted to hate him for potentially sickening Great Speaker, but he could not summon the energy. Nobody knew for certain how the Great Rash was spreading, or why, and he could not begrudge Anahuaca for doing what many would have done in his place. The bathhouses had long been a place for healing, and the Great Rash had only made them more popular. "You have a sharp mind, Milintica, and I am grateful that Cuitlahuac turns to you for advice. I will avoid the bath houses, and thank you for your wise counsel."

"Will you still take my wise counsel when you are Great Speaker?"

Cuauhtemoc huffed. "What makes you think I desire the position?"

Milintica narrowed his eyes. "What you desire no longer matters. Should Cuitlahuac die, the nation will need you to serve as Great Speaker. I hope you will be equal to the task."

Cuauhtemoc bit his tongue to keep from answering. He despaired that he might not be equal to the task, but he knew better than to admit as much. A Great Speaker could never admit to weakness.

~ ~ ~

Malintze placed a hand on her aching midsection. Her stomach had been in turmoil all day, and the onset of night had done little to calm her insides. Darkness had settled over camp almost an hour before, but sleep continued to elude her.

She sat up on her pallet, her sore muscles protesting every moment. The long march had exacerbated her menstrual cramps, and she ground her teeth as she waited for the pain to fade. Men would never understand the pain women suffered, nor would they ever want to.

She groped in the dark for her water gourd. After much shuffling and sorting, Malintze finally found it, only to discover there was hardly any water in it. She squeezed the gourd's neck in frustration.

The rough feel of her hands cooled her anger. A few days before, strange red bumps had developed on both of her palms. They were so faint few could notice them and were easy to ignore since they did not itch or fester. She fretted at first that she must have developed the Great Rash, but she did not develop pustules or lesions. Other than her menses coming unusually early, she felt hale and strong. Hopefully, the bumps would fade with time.

Malintze pushed herself to her feet and clambered toward the tent exit. Despite the dark, she managed to undo the tent flap. A cold draft rushed into the tent. She bit her lip in frustration and wrapped herself in a thick blanket. She rubbed her arms for warmth and sauntered past a dozing guard.

Sleeping on duty was a punishable offense, but Malintze bore the man no ill-will. He had spent all day marching and would be expected to march again on the morrow. If anything, she envied his ability to find respite. She suspected the night would be half gone before she finally succumbed to sleep.

She pulled her blanket closer and set off in search of a water barrel. Her cramps began to ease, and she sucked in a deep breath. The thin mountain air made her cough, and Malintze doubled over in pain. She hated traveling through the highlands.

No matter how much air she tried to draw, Malintze could never seem to capture enough. Some of the *teteo* had developed a rattling cough, and she worried the same would happen to her. Malintze was quite confident that most of them hated the mountain climes, but it mattered for naught.

Cortés was determined to meet with Ixtli, the dispossessed ruler of Tetzcoco, to forge a pact. If that meant leaving the safety of Tlaxcala to march into potentially hostile territory, she and the others simply had to make do.

As had been explained to her multiple times, winning Ixtli's friendship would be the masterstroke in the war. Not that she put much stock by those claims. Forging a pact with the Totonacs was supposed to be key to winning the war, then forging a pact with the Tlaxcalteca. Cortés had allied with both peoples, but still the war raged on.

A small whimpering caught her attention. She froze. Had a wild animal snuck into camp? No, that couldn't be possible. The *teteo* dogs were much too good at sniffing out intruders. She strained her ears. The whimpering was coming from her left, from behind Estrada's tent.

More intrigued than alarmed, she slowly made her way toward the sound. Careful not to make any sudden movements, she peeked behind the tent. What with the darkness, it took her a moment to realize she was staring at a person.

The person, a young boy, did not seem to notice her staring. He was curled in a ball and sucked on his thumb as if it were a milk teat. He had only a thin blanket to protect him from the cold, and the chattering of his teeth made her forget about her stomach pains.

Malintze tilted her head to the side. His face was familiar, she had seen him around camp a few times. Estrada had captured him during the Tepeaca campaign, but what was his name?

She could not say as she could put a name to only a few of the slaves. Hundreds had been added to the company's manifest in just the past few past few weeks, not to mention the countless numbers the company had purchased and captured early in the expedition.

Malintze frowned. Something about the boy's expression reminded her of the brother she once knew. For a moment, the resemblance was so stark she wondered if she were actually looking at her brother. That wasn't possible, though. Her brother was only a few years younger than her, and the boy in front of her was no more than half her age. She studied his face carefully. Save the ugly scar that marked him as a captured slave, he had few distinguishing features.

Malintze sighed and knelt in front of him "Why are you crying?" The boy said nothing, did not even acknowledge her presence. She laid her hand on his back. "What's your name?"

The boy stiffened. After a long pause, he said in a quiet voice, "I used to be called Pozon."

"That's a very nice name."

"I like it better than my Christian name," Pozon muttered. "But don't tell Estrada that."

Malintze bit back a laugh. "Your secret is safe with me." The boy mumbled his thanks. Malintze sat down next to the boy and wrapped an arm around him. The blanket wasn't big enough to cover both of them, and her garments provided little protection against the chill of night. "It's cold out. Why aren't you inside the tent with Estrada and Farfán?"

A hurt look flashed across Pozon's face. "They say I make too many noises in my sleep."

Malintze nodded. "I make many noises in my sleep, too."

Pozon stared at her in astonishment. "You do?"

Malintze smiled. "Of course, I do. It's not just children who dream, you know."

Pozon's face scrunched up. "Only some grown-ups dream. Tahtli never told me about his dreams."

Malintze shook her head and rubbed Pozon's shoulder. "Everyone dreams. Some of us do it during our waking hours, some of us when we're asleep, but it's something we all do. Without dreams, life would be dreary and dull, and who would wish for a thing like that?"

Pozon wiped his dripping nose. "What do you dream about?"

Being free. Malintze cleared her throat and said, "So many things. I often dream about butterflies. They come to me in my dreams now and again. I try to chase after them sometimes, but I can never catch them. Butterflies are such beautiful creatures, don't you think? I hear there are some places in the One World where butterflies are so numerous they cover entire trees, that they blot out the sky when they take to the air. I think that would be quite the sight to behold." Malintze sucked in a deep breath. There were so many things she wanted, but all of it would have to wait until the war was over. Until she was free. "What do you dream about?"

"My sister, Yaotl," Pozon whispered.

"You must love her very much. She probably dreams of you also."

"If she's still alive," Pozon said, his voice cracking.

Malintze sighed. She knew his pain all too well. The last time she saw her brother, she had been even younger than Pozon. "You know, I had a brother, when I was a little younger than you."

"Had?"

"I was taken from him when I was very young." A lump formed in her throat as the memories came back to her. Long as she lived, she would never forget the terrible traumas that had been foisted upon her when she was only a child. "Life can be very cruel. Sometimes, it's all we can do to survive, but you must never give up hope. Otherwise, life loses all meaning."

Pozon stopped shivering and rested his arm on her shoulder. "Why were you taken from him?"

"I used to ask myself the same thing," Malintze said. She gazed off into the distance, thinking about everything she had endured in Potonchan. All the men who had used her, all the women who had abused her. "All the time, over and over. After a certain point, I realized the why doesn't matter. All that matters is overcoming." Another tear dripped down Pozon's face, and she squeezed his shoulder. "Pozon, you are cold as ice! Here, take my blanket."

Malintze wrapped the blanket around Pozon. To her surprise, he scooted away from her as she tried to enwrap him. "I can't."

"Why not?" Malintze asked, genuinely surprised by his refusal.

"Someone will take it from me." Pozon sniffled and stared at the ground. "It's a nice blanket. I think you should keep it."

"I will keep it on one condition." Malintze held up her finger for emphasis and waited for Pozon to ask her what she meant. Much to her disappointment, Pozon did not oblige. She hugged him close and whispered, "I will keep the blanket if you agree to share my tent."

Pozon's eyes went wide. "You would share your tent with me?"

His disbelief caught her off-guard, and she turned away. "Pozon, my tent is very spacious," she explained. "The air is thin up here, and you will never get to sleep if you stay outside all night. Stay in my tent tonight."

Pozon's lip trembled. "I don't think Estrada would like that."

Malintze did not argue the point. Estrada was highly respected all throughout camp, both for her skills as a soldier and her bravery, and it would not be wise to attract her enmity. All the same, she could not leave Pozon alone. "I wake up very early," Malintze said. "When I wake up, I will wake you up so you can come back here. Estrada will never know."

Pozon's face brightened. "Promise?"

Pozon's sudden joy caught her off-guard, and she found herself returning his smile. "I promise."

Malintze stood and helped Pozon to his feet as he wrapped himself in the blanket. He took hold of her hand, setting her heart aflutter. When was the last time anybody had done that?

She ruffled his hair, drawing a small laugh from his pinched mouth. The beauty of that little laugh made her heart turn white, and a strange pride blossomed in her chest. Hand in hand, they made their way back to her tent.

Chapter 9

Cortés leaned forward and pressed the bloody handkerchief against his nose. The thin air had caused a blood vessel to burst in his nose, and he could not tilt his head backward without becoming nauseous.

He wished he were back in the valley. However, owing to Ixtli's intransigence, Cortés had been forced to abandon Tepeaca's pleasant clime to journey deep into the craggy mountains of Coatepec. *If Ixtli cannot make good on his promise of an army, I will hang him myself.*

While the distance between Tepeaca and Coatepec was not all that great, the rugged terrain made for difficult marching. The rigor proved too great for Doña Marina, and he had been forced to send her back to Tepeaca when she developed a fever.

Much as he hated not having her close, he knew it was for the best. Fever was no trifling matter. In the first few months of the campaign, he lost more men to sickness than he did to enemy Indians. He could not and would not lose Doña Marina, and he assigned her multiple physicians. Cortés hoped they could restore her health soon, but they seemed rather puzzled by her symptoms.

They were especially confused by the red bumps on her palms. He did not understand the fixation himself. Cortés had developed similar symptoms following a terrible fever almost ten years prior. He was tempted to tell them as much but decided against it. He had only hazy memories of the experience and would not clutter their heads with useless information.

Cortés pulled the handkerchief back to check for spotting. Stymied by cloth no more, a trickle of blood wormed its way into his mustache. He clenched his fist in frustration. What a time to be afflicted by a nose bleed!

A distant horn sounded, and he snapped his head toward the tent flap as Olea stepped inside. "An Indian party has been spotted. They are heading toward camp. Should we attack?"

"Most certainly not," Cortés replied, his voice steeped with anger. Olea had served him ably as his guard, but there were times when he had all the sense of a halfwit. "The party of Indians could be Ixtli and his retinue." Cortés dabbed his nose with his knuckle and was pleased to see only a few spots of blood. To have blood streaming out of his nose as he parlayed with Ixtli would be most unseemly. "Hail the Indians before they reach camp and determine their identity. Do not attack unless they have hostile intentions."

Olea nodded. "And if the scouts spot Ixtli? We can detain him before he reaches camp, if it pleases you."

Cortés shook his head. "I want Ixtli escorted to my tent with an armed guard. Detain him only if he offers resistance."

Cortés surveyed the tent interior. Other than his page and his secretary, he had nobody for company. *Perhaps I should send for others.* Whenever he met with Indian dignitaries, he made a point to surround himself with a cadre of loyal men.

He doubted Ixtli was the type to be easily impressed but knew it would be wise to have others present, if only to assist with translation efforts. He sent his page to fetch Andres de Tapia and a small detachment of guards.

A few minutes later, his page returned with Tapia and others in tow. "I am told you need my help with translating," Tapia said, a hint of a question in his voice.

"Yes. I believe Ixtli has been spotted near camp, and Olea will be escorting him to my tent."

Tapia nodded and ran a hand through his hair. If he was pleased to serve as translator, he hid it well. Cortés had done him a great honor by allowing him to partake in the conversation with Ixtli, but he looked as if he were readying himself for a tedious chore.

Scattered shouting let him know that Olea had returned to camp. Cortés straightened his back and checked his nose one last time. Satisfied that he would need the handkerchief no more, he tossed it aside and dropped his hand to the hilt of his sword.

A few moments later, the flaps of his tent were pulled back and a small party of Indians stepped inside. Every single one carried a *macuahuitl* and a shield, but only one of them wore a headdress. It was not nearly as ostentatious as the Great Speaker's diadem, the Quetzal feathers were no bigger than his hand, but Cortés understood that it marked the wearer as an important man. He had heard that Ixtli liked to wear such a headdress and knew, without even having to ask, that he was standing before the rightful ruler of Tetzcoco.

Appearance wise, Ixtli was most striking. Many of the Indians were tall and lanky, but Ixtli was short and stout. He was not blessed with a beautiful face any more than he was blessed with height. His ears protruded too far out, and his nose was sharper than a bird's beak. Ugliest of all were his eyes. His pupils were dark as pitch and moved about constantly, darting to and from like a sparrow between branches.

His countenance was not all that pleasing to look upon, but Cortés did not care overmuch. Even if he were as ugly as Satan, Cortés would not let that stop him from entering into a pact with him. He opened his mouth to give words to Ixtli but before he could utter even a single word, Ixtli shot out a rapid stream of words.

Cortés turned to Tapia for explanation. Tapia colored and stared at the ground. "Captain, Ixtli says you must do obeisance before him with a dirt-eating rite. Otherwise, he will not speak with you."

Cortés' eyes widened. The Indians had a habit of dropping to one knee, rubbing their fingers in the dirt, and then wiping their fingers against their lips to show obeisance. During all his time in the One World, no Indian had ever asked him to do the same. It was as outrageous as it was unseemly. "Tell Ixtli that I recently injured my knee and cannot humble myself as he wishes. Give him my sincere apologies, and let him know that I have the utmost respect for him."

Tapia frowned and stared skeptically at Cortés' knee. Cortés shot him a sharp glare, and Tapia averted his gaze. He coughed and passed on his words to Ixtli.

"Ixtli says you must find a way to humble yourself despite your knee injury," Tapia translated.

Cortés knew the value of yielding, or pretending to yield, when dealing with haughty, arrogant men. He also knew, however, that certain of his compatriots would be outraged if he humbled himself before an Indian. He glanced at Tapia and the others. Tapia was from Medellin, he could trust him to keep a secret. Many of the guards, however, hailed from elsewhere. *Can I trust them to do the same?* He certainly hoped so. He could not have it bandied about that he had prostrated himself for an upstart Indian.

Cortés sucked in a deep breath and dropped to a knee. Determined to make a good impression, he dabbed two fingers against the tent floor before gently pressing them to his lips. A ghost of a smile crossed Ixtli's lips, but it vanished by the time Cortés raised himself to full height.

"Ixtli is most pleased that you had the good sense to humble yourself," Tapia said. "He wishes to discuss a pact."

Cortés fought the urge to laugh. Often times, the Indian dignitaries liked to beat around the bush. He appreciated that Ixtli was more straightforward. "It pleases me to hear him say that. I, too, wish for the same."

"He says the evil traitor Motecuhzoma deprived him of his throne, and the people of Tetzcoco long for their rightful ruler. He has spent many years in exile, but all the greatest warriors have flocked to his standard. He commands an army of thousands and will soon march for Tetzcoco. He must know whether you will aid him in his cause."

"Of course we will," Cortés said in a warm voice. "We Spaniards have a deep and abiding love for justice, and we would be honored to restore him to his rightful position. Can we count on Ixtli to aid us in battle against Tenochtitlan?"

Ixtli's face darkened once he heard the translation, and he whispered something to his guards. They laughed and Cortés' hand tightened around his sword. The laughter died abruptly, and Ixtli gave new words to Tapia.

"Ixtli says there are some in Tetzcoco who do not share our love of justice. He says they happily serve traitors and would need to be killed once we take the city."

Cortés smoothed his beard. "Such is only natural. Once the traitors are dead, we ought to launch an attack on Tenochtitlan. We mean to take the city before the year's end."

Ixtli snorted and gave words to Tapia. "He says if you mean to attack Tenochtitlan before the end of the year, you must do so without the assistance of his army."

Cortés suppressed a flare of anger. "Why is that?"

"Ixtli says it will not be possible to take Tenochtitlan before the end of the year," Tapia said. "He says we must focus our energies on capturing Tetzcoco. It will be a great challenge but if the gods are kind, we will capture it before the end of the year."

Cortés had hoped Ixtli was a man of great ambition, but he had clearly taken his measure wrong. Ixtli, like so many others, did not seem to understand that victory favored the bold, not the timid. "The new year will be upon us in less than a month. Does Ixtli truly believe it will take multiple weeks to capture Tetzcoco? I thought the people longed to have him as their ruler."

Ixtli narrowed his eyes. "Almost sixty thousand people call the city home. Proving worthy of their affection is a process that will take a great deal of time. Political victories do not come to fruition as quickly as military victories."

Cortés forced a smile. "Forgive me for not putting more stock by your word. I have heard you are very brave, but now I know you're also wise. I would be honored to fight alongside you. Once we take Tetzcoco, the people of Tenochtitlan will know we mean to retaliate. We ought to attack as soon as we capture control of Tetzcoco."

Tapia flushed once he heard Ixtli's response and ran a hand through his hair. Cortés fixed his gaze on his friend from Medellin. "Tell me what Ixtli said, Tapia. I want to know exactly what he said."

"It would be difficult to translate what he said. He used many turns of phrase—"

"Then translate as best as you can," Cortés cut in. He clenched his teeth. Translations were always easier when Doña Marina was present.

"Ixtli says you must be a fool of the worst sort if you think it would be wise to launch an immediate attack on Tenochtitlan." Cortés blinked. Not even Motecuhzoma had ever dared to insult him so. For a moment, he thought about running Ixtli through with his sword, if only to wipe the smug expression off his face. But Cortés had a lifetime's worth of practice enduring insults and slights, and he drew upon that experience to check his temper. Nothing mattered more than winning the war against

Tenochtitlan and regaining the gold lost during the Sad Night.

Tapia cleared his throat and added, "He says we must take control of the lakeshore settlements before we can attack Tenochtitlan. The *altepetl* depends on trade and must be cut off from all trading partners. We must isolate the city before we lay siege to it."

Cortés flared his nostrils. Taking control of all the lakeshore settlements would take weeks, if not months. *Can I hold the army together that long?* Since his fever broke, he had to put down two different mutinies. None of them had amounted to anything serious, but he had no wish to try the patience of his men.

It pained him to admit it, but they did not love him as they once did. Despite the victories in Otampan and Tepeaca, many refused to forgive him the Sad Night. They would not forgive him until Tenochtitlan sued for peace, and they might not even forgive him then. Cortés sighed. He had never suffered for a shortage of detractors, and he would not let their pessimism thwart his ambitions. Forming a pact with Ixtli was more important than mollifying the malcontents. "Does Ixtli have any suggestions as to which lakeshore settlements we ought to attack first? We would be pleased to offer counsel in this regard as certain cities are richer than others."

Ixtli shook his head and spat out a rapid stream of sentences. "He says he has no use for our counsel," Tapia translated. "He will decide with his own warriors which cities ought to be attacked. He says he would be honored to receive our assistance, but he will take lakeshore settlements with or without our help."

A thunderous silence filled the room. Ixtli wasn't just rejecting an alliance; he was suggesting he had no need for Spanish aid. Cortés was nothing more than a lackey to him, a mere means to an end. Numb with shock, Cortés stared at Ixtli.

Ixtli grinned, clearly relishing his dismay. Embarrassed, Cortés turned away. When he still lived in Medellin, he spent many hours by the riverside. The Guadiana often froze come winter, and he ventured onto the ice to test its strength. One day, it cracked and splintered, forcing a profound choice on him: he could give in to panic and run, or he could heed the voice of caution and prostrate himself on the ice.

He chose the latter and slither-crawled his way to safety. A few days later, he developed a chill that left him bedridden for most of Easter week. He never told anybody how close he came to falling through the ice, never told anybody how close he had come to dying that chilly winter day.

Cortés sucked in a deep breath. It didn't matter what he wanted. He turned his gaze back to Ixtli and did his best to match his stare. "We will assist you in attacking some of the lakeshore settlements. In exchange, we ask your assistance when we lay siege to Tenochtitlan. Is Ixtli willing to agree to these terms?"

Tapia passed on his words and Cortés held his breath as he waited for an answer. "Ixtli wants to know what you will do after Tenochtitlan falls."

Cortés had been asking himself the same question of late. Not so long ago, he would have said he intended to stay in Mexico for the rest of his life. But that was before the Sad Night, before he realized the Indians had played him false. He was tired of campaign life, tired of always having to be on edge. He prayed every day for a swift end to the war, but God did not pay his incessant requests much mind.

"I will return home with my riches from Tenochtitlan and enjoy a life of leisure," Cortés said.

Ixtli nodded once he heard the translation and gave Tapia a new statement to translate. "Ixtli is honored to accept our aid. He promises to lead us to a glorious victory, and he is glad you have the good sense to let Tetzcoco play the lead role in the battles to come."

Cortés opened his mouth to correct him, to let him know that Tetzcoco actually served Spain, but he found himself unable to utter the words. They tasted false on his own tongue and would sound no better. Whether or not he was willing to admit it, he might only play a small role in the war for Tenochtitlan.

Chapter 10

Cotton Flower shivered as a gust of wind raced across Lake Tetzcoco's still surface. The open boat provided little protection from the elements, and her dress did not provide much either.

If Cuauhtemoc was cold, he did not show it. He radiated more heat than a furnace. She considered moving closer to him. Better not to. Such brazenness would be unseemly. She was a princess and had to observe a certain amount of propriety.

At least, that's what others told her. She herself was not convinced. The barbarians had wrought great change in Tenochtitlan, none of it good, and she found it ridiculous that so many expected her to keep with tradition. Tradition had done nothing to prevent Great Speaker Cuitlahuac from succumbing to the ravages of the Great Rash, nor had it done anything to prevent the fall of Tetzcoco.

Cotton Flower let out a deep breath. A part of her still could not believe the barbarians had taken the *altepetl* so fast. Tetzcoco boasted a mighty military, second only to Tenochtitlan, but the brave warriors of Tetzcoco did not lift a finger to stop the barbarians from entering the city. Instead, they welcomed the barbarians with open arms.

Once the *pilli* discovered their treachery, they fled the city for Tenochtitlan. Hundreds upon hundreds took to their canoes to escape, but many *pilli* dawdled too long and were captured as they tried to flee. She hoped the barbarians had taken mercy on them, but she knew from firsthand experience how cruel they could be.

"How long will it take to recapture Tetzcoco?" Cotton Flower asked.

A dark look passed over Cuauhtemoc's face. "It could take years."

Cotton Flower blinked. "But it fell to the barbarians so fast…."

"The barbarians had the Great Rash for an ally. And Ixtli."

Cotton Flower nodded. The Great Rash made for a powerful ally, but Ixtli made for an even better one. Were it not for Motecuhzoma's diplomacy, he would have become ruler of Tetzcoco long before. Had Father erred by meddling in the succession of Tetzcoco? At the time, nobody in Tenochtitlan thought so.

On the contrary, Motecuhzoma's intervention was hailed as political genius. But that memory belonged to a different time, a different world. One in which Tenochtitlan reigned supreme, and people not of the One World were as unimportant as they were unknown.

Something bumped against the side of the canoe, scattering her thoughts. She peered over the edge of the boat, heart in her throat. Some said crocodiles could still be found in Lake Tetzcoco. To her relief, she espied nothing of the sort. She settled back into her seat and chided herself for being ridiculous.

If there had ever been crocodiles in Lake Tetzcoco, they had long since vanished. She did not know if such things could happen naturally, but she suspected that able hunters and concerned *pilli* might have helped the process along. Crocodiles were majestic animals, but they were also dangerous. To live side by side with them would have been unthinkable.

Even more unthinkable, however, would be trying to do the same with the barbarians. There was once a time where it might have been possible, yet that time had come and gone, like the rains of the previous season. But as long as the barbarians held Tetzcoco, the people of Tenochtitlan would have to accustom themselves to having an avowed enemy as a neighbor.

"Do you think the barbarians will attack soon?" Cotton Flower asked, her gaze fixed on Tetzcoco's distant profile. In times past, the rowers would have gladly taken her to the shoreline. The aqueducts of Tetzcoco were famous throughout the One World, and the *altepetl* was renowned for its beauty. She suspected, however, the barbarians would care little for such matters. They cared only for gold and slaves.

"Princess, are you sure you wish to know the answer?" Cuauhtemoc asked.

Cotton Flower mulled his question. Cuauhtemoc had been chosen as Great Speaker shortly after Cuitlahuac died, and he received reports from every corner of the One World. Seldom did he share that information with her, but she suspected that little of it was good. "Yes, I am sure. I cannot prepare myself for the future otherwise."

"Tenochtitlan has never been taken by force. We have had months to prepare for an attack, and the barbarians will suffer greatly if they try to invade our city. Our allies, however, are not as safe."

Cotton Flower pressed her lips into a thin line. Refugees from the eastern lands had been pouring into Tenochtitlan for weeks, and they brought the most terrible stories with them. Some of the *pilli* were so unsettled by their accounts they agitated against their entry. Thus far, Cuauhtemoc had resisted such calls, but pressure was mounting for him to change course. Many of the refugees arrived with nothing on their backs save empty baskets and wailing children. Even in a time of plenty, they would have been looked upon askance but in a time of disrupted trade routes and food shortages, they were despised by many. Despite all his reasons not to, Cuauhtemoc continued to grant them entry and assured the malcontents the refugees would help protect Tenochtitlan against barbarian raids.

Cotton Flower turned toward Cuauhtemoc. Numerous weeks had passed since their marriage ceremony, but they were strangers in many respects. They had never shared a kiss, a hug, or even a longing glance, and she did not expect that to soon change. He married her for political gain, not romantic interest, and probably had little interest in her body.

At least, she hoped that was true. The prospect of sharing her body with him frightened her dearly. Cuauhtemoc helped rescue her from the barbarians and had been nothing but kind to her, but he was also ten years her senior and two heads taller than her.

Besides that, they were little alike. He had thighs as thick as tree trunks; her legs were thin as kindling. Her chest was flat as a board; his chest bulged with muscle. And his hands! They were big enough to cup a melon. *Will I ever welcome his touch?* She shook her head and dismissed those thoughts from her head. "Where will the barbarians attack next?"

"Whichever nations have not submitted to them already." Cuauhtemoc smiled sadly. "I do not intend to sit by as the barbarians consolidate their strength, though."

Cotton Flower's chest tightened. "What do you mean?"

"We are not strong enough to launch an offensive against the barbarians yet, but we cannot allow them free movement. I intend to leave the city on the morrow—"

"You cannot," Cotton Flower said.

Cuauhtemoc turned toward her. "Why not?"

Cotton Flower bit her tongue and cursed herself for being so impetuous. She had important information for Cuauhtemoc, the type of information best given in a private setting. She shot a quick glance at the men sitting in the canoe with her. Could they be trusted? Most of them were strangers to her, but she knew they had served Cuauhtemoc for many years. If Cuauhtemoc considered them loyal, she also had to extend them her trust.

She tucked her hair behind her ear and straightened her back. "Events of late have been most trying for the city." Cuauhtemoc clenched his jaw shut and Cotton Flower waited to see if he would say anything. He stayed silent, so she continued, "Many have given in to despair and wish for peace."

Cuauhtemoc snorted. "How can we have peace with a people who mean to enslave us?"

"We cannot," Cotton Flower said, surprised by the certainty in her own voice. "Unfortunately, my brothers do not understand that."

"Your brothers?"

"Yes, my own kin." Cotton Flower looked down at her wrists, still scarred by the manacles that had been forced onto her so long ago. She had tried so very hard to see things as her brothers did, all to no avail. "My brothers are convinced battle would be calamitous and believe we must surrender to the barbarians. They believe if we give them our gold and our jade, we can prevent them from sacking the city. They mean to marry me, and others, to any barbarians willing to have us."

Cuauhtemoc's eyes bulged out as if he had swallowed a wasp. "Your brothers would have you marry a barbarian even after…"

Cotton Flower nodded, thankful he did not say the words. "My brothers think that I should welcome such a match. They believe it will help save Tenochtitlan and tell me I should be pleased by it. They were kind enough to remind me that a dishonored princess cannot expect choice pickings."

"A drooling babe knows more about honor than any of your brothers."

Cotton Flower sighed. Not so long ago, she would have risen to their defense. But the love she once bore them was no more. Treason could not be forgiven nor forgotten. "If you leave the city, they will take advantage of your absence to send peace envoys to the barbarians. They are convinced we will suffer even worse than Tepeaca if we fight them."

"It is because of Tepeaca we must fight!" Cuauhtemoc shouted. "No people are safe from the barbarians, and I will kill the fool who says otherwise. How many villages need to be raided, how many more settlements need to be destroyed for others to understand? Tepeaca was attacked simply for daring to exist."

"Cuauhtemoc, I know," Cotton Flower said, her tone more curt than she intended. She laid her hand on Cuauhtemoc's scarred hand. "Why else would I tell you of my brother's intentions?"

"Forgive me for losing my temper. I know you speak true, and thank you for the news you have brought me." Cuauhtemoc let out a deep breath, his voice heavy with dejection and regret. "What your brothers are contemplating is treason. An offense that extreme can only be punished one way."

Cotton Flower stiffened. There was once a time when she would not have understood what Cuauhtemoc was implying, but those days were long past. The barbarians had degraded her in the worst possible ways, and she understood the ugliness of the world better than men twice her age. Her brothers played at wisdom, but they would never understand what she had endured, nor would they want to.

A pang of guilt extinguished her budding indignation. Her brothers were misguided, but she knew they were not motivated by malice. Was she wrong to betray them to Cuauhtemoc?

She hoped not. More than anything, however, Cotton Flower hoped for victory. The Great Rash had finally abated, and Tenochtitlan was slowly recovering. Whether it took weeks or months, the Mexica would regain their former supremacy and destroy the barbarians once and for all. Cuauhtemoc would not allow Tenochtitlan to fall to the barbarians, she was sure of it.

"Do what must be done, husband."

~ ~ ~

Pozon carefully set his foot down on the next stair. He strained his ears for anything amiss. The *teteo* were rifling through the downstairs section of the house, but the upstairs portion was dead quiet.

He took another step forward. A loud clattering made him freeze. After a moment, he realized the sound had been caused by Estrada and Farfán. He took a deep breath. His *teteo* masters had ordered him to search the upper floor for loot, and he needed to put aside his fear. He needed to be brave. Like Yaotl, right before the *teteo* cut her hand off.

Pozon marched up the rest of the stairs and advanced toward the closet room. What if a Mexica warrior was hiding inside? They were nothing if not sneaky. Earlier in the day, they had launched a surprise attack as the *teteo* and their allies marched for Iztapalapa. They had not attacked in great enough numbers to prevent the *teteo* from reaching Iztapalapa, but they did succeed in irritating them greatly.

By the time the *teteo* reached Iztapalapa, they were so wroth they ransacked everything in sight. The Tlaxcalteca and the Tetzcocans were all too eager to join in and seized everything they could get their hands on. Try as they might, they could not find any slaves to capture, though. The locals had fled the city long before the soldiers arrived, leaving behind almost everything they owned to the *teteo* and their allies.

Pozon stopped outside the room. He needed to be certain there was nothing scary on the other side of the wall. Careful to keep most of himself hidden, he peeked around the corner. Something gray and large caught his eye, and he hid once more.

Unless his eyes were playing tricks on him, somebody was inside the room. He took a step backward, then another. His heart was thumping against his chest like a mallet. He let his heartbeat slow and tried to think of what he should do. Perhaps he should alert the *teteo* downstairs?

He shook his head. No, that would be folly. He had to make sure there was someone in the room before he went to them for help. If he distracted the *teteo* from their looting for nothing, they would lash him without mercy. Pozon squared his shoulders. He would have to investigate the room himself. He stole forward on the balls of his feet and pressed himself against the wall. He crept toward the door and craned his head to the side so he could peer inside the room again.

Not a warrior in sight, no matter where he looked. His gaze drifted to the bed. A pile of bones lay atop the blankets. No, not a pile; a skeleton. Of a person. Curious, he crept forward.

When he had been much younger, he and Yaotl had found the skeleton of a massive bird in the grasslands near their house. The skeleton became their shared secret and they visited it together for weeks on end, carefully unearthing every bone. They discovered it had a beak as long as an oar and a wingspan that stretched the length of a canoe from tip to tip, something that seemed both impossible and wondrous. Then the rains came and washed all trace of it away, leaving him with a strange ache in the pit of his stomach.

Pozon squatted in front of the skeleton. It was small, only a little bigger than him. The ornate bed frame made it clear, however, the person belonged to the *pilli* class. The reed mat wasn't one mat so much as many mats woven together, and the thick blankets were nicer than any Pozon had ever possessed. *Pilli* were usually immolated upon death. Why hadn't this one been given that honor?

He scanned the room for clues. There was a shallow pan at the foot of the bed for night soil, and the walls were adorned with greenstone masks and mosaic discs. He studied the items close at hand. Next to the bed, there was a three-legged bowl. He leaned forward so he could see inside it. His stomach dropped. The bowl was full almost to the brim with crushed beetles.

Pozon rose to his feet. Crushed beetles were often used to treat victims of the Great Rash. He retreated toward the hallway and did not stop until he felt his back press against solid stone. He exhaled and clenched his teeth to keep from shivering. His gaze wandered to the other rooms. Would there be skeletons in those rooms also? Perhaps the whole household had succumbed to the Great Rash. He had heard of such things happening and had seen firsthand what the Great Rash could do to its victims.

Yaotl, please take me from this terrible place. Yaotl, please guide me home.

The loud blaring of a conch grabbed his attention. He stopped shivering and tried to focus his thoughts. The sound had come from outside the house. Was it a call to arms? Perhaps the Mexica were attacking. Another conch sounded, and another one after that.

Pozon turned so he could stare out the window. Like Tenochtitlan, Iztapalapa was built on the water and crisscrossed by an intricate system of canals. Most were so wide they could accommodate multiple canoes, and could hold incredible amounts of water. Today, they were full to the brim. He glanced up at the dark clouds overhead. A light rain was coming down, but nothing heavy enough to cause a flood. So why were the canals so full?

Another conch shell sounded, and loot-bearing soldiers streamed into the streets. After a few moments, Estrada and Farfán wandered outside. Estrada turned around and quickly fixed her gaze on him. She motioned for him to come, and he trudged toward the stairs. A treacherous thought occurred to him as he descended the steps: the house was very big and had many hiding places.

He stopped in the middle of the stairs and glanced behind him. None of the *teteo* had followed him up, and there were only a few downstairs. Would they search for him, if he tried to hide? If an attack were truly imminent, they would be concerned only for themselves. They would probably spend no more than a few moments searching for him, if that.

But if he abandoned the *teteo*, he would be abandoning his sister also. He had no idea where she was, if she was even alive, but he knew he would never get the answers to those questions if he stayed in Iztapalapa. No matter how much the *teteo* abused him, he had to keep faith. Otherwise, he would never learn their language or their ways. And without that information, he would never find out what had happened to Yaotl.

Having made up his mind, Pozon hurried down the stairs and ran outside to find his masters. Estrada—deep in conversation with her husband, Farfán—had not moved from her spot beneath the window. She spared Pozon not one word as he approached and did not even deign a glance his way.

A powerful anger took hold of him. He was nothing to Estrada and Farfán. He would never merit their attention, not unless he did something wrong. Or tried to run away. Pozon clenched his fists. He needed to stay loyal to the *teteo*, but that did not mean he had to stay with Estrada and Farfán forever. One day, he would find a way to escape them.

Another conch shell sounded. Farfán and Estrada began talking more loudly, but he could not make out their words. Pozon hissed in frustration. If they just spoke a little slower, he would understand them!

Teteo on the other side of the canal started shouting at one other. They seemed more confused than alarmed, but the shouting made Pozon uneasy. A few of them pointed at the canal. It was *spilli*ng over on both sides now, submerging the hard-packed walkways.

Off in another section of the city, the Tetzcocan warriors and the Tlaxcalteca shouted warnings in Nahuatl. One refrain cut through the rest: the dike has been sabotaged.

The air rushed from Pozon's lungs. Of course, the canals were flooding; if the dike was sabotaged, it would not be long before water reclaimed the city completely. In a matter of hours, it might become impossible to escape on foot.

Pozon tapped Estrada on the arm. Before she could react, Farfán wheeled around and grabbed him by the ear. He yanked downward and screamed, "You do not ever touch my wife! Do it again, and I will cut your hand off." Farfán yanked again, and the pain was so intense it robbed Pozon of his breath. "Do you understand?"

He squeezed his ear. Pozon grimaced and said in Spanish, "Staying here not safe."

Farfán released his ear and took a step back. He glanced at Estrada, then back to him. "What mean you?"

"The dike is broken," Pozon said, his ear still throbbing. "The water going to keep rising—"

"And it will become impossible to escape the city," Estrada finished.

Farfán and Estrada exchanged a worried glance. More conch shells blared to life, prompting shouts in Nahuatl and Spanish. More *teteo* came stumbling out of the house Estrada and Farfán had been looting.

"Leave the loot," Estrada ordered. "The city is flooding, and we need to make haste if we are to escape." Estrada began rummaging through one of her husband's bags. She pulled out a cotton gambeson and threw it to Pozon. "Put this on. The Mexica might try to attack us as we retreat to high ground."

Pozon rubbed the material. A cotton gambeson was almost as valuable as steel mail. Some of the *teteo* even preferred it to mail as it was much lighter but still effective against darts and the like. He tried to think of something to say, yet his tongue failed him. He had never owned anything near as fine, nor had he ever expected to receive such a splendid gift from Estrada of all people.

"You made yourself useful today," Estrada explained. "Put that on and stay close to us; you might survive that way. But remember my husband's warning. Because if he does not cut your hand off, I will."

Pozon did not doubt that Estrada or Farfán would follow through on their threats. He slid the gambeson over his head and slipped his arm through the sleeves. It was far too big, but he did not mind. He did not care how it looked, only that it protected him darts and arrows. He forced a smile and looked up at Estrada.

"Thank you, Master. I will remember your kindness always."

Chapter 11

Cuauhtemoc inspected the ransacked village with a handful of warriors. It had once been a home to hundreds of people, but not a single person had been found within any of the wattle and daub homes. At least, none that were alive.

He had inspected enough ransacked villages to know the barbarians rarely left survivors. He also knew they had become much more careful as of late. No longer did the barbarians lay siege to the large settlements built on the water; instead, they raided the small and medium-sized settlements that dotted the lakeshores. It was a cautious strategy, but a smart one. And one they had hewed to most closely ever since their near-defeat at Iztapalapa.

Cuauhtemoc ground his teeth together. He wanted to hit something whenever he thought about Iztapalapa. They had come so close to killing Ixtli and Cortés that day. Unfortunately, both had escaped, and they were now wreaking havoc throughout the One World.

A strong gust of wind carried the stench of death and panic to his nose. He wrinkled his nose in disgust. Many of his warriors had covered their faces with cotton garments to block the terrible smells, but he could not bring himself to do the same. He needed to experience the carnage firsthand, needed to see what happened to settlements that fell to the barbarians. Otherwise, he might succumb to the wishful thinking that Motecuhzoma's sons had given in to. He mourned for them, but he did not regret killing them. Infections were deadly when they were allowed to spread, and he had learned from years of battle that it was better to remove an infected appendage early on.

Cuauhtemoc rubbed his temple. He could feel a headache coming on and slowed his pace. He had not been sleeping much of late, a marked change for him. Usually, he slept best on campaign, but his sleep had taken a turn for the worse since leaving Tenochtitlan.

Much as he wished otherwise, the lakeshore settlements had proven difficult to defend. Oftentimes, he did not know which settlement the barbarians would attack until it was too late. Worse yet, many of the lakeshore settlements were voluntarily submitting to the barbarians to spare themselves the indignity of invasion.

To prevent others from doing so, Cuauhtemoc had offered loyal vassals a years' exemption from tribute. Unfortunately, the enticement did not seem to matter much, and it seemed a new *altepetl* defected to the barbarians every week. Once the barbarians gained a secure foothold in the lakeshore settlements, they would be sure to launch an attack on Tenochtitlan. Cuauhtemoc clenched his fist. He felt as if a cord were being tightened around his neck, and it frustrated him to no end that he could not do more to protect Tenochtitlan.

The honk of a gibbon split the air. Cuauhtemoc glanced over his shoulder. Somebody was signaling for attention, but they would have honked twice if an enemy was nearby. Unsure what to expect, he made his way toward the sound.

Cuauhtemoc turned the corner of a building, his hand wrapped around the hilt of his *macuahuitl*. A group of his warriors were conferring with one another, and their lack of alarm put him at ease. One of the warriors, Ollin, turned his way as he approached and broke off from the group to intercept him.

"Did somebody signal for attention?"

"Yes," Ollin replied. "A relay runner has arrived with a message from the *teteo*."

Cuauhtemoc narrowed his eyes. A sour taste filled his mouth. A message from the *teteo* did not bode well. "Bring him to me."

Ollin nodded and hurried off. Cuauhtemoc sighed and wiped his brow. Tonatiuh had already set, but the day's heat still lingered in the air. *What I would give for a cold downpour or a small breeze.*

The relay runner, directed by Ollin, trudged toward Cuauhtemoc. He was drenched with sweat and completely unarmed, but Cuauhtemoc's guards huddled closer as he approached. Once he came within five paces of Cuauhtemoc, the guards ordered him to humble himself.

The weary runner did so without hesitation and rubbed his fingers in the dirt. He brought them up to his lips to show obeisance, but Cuauhtemoc lost his patience and ordered the man to stop.

"Tell me your message," Cuauhtemoc commanded.

The messenger stared at the ground. Whether he did so out of fear or respect, Cuauhtemoc could not tell. After a long pause, he finally said, "Your envoys to Willow Grove and Snake Den have been captured."

Cuauhtemoc sucked in a sharp breath. He felt as if he had been kicked in the stomach. He had handpicked each envoy, confident they could evade enemy patrols. They had served him ably in times past, having braved the jungles of the Near South and the highlands of the Far East, and he could not fathom how they had been captured.

"When did the barbarians capture them?"

"They were not captured by the barbarians," the messenger replied. "The people of Willow Grove and Snake Den took them hostage to please the barbarians."

Cuauhtemoc cursed inwardly. He had been warned that Willow Grove and Snake Den might make common cause with the barbarians, but he had paid little heed to those warnings. Blood pounded in his ears, and he squeezed the hilt of his *macuahuitl* until his heartbeat calmed.

"Are they still alive?" Cuauhtemoc asked.

"Yes," the messenger said. "Cortés has a message for you, if you wish to hear it."

Cuauhtemoc stiffened. "I do not wish to hear it… but tell me all the same."

"The *teteo* say they will release the envoys if Tenochtitlan surrenders before the next moon. If we honor them as our masters, Tenochtitlan will be spared attack. Should we refuse to surrender, they will lay siege to the city. None will be spared if they have to take the city by force."

Cuauhtemoc clenched his teeth. *The barbarians must think me a complete fool.* Even if he were to surrender on the morrow, it would count for little with the barbarians. *The Tlaxcalteca will never forgive us the sanctions, the teteo will never forgive us the Night of Glory, and the Tetzcoco will never forgive us our past glories.* Only victory would prevent Tenochtitlan from suffering the same fate as Tepeaca. It did not matter that victory became less likely with each new moon; he had to fight anyway.

"Thank you for bringing me this message," Cuauhtemoc said, forcing some cordiality into his voice. "You have done the nation a great service."

The messenger nodded. "Do you have an answer for the *teteo*?"

Cuauhtemoc glanced at the ruins of the ransacked town. Had the people tried to surrender? Perhaps they had, perhaps they hadn't. Impossible to know either way. His people had searched all evening for survivors and found nothing besides picked-over corpses and ash. "My answer is no. Tenochtitlan has never been taken by siege, and the barbarians will suffer greatly if they try to take our city by force. Do not worry about carrying a message back. They will have my reply soon enough."

Cuauhtemoc lifted his *macuahuitl* to study its edge. He replaced the obsidian shards after every battle, but there had been few major engagements since the battle at Iztapalapa. Much as he wanted to attack the barbarian camp at Tetzcoco, he knew better than to attack a fortified position with a small force. He did not dare assemble a large force for an attack, either; the memories of Otampan were still too fresh.

Nonetheless, he had no intention of allowing the barbarians a free hand. They had become accustomed to easy victories against defenseless settlements, and he had intended to use that arrogance against them. The barbarians could not always travel in large parties. When they made the mistake of venturing off by themselves, they would be vulnerable.

Ambushing small parties was a terrible, cowardly way to win a war, but he did not care. So long as Tenochtitlan triumphed, nothing else mattered.

~ ~ ~

Xicotencatl scooted closer to his countrymen as Sandóval, seated upon a chestnut horse, raced alongside the column bound for Tlaxcala. Sandóval seemed more comfortable in a saddle than he did on his own feet and never missed a chance to clamber onto a mount. He seemed to prefer horses to people, but the same held true for many of the *teteo*. If Xicotencatl lived to twenty times five, he would never understand all their customs, nor would he want to. Nonetheless, he would not deny they had good reason to love their horses.

Mounted men, when given an open field and level ground, were practically invulnerable if they took the time to put on armor and stayed in formation. They could wreak havoc against an enemy army, but they were even more deadly when deployed against a defenseless settlement. People throughout the One World were learning that terrible truth, and Xicotencatl pitied the poor fools who thought they were safe from the *teteo*.

His own people, the mighty Tlaxcalteca, were convinced they were safe from the *teteo* because they had been such faithful allies, but he knew a day would come when they would rue the alliance. The only question was when.

People like Father disagreed, however. They were sure only good things would come of the alliance with the *teteo* and rejoiced every time a new water-house brought more *teteo* from beyond the mists. Xicotencatl was willing to concede that Tlaxcala had gained a great deal of power on account of the *teteo*, but he did not care for the alliance. He liked even less that the Tlaxcalteca had agreed to help the *teteo* construct a fleet. Helping the *teteo* build siege weapons struck him as foolish, dangerous even. The more weapons the *teteo* acquired, the more difficult it would be to expel them from the One World.

Xicotencatl coughed and wiped his nose. The column was kicking up an incredible amount of dust, and he would be most glad once they reached Tlaxcala. He wished he did not have to suffer the presence of the *teteo*, but he would not deny they made for useful guards. He had heard too many stories about small groups of men disappearing when they ventured off by themselves.

The *teteo* were outraged the Mexica would make use of such cowardly tactics and cursed them to that place they called hell. Xicotencatl could not muster the same outrage himself. Were he in the same position as Cuauhtemoc, he would have done the same.

"Movement ahead," shouted a Tlaxcalteca warrior.

Xicotencatl shaded his eyes. He had been so lost in his thoughts he had not noticed the dust cloud further up the road. Even a large caravan would not kick up half as much dust. It could only be an army that was approaching them, and a large one at that.

Xicotencatl reached for his bow. He doubted the Mexica would attack the column—not in the middle of the day, not in the middle of an open field—but he knew that desperation could drive warriors to all kinds of madness. His guards began readying their own weapons. If the Mexica meant to attack the formation head on, they would soon regret it.

Sandóval raced ahead to intercept the scouts hurrying back to the column. He exchanged only a few words with them, nothing Xicotencatl could hear, before he turned around and shouted something in his strange tongue.

A great cheer went up at the sound of his voice. Xicotencatl relaxed his shoulders. He understood little of the *teteo* tongue, but he knew they would not cheer for a Mexica army.

Xicotencatl glanced to his right. He wanted to get a better view of the approaching army and could not do that on level ground. None of the trees nearby had branches low enough for climbing, but the trees up ahead would suit his needs just fine. He whispered a few commands to men nearby and peeled off from the main column.

Two men trailed behind him, young Otomis whom he only recently accepted into his service, as he made his way toward the grove of pine trees. Without saying a word to either of them, he jumped for a nearby branch. Before either of his guards could offer assistance, he planted both his feet against the trunk and scrambled upward.

The sudden exertion winded him, and he perched himself on a thick branch to catch his breath. A smile crossed his lips. One of the guards seemed rather upset the tree lacked for footholds. He stared upward. The tree had plenty of footholds, if one knew how to look for them. Nature offered its bounties free to everyone, but only the learned knew how to appreciate them.

Xicotencatl wrapped his hand around a nearby branch and looked for another branch to latch onto. A sharp stinging distracted him, and he glanced at his hand. A large red ant had crawled onto his finger and bitten him on the knuckle. He raised his other hand to crush it but mercy stayed his arm. The ant was only trying to protect its territory.

He flicked the ant off and resumed his climb. The branches thinned as he climbed higher, but he did not stop until he was almost eighty hands high. He closed his eyes and sucked in a deep breath, flooding his nostrils with the pleasing smell of sap and resin. A man could feel strong when surrounded by his countrymen, but he could only feel at peace when surrounded by nature.

The sound of his Otomi guards disturbed his reverie, and he opened his eyes. A brilliant array of colors flooded his vision, and he waited for his eyes to adjust to the mid-day brightness. A vast expanse of grasslands and foothills and mountains stretched out before him. It would have been a beautiful sight, were it not for the giant army marching toward him.

If he squinted, he could spot individual faces amongst the vanguard. Most of them appeared to be Tlaxcalteca, and few of them carried weapons. Instead, they carried crates and barrels and ropes and a litany of other items. The vast majority, however, carried heavy cuts of timber that curved like giant rib bones.

Somehow, all those items would be combined together to make the double-decked water-houses. A knot of dread formed in his stomach. The fleet wasn't supposed to be ready for transport yet, wasn't supposed to be ready for another moon or so. A sudden wave of dizziness grabbed hold of him. Once again, he had underestimated the *teteo*.

He tightened his grip on the branch above him. Once the fleet could be put to water, the *teteo* could use the water-houses to attack Tenochtitlan. If the water-houses were as powerful as they claimed, the Mexica would not be able to hold out for long. Sooner or later, Tenochtitlan would fall. And once that happened, the *teteo* would be sure to cast their greedy eyes elsewhere. To Tlaxcala perhaps.

One of his guards clambered onto a branch next to him. Xicotencatl did not even spare him a glance, his gaze affixed to the twisting, snaking procession of porters and warriors.

The guard next to him coughed. "I hear the procession is being called a wooden serpent."

Xicotencatl squeezed the branch above his head. Yes, that's exactly what it was. And soon it would be released into the waters of Lake Tetzcoco.

"It's beautiful," the other guard said, his voice colored with awe.

Xicotencatl could think of many words to describe the wooden serpent splayed out before him but beautiful was not one of them.

Chapter 12

Pozon smashed his wooden sword against the ribs of his defenseless dummy. The cloth dummy, fixed in place with an oak stake, did not budge.

He retreated a few paces and adjusted his helmet. Farfán and Estrada said it was unfair that the others had Indians to protect them and insisted he learn how to use a sword. They were, of course, too important to give him lessons, but they assured him he could learn on his own. After all, Estrada had little in the way of formal training and she was one of the best sword hands in all the crew.

Pozon squeezed the sword hilt and stabbed it into the dummy's torso. He twisted the sword, but the fabric caught the blade mid-turn, sending a sudden pain through his forearm. He dropped the practice weapon. It landed next to his feet, and he kicked outward in a fit of rage. The wooden sword sailed through the air and landed amongst the corn stalks.

He turned his frustration on the dummy and pummeled it with his bare fists. He poured all of his pent-up fury into each hit, pounding with all his might. By the time he was finished, his arms were burning like fire and felt heavy as copper weights. The dummy, however, looked none the worse.

A bead of sweat rolled into his eye, and he adjusted his helmet to wipe the sweat from his brow. The snapping of a stick caught his attention, and he dropped into a crouch.

Was somebody watching him? He glanced over his shoulder. He had set up the dummy next to a stand of pine trees, and the nearest tent was fifty paces away. His goal had been to find a place far enough from camp for privacy, but close enough that he could make it back easily. *Perhaps I should have stayed closer.*

Pozon scanned the corn field for danger. The immature stalks did not rise much higher than his head, but he could hide among them if he needed to. A bead of sweat trickled down his face. What good would hiding do if the Mexica attacked with a full army?

His heart pounded in his ears. The thought of being taken captive by the Mexica made his knees shake. They did awful, terrible things to their captives. All the *teteo* said so, and so did Yaotl.

A lump formed in his throat. It had been so long since he had seen his sister, Yaotl. He missed her every day. He tried to think of what Yaotl would do if she were with him. It was pointless, though. Yaotl would have never allowed herself to become a slave. He closed his eyes and pushed those thoughts from his head. It would not help to think like that, not right now.

Yaotl would find a way to defend herself, that's what she would do. Pozon gritted his teeth and cursed himself for kicking his sword. Sure that no good would come from hiding, he waded through the thick stalks in search of his sword.

He wiped his clammy hands on his shoulders. The *teteo* pretended there was no reason to be scared of the Mexica, but they were wrong. The *teteo* were very good at their lightning attacks, they could reach almost anywhere with their hornless stags, but that did not mean they were safe from sneak attacks. Juan Yuste tried making his way through the mountains with a force of fifty men, but not one of his men made it through safely. Some of the *teteo* said Yuste and his men had been skinned alive. A frisson of fear stole up his spine.

Voices drifted toward him. Pozon tensed. Somebody was speaking Nahuatl, but they were struggling to get their words out. A woman with a soft voice interjected, and the sound of her voice banished Pozon's fears. He knew that voice well; it belonged to Malintze. That other voice must have been one of her guards. He straightened his back and chided himself for being silly. Malintze had been nothing but kind to him, and there was no need to be afraid of her.

Malintze's guards said something about feathers and made a hushed raspy sound. Pozon scratched his neck. Why would they mention feathers?

Pozon reached for his helmet. The plume! He had forgotten all about the feathers sticking out of his helmet. If they were poking above the corn stalks, the guard must have seen them.

Pozon smiled. He was no good at hiding. Thankfully, there was no need to hide from Malintze. She was always so nice and kind.

A *teotl* grabbed Pozon from behind and threw him to the ground. He tried to scramble to his feet, but a knee pressed into his neck with so much force it drove the air from his lungs. The *teotl* grabbed his helmet and ripped it off.

He shouted strange *teteo* words, but his speech was garbled and nonsensical. He smashed the helmet into the ground, right next to Pozon's face. Pozon tried to wriggle out from underneath the *teotl's* knee. The *teotl* responded by pressing his knee down harder. Pozon went still. The *teotl* muttered the word slave, grabbed Pozon by the nape of his neck, and pulled him to his feet.

The *teotl* hauled him onto the walking path and forced him into a kneeling position. The *teotl* shouted the word runaway, and a heated argument ensued between him and Malintze. Pozon kept his eyes fixed on the ground, wishing he was anywhere else. The *teotl* dug his foot into the back of Pozon's knee, and Pozon had to bite his lip from crying out.

Malintze shouted at the *teotl* in Spanish, and he went stiff as a board. He let go of Pozon's neck and threw the helmet to the ground before storming off. Malintze dismissed her other guard and squatted in front of Pozon.

She put her finger under his chin and lifted his head. "How fare you?"

Pozon turned away, too shamefaced to make eye contact. He wished he could dredge the tears in his eyes. Grownups could always tell when he was upset, and he hated the pitying looks they gave him. He clenched his eyes shut and sucked in air through his nose until his heart calmed.

When he opened his eyes again, Malintze handed him a water gourd and he accepted it with some trepidation. He took only a small sip before handing it back.

"My guards should not have been so rough with you," she said. "They thought you stole the helmet and that you were running away—" Pozon gaped at Malintze open-mouthed, too scared to form words. Runaways could be punished in a variety of ways, but they were often punished with the axe. "They are not going to hobble you," Malintze added hurriedly. "I explained to them you weren't running away and won't let them hurt you."

Malintze smiled at him and rubbed his back. Her gentle touch put him at ease, and he moved his hurt leg so he was no longer sitting on it. He could feel a bruise forming already and did not think he could walk just yet.

"What are you doing out here by yourself?"

"Estrada and Farfán told me to practice fighting." Pozon wiped his runny nose and swallowed the lump in his throat. "I set up a dummy to practice by the oak tree."

Malintze nodded. "You want to be a warrior, then? Like all the other boys."

Pozon shook his head. "Estrada and Farfán told me I had to practice sword fighting. They gave me the dummy and told me to come back at dark. I'd rather be at camp. I want to be a translator one day. Like you."

Malintze's face darkened. "Trust me, Pozon. You do not want to be like me."

Pozon furrowed his brow. Why would she say something so strange? Of course he wanted to be like her. He would never want to be like Farfán and Estrada. They were cruel and spiteful, and he hated everything about them.

Unsure what to say, Pozon grabbed the helmet and checked it for damage. The plume was a little ruffled, but it looked fine otherwise. He turned the helmet over. The chin strap was broken! His mouth went dry. When Estrada found out, she would be sure to punish him. The only question was whether she used a switch or a whip.

"What's wrong?" Malintze asked.

"The chin strap," Pozon whimpered.

"Here, let me see it. Perhaps I can help."

Pozon handed it over with some reluctance, and watched as Malintze inspected the helmet. She froze once she took in the feathered plume.

"Where did you get this?" Malintze asked, her voice choked and small.

"Farfán got the helmet from one of his Sevillo friends. They took it from a Choluteca slut."

Malintze's eyes went wide. She stared at him as if he had mortally offended her, and the intensity of her gaze made him want to squirm. "What did you say?" she asked, her voice louder and more authoritative.

"He took it from a slut—"

Malintze's hand shot out fast as lightning and slapped him full in the face. Pozon reeled backward, shocked and angry.

Her composure cracked, and she broke down in tears. "I thought they would be safe," she whispered. "I thought the soldiers would spare them."

Malintze cried as if her life were ending. Too angry to offer her solace but too scared to leave her, Pozon stood and waited for her to stop crying. He sniffled, and the small sound prompted her to look up. Before he could retreat a single pace, Malintze wrapped him in a hug. "I'm sorry, Pozon. I should not have slapped you. Please forgive me."

Pozon scooted away from her. "Why did you hit me?"

"That word you used, it brings back very bad memories."

"What word?"

Malintze wiped her cheek. "Slut."

"But everyone—"

"It doesn't matter," Malintze said. "It's a mean word, and you shouldn't use it. Promise you won't speak like that anymore."

Pozon nodded. He had no idea why Malintze cared so much.

Malintze brushed dirt off his forehead. "Are Estrada and Farfán good to you?"

Pozon tensed, unsure what to say. Estrada and Farfán were anything but good to him, but he could not bring himself to say the words out loud. If he said anything bad about them, they would be sure to punish him.

"Do you want to stay with them after the war is over?"

Pozon shook his head.

Malintze brushed her hair back and cleared her throat. "After the war is over, I will be free. Cortés has promised me many riches, and I will have my own household. Would you like to have a place in my household?"

Pozon rubbed his shoulder. "What would that mean?"

"I do not know," Malintze admitted. "I have never run a household. You will be free, though; I can promise you that."

Pozon's hand flew to his cheek. "But my scar..."

"I don't care about that," Malintze said. "If you join my household, you will do so as a free person."

"Do you think Estrada and Farfán will release me?"

"Cortés owes me a great deal. If I cannot convince them to release you, I will have Cortés act on my behalf. However, I cannot do anything to help you before the war is over. You understand why, right?"

Pozon nodded. Malintze wore fine dresses and had her own detachment of guards, but she could not leave the *teteo* any more than he could. But after the war, she would be a free woman. As long as Cortés made good on his promise.

"When will the war end?" Pozon asked.

"The *teteo* think the Mexica will surrender once we take Xaltocan."

Excitement bubbled in Pozon's chest. "Estrada says we are very close to Xaltocan and that it will be easy to take the city."

"Soldiers never lack for confidence." Malintze smiled grimly and added, "Estrada is right that Xaltocan will not be able to hold out long. Tenochtitlan, however, is a much bigger *altepetl*. They have more warriors who can defend the city, and they know we will soon attack. They are probably restocking their food supplies as we speak."

A dull anger seized Pozon. Why did the Mexica insist on fighting? Life would be so much better once they stopped fighting a war they couldn't win. "When will they surrender?"

"Not for a long time, Pozon. Not for a very long time."

Chapter 13

Xicotencatl took a swig from his drinking gourd and swished the water around his mouth to clean the grime from his teeth. He leaned to the side and spat, splattering water on the spectators standing closest to him. A sharp hiss let him know that his uncouth behavior had not gone unnoticed, but none dared to openly censure him. Distinguished warriors did not have to abide by social mores, even if they came from Tlaxcala.

His heart fluttered at the thought of home. Months had passed since he last set foot in Tlaxcala, and each new battle took him farther from home. He had no idea when the campaign would end. If it ever ended. Every day it seemed a new *altepetl* was dragged into the war, and many of the warriors were shamefully giddy about the never-ending, ever-expanding nature of the conflict.

They thanked the gods battle was no longer confined to the narrow alleys of Tenochtitlan and berated him for a lack of cheer. Xicotencatl did not care. He had no wish to attack small useless islands like Xaltocan and would not pretend otherwise.

A loud chanting pulled him out of his reverie, focusing his attention on the duel in the fighting ring. Ixtli had challenged a warrior to single combat in a fight to the death, and his opponent was faring poorly. Such was to be expected. Xaltocan never boasted a great military and fell to the joint forces of the *teteo*, the Tetzcoco, and the Tlaxcalteca after a day's worth of fighting. Truth be told, Xaltocan never boasted a great anything. It was a smaller, less impressive version of Tenochtitlan and had little to offer in the way of loot.

Ixtli's opponent pushed himself off the ground and wiped away the blood dribbling down his chin. Instead of pressing the offensive, Ixtli smiled at the man and asked him if he needed a cleaning cloth.

The audience howled with laughter, and the warrior shot a baleful glare at Ixtli. He did not dare advance toward him, though. Ixtli had never been bested in single combat, and the Xaltocan warrior could not match him in strength or skill. Nor could he hope to escape. The fighting ring, a dry patch of dirt surrounded by a stone wall, afforded no place to hide. Whether he fought bravely or not, the Xaltocan warrior had little cause for hope.

Ixtli said something in a low voice, something only his opponent could hear, and the Xaltocan man went rigid as a board. To the surprise of everyone, the Xaltocan warrior threw his *macuahuitl* to the ground and dropped to a knee. The crowd went quiet. A warrior could not simply relent in the midst of a duel; it was unheard of, it was outrageous.

Ixtli flushed and screamed at the warrior to stand. The warrior stayed on his knee, silent as stone. Ixtli cursed the warrior and all his family to the worst levels of the Underworlds but still the warrior did not respond. Incensed, Ixtli advanced toward the warrior and raised his *macuahuitl* high in the air.

Before he could bring it down, the warrior did something as devious as it was genius: he threw a handful of dirt in Ixtli's face. Ixtli jumped backward to cover his face, but his pained cry made it clear he had been taken unaware. The warrior scrambled toward his discarded *macuahuitl* and shouted a challenge at Ixtli.

Ixtli, honored leader of the Tetzcoco forces and distinguished heir, did not honor him with an answer. Instead, he dropped into a squat and retreated toward the edge of the fighting ring. He extended his arm far out behind him and did not stop until he touched the stone barricade. Once he reached it, he tightened his grip on his *macuahuitl* and straightened his stance.

Xicotencatl smiled. Ixtli was an arrogant haughty man, but even his detractors did not deny his intelligence. So long as Ixtli had the barricade behind him, it would be impossible for anyone to sneak up behind him. He would be blind as a hatchling until he cleared the dirt from his eyes, but he could defend himself, somewhat at least, if he knew which direction an attack would come from.

The Xaltocan warrior, still standing in the middle of the ring, shouted, "Come fight me, you coward!"

The crowd shouted their derision at the warrior, and one spectator even had the temerity to throw a rotten tomato. It exploded on contact with the warrior's shoulder blade, and he wheeled around to hurl insults at all the spectators. Once he concluded he would not be able to identify his assailant, he turned his attention back to Ixtli.

The Xaltocan warrior wiped the sweat from his eyes and advanced toward Ixtli. The crowd shouted a warning at Ixtli, but they went quiet when Ixtli raised two fingers in the air and pressed both of them against his lips.

The warrior stopped five paces short of Ixtli. Xicotencatl tried to think of what he would do if he were in his place. The warrior had lost his dagger earlier in the battle but still had his *macuahuitl*. If he were to throw it, he could catch Ixtli by surprise and strike a lethal blow. But if he missed, he might lose his weapon for good.

The warrior must have concluded that idea was not risky enough as he did something even riskier: he threw himself at Ixtli. He swung his *macuahuitl* out as he sailed through the air and screamed like a crazed man. Ixtli, quick as lightning, dropped into a crouch, and the weapon missed his scalp by a hair's breadth.

Ixtli drove his shoulder into the man's midsection, and the two of them fell to the ground in a messy tangle.

Ixtli, however, proved stronger and quicker and pinned the man to the ground in the flutter of an eyelid. With his one free hand, he reached for the stone dagger hanging from his hip. Before the warrior could even cry for help, Ixtli drove it deep into his groin.

Xicotencatl stiffened. Nothing was as agonizing or humiliating as a groin wound. In the rare instance a warrior survived a wound like that, they could never go back to life as it used to be. Siring children became impossible, along with running and fighting. Xicotencatl shuddered. Death seemed a better fate than that.

Had Ixtli left the knife in, the healers might have been able to save the man. But Ixtli was determined to have the man's life and yanked the knife free. A dark spout of blood poured forth, staining the sand and Ixtli. The sudden rush of life water might have perturbed some men, but Ixtli seemed to revel in it and plunged the knife into the man's innards once more.

He stabbed again and again, and the dark puddle of red spread outward. By the time Ixtli stopped, his arms were lathered with sweat and blood. Satisfied his enemy no longer posed a threat, Ixtli stood and held up his bloody hands for all to admire. The crowd erupted with wild cheers and applause, but Xicotencatl took part in none of it.

The Xaltocan warrior deserved a better death than he had been given. He had not fought honorably, but the fight had never been honorable to begin with. Xaltocan was an insignificant island and had no practical value to the war effort. The people of Xaltocan had never done anything to harm the people of Tlaxcala, and the spoils would be sure to go to Ixtli's warriors before his own.

Xicotencatl was ashamed he had helped lay siege to the *altepetl*, and he was ashamed the Tlaxcalteca had done so much to help Ixtli and Cortés. They feigned friendship, but neither had any great love for Tlaxcala.

His people were only useful to them in their willingness to fight and die in battle. And the campaigns would never end for there would always be another *altepetl* to topple, another province to raid. They would bleed Tlaxcala dry with their wars of conquest, and he would assist them no more. Come what may, he was going home. To Tlaxcala.

~ ~ ~

Cuauhtemoc quietly nocked his arrow as the first warrior came into range. Dressed in light cotton armor and covered in decorative paint, the man stifled a yawn as he trudged forward with the rest of his countrymen in a single-file line. All told, they were about forty in number which meant they outnumbered Cuauhtemoc's party by a factor of two to one. Cuauhtemoc did not like those odds, but he was confident the ambush would be a success.

He shot a glance at a pine tree on the other side of the walking path. Three of his archers were hiding amidst its voluminous canopy, but he could not see any of them. Cuauhtemoc let out a relieved breath. If he could not spot his own men, the enemy certainly would not be able to.

A small creaking made him go still. He shifted his weight slightly to better balance his weight on the branch. He glanced at his sandaled feet. *Should have chosen a thicker branch.* He turned his attention to the enemy warriors once more. The first one would pass his tree soon; it was too late to find a new perch.

He slowly pulled the bow string back and searched for a target. None of the men would shoot until he did, so he had to select his victim with care. An odd thing, deciding who would die first. A great responsibility, too.

What with the imbalance in numbers, most of the barbarians would survive the first volley. The brave ones would try to stand their ground, but the smart ones would flee to the woods for cover. If enough of them evaded capture, they could rally for a counter-attack.

His gaze landed on a thick-set man with wide shoulders. Like so many of the distinguished warriors of the One World, his head was shorn of all hair except for one braid tucked behind his ear. He carried a round shield decorated with an array of bright feathers, and his confident bearing made it clear he held a position of command. Cuauhtemoc aimed his weapon at the man's chest. He asked the gods to guide his aim and released the bow string.

The flint-tipped arrow blurred as it cut through the air and lodged itself deep inside the man's sternum. His eyes bulged out as if he had swallowed a mouthful of chilli seeds, and he fell to his knee. Arrows flooded the air, and the barbarians threw themselves flat against the ground. Two young warriors rushed to their leader and tried to help him to his feet. One was felled by a throwing sling, the other by a spear.

The leader tried to shout something, but a sudden spasm seized him. He managed nothing besides a choked cough before he fell over. Cuauhtemoc nocked another arrow and took aim at a warrior who had dropped his pack to flee for the woods. The arrow lodged itself in his elbow rather than his back. The man stumbled but did not fall.

Cuauhtemoc cursed and reached for his quiver. A loud whirring alerted him to danger, and he turned as a throwing sling smashed into his bow. The clay balls exploded as they smashed into each other, and he raised his hand to cover his face. The sudden motion left him unbalanced, and he fell from his perch.

The fall lasted only a heartbeat or two, and he rolled as he hit the ground. A sharp pain in his hand let him know that he had landed wrong, and he prayed he had not seriously injured himself. He did not have time to check and leapt to his feet as he reached for a discarded club. Cuauhtemoc had just barely wrapped his hand around the hilt of his weapon when something knocked him to the ground and jolted the club from his hand. A bewildered warrior landed on top of him, and they stared at each other in confusion.

It took both of them a moment to come back to their senses, but that was enough time for Cuauhtemoc to grab a rock. He smashed it into the warrior's ear and rolled over so he was on top of the man. He smashed the rock into his mouth and raised it up again to deliver the final blow.

The warrior's bloody maw gave him pause. His mouth was hanging open at an odd angle, and his eyes had rolled backward. A loud hoot, the signal to stop fighting, made him start. He took a deep breath, elated but spent. The skirmish was over. It was time to look for survivors. He let the bloody rock tumble from his grip and glanced at the man who had knocked him over.

He had assumed the man had been a warrior of some kind. In taking a closer look at his victim, he could now see that was not the case. Judging by the ugly burn mark on his cheek, he was nothing more than a captured slave. His elation curdled, and he tore his eyes away from the macabre sight.

Cuauhtemoc stood and raised his hand to his head. A sudden pain made him wince, and he glanced at his hand. A gash had opened in the middle of his palm, but it was a shallow wound. He tried to think of when it had happened. Probably when he fell from the tree. He tried to close his hand. A fresh wave of pain rolled over him. He hissed in frustration. Hand wounds were the worst. Until it recovered, he would not be able to wield a *macuahuitl* or a club properly.

A flushed and out-of-breath Ollin came running toward him. "We have a survivor."

Cuauhtemoc nodded and fell into step behind Ollin. His trusted deputy led him to a pine tree on the other side of the walking path. A group of warriors had gathered around the base of the tree but they parted as he neared, allowing him his first glimpse of the wounded man.

Not only did he have an arrow sticking out of his shoulder, he had a large knife protruding from his midsection. His eyes were sunken and glassy, and a light sheen of sweat covered his torso. He looked as if he might keel over at any moment, and Cuauhtemoc was glad somebody possessed the foresight to prop him against the tree.

Cuauhtemoc squatted beside the man and tried to ignore the stench of fresh-spilled blood. Gut wounds were as painful as they were fatal. The man probably only had another day to live, and his last hours would be filled with unimaginable anguish. "What's your name?"

The warrior clenched his mouth shut and glared at him as if he were a pile of offal. "Why would I give my name to a hand-dipper like you?"

"I could have your tongue torn out for speaking to me that way."

"Better to cut my ears off. That way I don't have to hear your drivel."

Cuauhtemoc shrugged and beckoned to Ollin with a small gesture. Ollin dropped into a crouch, and Cuauhtemoc leaned over so he could give Ollin instruction. A look of confusion flashed across his face, but he did as commanded and quickly procured a jug of *octli*. Ollin removed the rubber stopper and guided the drinking gourd to the warrior's feeble lips. He accepted only a mouthful or two before he pushed Ollin away. He wiped his lips with the back of his hand and suppressed a cough.

"You are quite the word-dragger. Is that how I should refer to you?" Cuauhtemoc asked.

The wounded warrior grunted, causing the knife in his gut to quiver. He grimaced and drew in his breath in short gasps. "I am Nochtli."

Cuauhtemoc laid his *macuahuitl* on the ground in front of him. "Where are you from?"

"Tetzcoco."

Cuauhtemoc's warriors muttered angrily amongst each other. It felt as if a new *altepetl* defected from the Mexica Confederacy every week, but none of those defections had been half as painful as Tetzcoco's.

"A beautiful *altepetl*," Cuauhtemoc said. "I have only had the chance to visit on a few occasions. I fear it may be some time before I can visit again, though."

Nochtli scowled. "You Tenocha are too arrogant. Why would Tetzcoco wish to welcome a Great Speaker into the city?"

"Tetzcoco and Tenochtitlan have a long history of friendship," Cuauhtemoc said. "Surely, this trouble with Ixtli cannot negate all that. Tetzcoco gained great riches through the Triple Alliance."

"The Triple Alliance is no more," Nochtli said, his teeth gritted and his face twisted with pain. "Tetzcoco and Tenochtitlan are enemies now."

"Perhaps it does not need to be that way. I think there can be peace between our people. Things can go back to the way they used to be."

Nochtli shook his head. "So long as there are *teteo* in the One World, things will never be as they once were. The reign of Tenochtitlan is over. From now on, Tetzcoco will rule the One World."

"Tetzcoco has never lacked for grand ambitions. Why can't Tenochtitlan and Tetzcoco rule together?"

"Since when is the moon allowed to shine as brightly as Tonatiuh?" Nochtli asked.

Cuauhtemoc smiled. The creation legends held that the moon was once as bright as Tonatiuh, but none could remember the time when that was true. "What makes you so sure the reign of Tenochtitlan is over?"

"Tenochtitlan is nothing without the Mexica Confederacy, and the confederacy grows weaker every day. Soon all the lakeshore settlements will fall to Tetzcoco."

"It matters not," Cuauhtemoc said. "Tenochtitlan will still be independent. We will sabotage the causeways to prevent entry into our city, and we will patrol the waters with our canoes to guard against ambush."

"Cortés does not mean to storm the city. He will starve Tenochtitlan into submission."

Cuauhtemoc laughed drily. "Is he going to find a way to make rocks fall upward also? Tenochtitlan will never lack for food; the lake provides all we need. Trust that I speak with wooden lips when I say that hunting and trading brings—"

"You won't be able to." Nochtli coughed quietly. "The trench..."

Cuauhtemoc's blood ran cold. "What trench?"

Nochtli wiped away the red-tinged saliva dribbling down his neck. "You'll discover.... soon enough. Once it's finished, the *teteo* will gain control... the entire lake system. Canoes are no match for water-houses. No hope, any of you. Surrender... better for everyone."

The warriors standing next to Cuauhtemoc stiffened. None of them needed to be reminded how dangerous water-houses could be. If the barbarians could put an entire fleet in Lake Tetzcoco, securing aid from the lakeshore settlements would become far more difficult. Perhaps impossible.

Cuauhtemoc shuddered. Never in anyone's lifetime had Tenochtitlan gone to war without the assistance of allied peoples. Not since their days as a wandering people had they been forced to fend for themselves.

"We have destroyed their water-houses before, and we will do so again," Cuauhtemoc said. "We will triumph on our own and our victory will be all the greater for it."

Cuauhtemoc stood. He held out his hand. A nearby warrior obliged by handing him a heavy club. "You have shown great bravery in the face of death. I pray your journey through the underworlds ends well."

Nochtli managed what almost looked like a smile and tilted his head forward. "Thank you for your kindness."

Cuauhtemoc raised the club high above his head and smashed it against Nochtli's temple. His head hung limp afterward, and Cuauhtemoc handed the club back to the warrior. What he had done was highly improper. Warriors were supposed to be tested in their final moments or given to the gods as tribute, but he trusted his warriors would not think less of him for ending Nochtli's suffering. Sometimes, even an enemy deserved mercy.

Chapter 14

Xicotencatl stared into Noyollo's face. If it were light out, he might have been able to make out the small birthmark on her chin or the dimples in her cheeks, but it was much too dark to do that now. Not that it mattered anyway. Noyollo's features were so familiar he could draw them from memory.

Noyollo was the only woman he had ever truly loved. He had coupled with many women, but she was the one he always came back to. *I should have married you long ago.*

Xicotencatl tucked a strand of her hair back. She mumbled something incoherent, but made no response otherwise. He smiled. Noyollo could say the strangest things when she was sleeping. She told him one time that butterflies were prettiest when they were swimming upstream and the memory of it still warmed his heart.

The smile faded from his face as he thought about all the reasons they had never married. Father had encouraged Xicotencatl to take many wives, but he would have disowned him had he taken her for a wife. Noyollo was nothing more than a barren house servant and three years his senior. It would have been an insult to everything proper to marry such a woman, and he had never seriously considered it. Much as he enjoyed her company, he had never been willing to jeopardize his social standing for her sake.

A small sigh escaped his lips. What a fool he had been. They had lost out on so many years together, all so he could play at importance. She had good reason to resent him, but she was too good a person to give in to something as petty as hatred.

Noyollo rubbed her head against his forearm. She had been resting her head on his arm for so long that he had lost sensation in his fingertips. He knew he would eventually have to move, but he did not want to disturb her sleep. Not yet. Not until he had to.

Off in the distance, a wolf howled. In times past, he might have taken fright at the sound. Tonight, however, he found the piercing cry oddly comforting, a reminder that he and Noyollo had only animals and plants for company. On campaign, nights were filled with the snores of tired porters, the whispering of disgruntled warriors, and the shuffling of drowsy sentries.

He would not miss that aspect of campaign life. Truth be told, he was not sure he would miss any of it. He had long ago tired of that life and wished only to live the rest of his days in peace. With Noyollo.

He knew, of course, peace would not be easy to find. Once news of his defection became widespread, outrage would follow. Father would be most outraged of all and would agitate loudly for his capture. Deep in the ancient forests of Tlaxcala, however, he was safe. He knew that would not always be the case, but he trusted that he would be able to find a new sanctum when the time came. He could be happy anywhere, so long as he had Noyollo.

Perhaps sensing his thoughts, Noyollo stirred and opened her eyes. "My love, how are you still awake?" she asked, her words slurred and formless.

"One of us has to stay alert." Xicotencatl wriggled closer to Noyollo and kissed her on the lips. She responded with unexpected enthusiasm, and he pulled her closer.

Noyollo laid a hand on his chest and locked eyes with him. "Are we in great danger?"

"Worry not, my love. You are in no danger at all."

Noyollo scoffed. "You can protect me from all the creatures of the night, then? Will you turn into a bear to scare away the wolves?"

Xicotencatl smiled. "I would summon the power of our gods and the Christian gods if that's what it took to keep you safe from the night creatures."

"And what about other dangers?"

Xicotencatl went quiet. He had spent all night thinking about those other dangers, not that he would admit as much. He owed Noyollo peace of mind, even if he did not deserve it himself. "You are the only one who knows I am back in Tlaxcala. They will not think to look for us in the woods."

"But what if they do?"

"They won't—"

"But what if they do?" Noyollo asked.

Xicotencatl sighed. He had hoped to put off this conversation a few more days. "Are you sure you wish to know?"

Noyollo nodded. He could not make out her features in the dark, but he could tell from her rigid posture that she would not soon relax.

"If we are captured, you must tell them that I took you by force," Xicotencatl said. "It will be much worse for you if you tell them otherwise."

Noyollo's breath caught. "I can't do that, Xicotencatl."

"Yes, you can. You are so strong, Noyollo. Stronger than you know."

Noyollo sat up. She hugged her knees to her chest and fixed her gaze on the tent canvas. "I wish that were true," Noyollo whispered. "I always wanted a child, a little warrior to call my own. Did you know that?"

Xicotencatl reached for a strand of her hair. Noyollo had hair even longer than his daughter. His heart skipped a beat. He would never again see his daughter. *It is for the best.* His daughter was a stranger to him to these days, a mere trading good who helped broker peace between the *teteo* and the Tlaxcalteca. He rued the day he had allowed her to marry Pedro de Alvarado, the vile *teotl* who defiled everything he touched, and wished every day his people had never allied with the *teteo.* "The gods are as whimsical as they are powerful," Xicotencatl said. "Keep them in your prayers, and they may bless you with a child."

Noyollo laughed drily. "If the gods meant for me to have children, they would not have given me a barren womb." Noyollo brushed her hair back and cleared her throat. "Forgive me if I seem tart. I have much to be grateful for. The gods have blessed me with many cousins and many siblings." Noyollo slipped her hand in his. "And a brave warrior."

Xicotencatl squeezed her hand. "I am the blessed one."

Noyollo smiled weakly and laid down.

"Will you miss your family?" Xicotencatl asked.

"Of course I will. My cousins and my siblings were my first playmates, and my parents, and their siblings, have always taken care of me. My uncle is the reason I was able to get a place in your Father's household. I have disappointed them greatly…" Noyollo trailed off. Xicotencatl did not need to ask to know what she was thinking of. Women were supposed to help their families by making advantageous marriages and carrying on the family line. Much to her eternal shame, Noyollo had done neither of those things. "But I would like to see them again. Some day. My cousin says I am welcome to return whenever I want—"

"You told your cousin?" Xicotencatl asked.

"I had to tell my cousin," Noyollo said, a hint of anger in her voice. "You told me we would be gone from Tlaxcala a very long time, that we might never return. I had to let someone know why I was leaving. My family would never forgive me otherwise."

Xicotencatl ground his teeth, unsure whether he should be angry with himself or Noyollo. He had taken a great risk by seeking her out when he returned to Tlaxcala, but he had trusted that she would tell no one of his return. Perhaps he had asked too much of her.

A dark thought popped into his head. *What if Noyollo's cousin betrays her confidence?* Xicotencatl scratched his chin. He had only met her cousin on a few occasions. He did not have that many distinguishing qualities, other than a weakness for gambling. Or was he remembering that wrong?

"Noyollo, does your cousin like to gamble?"

"More than he enjoys breathing. He is perhaps overly fond of *octli* and *patolli*."

Xicotencatl's chest tightened. "Has my father ever provided him… assistance?"

Noyollo yawned. "I believe so. He lost an important bet, and I think he asked your father for help. I am not certain, though. It was a very long time ago."

Xicotencatl grabbed Noyollo by the shoulder. "Concentrate. Is it possible he owes my father a debt?"

"Yes, Xico. What does it matter?"

Xicotencatl's mouth went dry. "Let's find a different place to sleep tonight," Xicotencatl said, forcing calmness into his voice. "The brook will attract animals."

"Why the questions about my cousin?" Noyollo asked.

Xicotencatl reached for his loincloth.

"Answer me, Xico."

"First, we move." Xicotencatl reached for his sandals. "Then, I will explain."

Noyollo grabbed his arm. "Why are you so worried?"

Xicotencatl grimaced. Only a few moments ago, her touch would have sent shivers of excitement through him. Now he struggled just to keep his anger in check.

"Please, Xico. Tell me what's wrong."

"Your cousin is what's wrong!" Xicotencatl snapped. "I trust him to keep a secret about as much as I trust a *teotl* to keep faith."

"My cousin—"

"Is a degenerate," Xicotencatl said. "If he knows I am back in Tlaxcala, then my father also knows."

Xicotencatl reflected on his final words with Father. He had warned him not to come back to Tlaxcala before the war ended. Would Father know to search for him in the woods? *Of course he will.* Father was the one who taught him how to hunt forest game.

"You can't know that, Xico," Noyollo said, her voice pleading and panicked.

"Yes, I do. Father explicitly forbade me from returning to Tlaxcala before the war ended. He will put me to death for defying him."

Noyollo's eyes widened. "Don't even think such a thing. Your father loves you."

"That's why he will be so wroth," Xicotencatl replied. "Father will enlist the help of every man in Tlaxcala to find me and will offer a large bounty to any who aid him. Tell me, do you think your cousin will keep his mouth shut if Father offers enough to cover all his debts?"

Noyollo's mouth dropped open.

"Grab everything you need," Xicotencatl ordered. "We need to move."

"Xico, I'm sorry. I had to tell someone…." Noyollo trailed off. Xicotencatl pulled his sandal on and crooked his head to the left. The forest had gone quiet. The owls were no longer hooting, and the crickets were no longer chirping.

"What do you hear?" Noyollo whispered.

Xicotencatl pressed a finger to his lips and put his other sandal on. Careful to not make any noise, he leaned forward to grab his quiver. He took a quick count of the arrows inside. Only six.

He cursed himself for not fashioning more arrows. He had been confident he would be able to make more on the morrow, but he doubted he would get such an opportunity now. Xicotencatl slung the quiver over his shoulder and patted the tent floor to find his knife. By the time he finally found it, his heart was pounding and his fingers were trembling. He unwrapped his knife and stared at the knotted tent flap. The full moon provided enough light to know there was no one standing right outside the tent, but that provided him precious little comfort. For all he knew, a group of archers may have already encircled the tent. He reached for the knots that kept the tent flap closed. He undid the first one and waited.

Nothing happened, and he reached for the second one. His hand trembled, and he bunched it into a fist. He had to be strong, he had to be sure of himself. Noyollo was counting on him. He banished all thoughts of weakness and undid the rest of the knots. Off in the distance, a bird cried out.

Xicotencatl readjusted his quiver. It was possible the bird had been startled by something innocuous; there was no need to assume the worst. But try as he might, he could not stop himself from doing just that. *If Father knows I am back in Tlaxcala, he will have men searching for me.* He cursed. He needed to gather more corn and fashion more tools before he could disappear into the forest completely.

How would he do that now, if Father already had men searching for him? Xicotencatl glanced at Noyollo. The terror etched across her face was so profound it made his stomach twist in knots.

He motioned for her to stay quiet and to hide under the blanket. It would do nothing to protect her from a determined intruder, but she was safer inside the tent than outside. Probably.

He put his lips next to her ear and whispered, "If you hear anything loud, run away as far as you can."

She nodded, and he let out a relieved breath. Still crouching, he made his way toward the tent flap and peeked outside. He surveyed the landscape, searching for anything amiss. The clearing offered precious few places to hide, but an archer could easily conceal himself in the undergrowth. The nearest stand of trees was a stone's throw away. At that distance, almost any archer could hit a still target.

He glanced at his bow. Xicotencatl had hidden it next to a nearby tree, along with some other provisions. Had he any sense, he would have hidden the bow inside the tent. He had been concerned there would not be room in the tent for him, Noyollo, and the bow, but that worry seemed risible now.

He checked the lacings on his sandals. Tight, just like he needed them to be. The tree was only twenty paces away, and he would need to move quickly if he was going to reach his bow in time to nock it. His hand hovered above his ankle. It had never truly recovered from the Sad Night, but he trusted the distance was short enough to sprint.

He burst out of the tent like a spear launched from an *atlatl*. Rather than running directly toward the tree, he veered to the side so he could approach the tree from behind. If he came at the tree from just the right direction, he would be able to grab the bow without breaking stride.

Xicotencatl extended his arm outward to grab the handle. A muffled creaking alerted him to danger, and he jumped to the side as an arrow slid past his hip. He crashed into the tree and darted toward cover. An arrow slammed into his quiver, pinning it against the tree, and he fled for the undergrowth.

Branches and brambles tore open his skin. He charged forward anyway, armed with nothing besides his knife and a certainty that he needed to draw the archer away, far away from Noyollo. His energy was flagging, but he pushed himself to keep running. Out of breath and disoriented, his foot caught on an exposed root, and he fell to the ground.

His knee smashed into something hard, and he had to bite his tongue to keep from crying out. He drew in deep shuddering breaths and covered his mouth to muffle the sound. After a few moments passed, he tried to bend his leg. A new wave of pain enveloped him, forcing him to stop.

He rested his head in the dirt. Something was crawling along his leg. He pressed a hand against his hip. It came away wet and sticky. He stifled a groan. The arrow had cut his hip, and he was surprised he had been able to run at all.

Xicotencatl stared into the night sky. The stars were so bright in Tlaxcala, and the trees were so tall… how a man could be happy anywhere else, he did not know. He knew his end was near but he was glad he would spend his final moments in Tlaxcala. Not every man was so lucky.

His breathing slowed, and he pushed himself to his feet. His leg had gone numb, but he trusted that could make his way back to the tent. If the archer was no longer there, it might be safe to grab his bow now. He could not save himself but he could at least help Noyollo escape. He managed only a few steps before something sharp pressed into his back. He froze, unsure how to react.

"Put down the knife," Chichi ordered.

Xicotencatl's eyes widened. To be apprehended by Chichi, his former deputy, of all people! They had their differences in times past, but he trusted that Chichi did not wish any harm on him.

"Do you remember the raid on Motecuhzoma's palace?" Xicotencatl asked.

Chichi said nothing, but he pulled the rapier back a hair's breadth. Xicotencatl straightened, hope welling in his stomach. Chichi would not forsake him, not after everything they had been through.

"When we jumped from the balcony, you hurt your ankle," Xicotencatl said. "I went back to help you. Do you remember that?"

Chichi snorted. "Of course I remember."

"What do you think would have happened to you had I not come back for you? Had the Mexica guards captured you?" Xicotencatl paused, waited for Chichi to say something. He did not oblige. "I have never met a people as practiced in torture as the Mexica, save perhaps the *teteo*—"

"My life is but a little thing compared to the well-being of Tlaxcala."

Xicotencatl furrowed his brow. "You think I am a danger to Tlaxcala?"

"I think you are a traitor," Chichi snarled. "You abandoned the field of battle to bed your father's servant. Do not expect mercy from me you treacherous whoreson."

Xicotencatl went rigid as a board, the pain in his leg forgotten. He tightened his grip on his knife. "My father is the one who betrayed Tlaxcala, not me. We never should have made common cause with the *teteo* or the Tetzcoco. Our people will regret it one day, I promise you that."

"Perhaps," Chichi said. "I promise you will not live to see that day—"

Xicotencatl wheeled around and knocked aside Chichi's rapier with his forearm. Before Chichi could shout or even retreat, Xicotencatl plunged his knife into his midsection. Chichi's eyes bulged out, and Xicotencatl pressed the knife in deeper. To his surprise, the knife veered sideways.

Xicotencatl looked down in confusion. The knife had been stopped by Chichi's armor! He had assumed Chichi had nothing underneath his quilted cloth, but he realized now that Chichi had simply slipped a much stronger layer of armor underneath it. *Teteo* armor.

Chichi kneed him in the stomach, driving all the wind from his body. Xicotencatl stumbled backward and slumped against a tree, too stunned to speak. How had Chichi acquired a *teotl* sword and *teotl* armor? Did they trust him that much?

A glowering Chichi advanced with rapier in hand. He grabbed Xicotencatl by the throat and pinned him against the tree.

"Our nation's best days are ahead of us. I regret that you will not live to see the folly of your actions."

Chichi pressed down with all his might and raised the rapier high. Xicotencatl tried to think of something, anything, to say, but the hilt of the weapon smashed into his face and everything went dark.

Chapter 15

Garrido slumped against the dirt wall and rested a hand on the wooden spade. A crack had formed near the haft; he would need to find a replacement soon. Wooden spades, even when they were fitted with iron shoes, made for poor digging implements, but they were far better than the Mexica tools.

For reasons he could not understand, the Mexica made do with small digging sticks called *coas*. Owing to its thick hooked head, it could not carry much dirt and seemed far more suited to seed planting than trench digging. Despite the limitations of their tools, the Mexica had erected architectural wonders finer than anything he had ever seen. God may not have blessed the Indians with proper tools, but He had not cursed them with an indolent nature.

He wished he could say the same for his fighting companions. Finishing the trench was essential to the war effort, but few of the Spaniards were willing to lend their labor to digging efforts. Joining the raids against the lakeshore settlements had proven far more lucrative, and Martin López offered little that could compete with the lure of slaves and trading goods. Were it not for the porters and the servants, the trench would be nothing more than a latrine pit. It still needed to be widened, otherwise López would never be able to safely launch the brigantines, but Garrido trusted there would still be time to complete it before the rains returned.

Garrido glanced at his digging companions. They had also decided to take a rest, despite not having done much to exert themselves thus far. Were it not for López, he doubted any of them would have assisted with digging. He would not fault them for a lack of loyalty, however, and was glad that "Martin's Disciples" had accepted him into their confidences.

Narices was the group's unofficial leader and took after López in many respects. Not only did they both hail from Seville, they had both been a part of Cortés' initial crew. Narices had a well-deserved reputation for levity, and Lázaro was just as good-natured. The Mafla brothers, Piero and Miguel, were less outgoing, but they seemed friendly enough.

Narices shaded his eyes and peered up at the clear blue sky. "There'll be rain tonight, I'm sure of it."

Garrido hid a smile. Narices' weather predictions rarely came to pass, and he had to marvel at the man's ability to make such fanciful predictions with utter certainty.

"A downpour to wash away all our sins," Narices said. "The type of flood Noah warned of—"

"Quit your nattering already," Lazaro grumbled. "I'd sooner trust a whore than you when it comes to weather. As I recall it, you said we'd have hail last month."

"We did have hail!" Narices objected.

The Mafla brothers shared a laugh. "And what day did this blessed miracle occur?" Miguel asked.

"The night after Easter," Narices said confidently.

Lazaro laughed. "The day this valley gets hail is the day the Pope makes Luther a saint. If it's miserable weather you want, hurry back to the mountains."

"Or back to Spain," Garrido interjected. "A winter in Badajoz would make any man long for the heat of the Maghreb."

Martin's Disciples went quiet. They exchanged surprised glances and looked to one another for assurance. "You've wintered in Badajoz?" Miguel asked.

Garrido nodded. "Not by choice if I am to be completely honest. For a time, I served a traveling priest and I had little say in his..."

"Itinerary?" Narices offered.

"Exactly," Garrido said.

"How did you end up here?" Miguel asked.

Garrido tucked his tongue in his cheek. He had lost count of all the times he had been asked that very same question. Many of the Old Christians were convinced that he must have come to the New World for different reasons than them, an assumption he found strange.

Iberia was a land favored by God, but he understood as well as any of the Old Christians he could never make something of himself if he stayed there. Of course, there was a time in his life when he thought otherwise. When he first joined Father Jerez, on his travels, he had been stunned by Iberia's beauty. The ancient castles, the sweeping plains, the rugged cliffs, the towering churches; it spoke to something deep inside his soul that had always needed nurturing.

But the more time he spent in Iberia, the more he realized it could never be home. Father Jerez was kind enough, but Garrido was nothing more than a performing pet to him, an exotic lure who could draw a crowd in any town. He thought he could tolerate the incessant staring. But when Father Jerez began to refer to him as the Son of Ham, he knew he could stay with him no longer.

"I gave the priest the slip once I was old enough to join a sailing crew," Garrido said. "God was kind enough to grant me safe passage to the New World, but I must admit there are times when I miss Spain. I have never traveled to another country with so many churches, and I miss morning mass dearly."

"I love Jesus as much as any cardinal, but I take far more joy in the blood of Christ than any long-winded sermon," Narices said.

"Wine is for choir boys," Lazaro said. "I prefer a good strong cider any day. Cider and ham, that's what I miss the most."

Miguel laughed so hard he brayed like a donkey. "You miss ham? Be sure to tell the captains quick. We had ham last week, and the week before, and the week before that, but there's a chance they may forget to give us ham this week."

Lazaro waved his hand dismissively. "The dross they give us isn't fit for dogs. More maggots in it than fat. I miss real ham. Extremadura is a cold and miserable place, but there's no better place to find a good ham."

Garrido's stomach grumbled. Meat was hard to come by on campaign, and he subsisted mostly on yuca bread and New World staples. Like many of the men, he suffered recurring bouts of indigestion and looked forward to the day he did not have to gorge himself on fruits and vegetables with names he could not pronounce.

Lazaro's expression turned serious. "What is it you miss the most, Miguel."

Miguel scratched his head. "Whorehouses," he said simply.

Martin's Disciples doubled over with laughter, but Garrido could only feign a laugh. "Do you mean to spend all your gold on whores, once the war is over?" Narices asked.

Miguel shrugged. "Perhaps. If the captains are kind enough to grant me a pretty servant or two, I suppose I could be persuaded to go on campaign again."

Lazaro shook his head. "Don't count on it. The captains took all the prettiest captives for themselves, and they won't be sharing their Indians with low-born folk. Once the war is over, some of the captains will have hundreds of slaves. We'll be lucky to have our lives."

Lazaro spat on the ground and cursed fate with a string of colorful invectives. Garrido flushed in embarrassment and turned away, prompting much laughter from the group.

"Oh Garrido, you mustn't be embarrassed," Narices said. "Surely you must have learned by now that priests and soldiers are cut from different cloths? You must get used to these things. Otherwise, you'll never be able to enjoy life on campaign, and I know you wish to take part in more campaigns."

Garrido frowned. "How do you know that?"

"Have you gained a great deal of gold since you joined this expedition?" Narices asked.

"Only a little," Garrido admitted. "I lost most of it during the retreat. But when Tenochtitlan surrenders—"

"All the winnings will go to the captains and their favored men," Narices said. "Perhaps they'll remember we dug a trench for them, but I think not. Be prepared to take part in many expeditions if you intend to leave these lands a rich man."

"I do not intend to leave these lands," Garrido said.

"You love the Indians that much?" Lazaro asked.

Garrido smiled. "I care only for their souls. God as my witness, I find them a confounding bunch."

"Stubborn, that's the only way to describe them," Narices said. "Did you hear what the Indians said during the parley at Tlacopan?"

Garrido nodded. The parley at Tlacopan had acquired almost mythic importance amongst the company members. Despite being deprived of food and besieged on all sides, the Indians at Tlacopan had boasted they would never need to surrender because they could feast on captured warriors. To prove just how little they needed traditional foodstuffs, they even delivered a sack of corn cakes to Cortés' translators. "I fear it may be some time until the Indians are ready to accept Jesus into their hearts," Garrido said.

"Then why do you wish to stay?" Miguel asked. "Surely you wish to go back to…"

Garrido shook his head. "My future belongs with the New World. I mean to establish true religion in this part of the world. When I have an *encomienda* of my own, I will build a church for the faithful."

Martin's Disciples stared at him as if they were seeing him anew. Unsure what to say, Garrido picked up his spade and resumed digging. Regardless of what the Old Christians thought of him, Garrido knew that God loved him and that was all that mattered. He reciprocated the love with all his heart and would do anything to make himself worthy of it. If that meant forsaking family and home, that was a small price to pay.

~ ~ ~

Xicotencatl stared at the crowd that had gathered in the town square for his hanging. Men made up the bulk of the group, but he recognized few of the faces. As far as he could tell, most of the spectators did not hail from Tlaxcala. Many hailed from Spain, but the majority of them appeared to be merchants from Tetzcoco.

If the Tetzcocans bore him ill-will, they hid it well. Truth be told, they seemed only mildly interested in him. Boredom had probably drawn them to his hanging, and boredom had already driven some of them back to their stalls. Then again, it could have been simple exhaustion.

Tonatiuh was bearing down with a fierce intensity, and the crowd had thinned as the heat thickened. A part of him felt insulted the spectators could only muster a superficial interest in him, another part of him felt relieved.

A bead of sweat rolled down his neck, wending its way along blisters and welts with abandon. He had been wearing the noose for so long his skin had begun to chafe, and he cursed the *teteo* for their lethargy. He had been standing all morning, waiting for them to carry out the hanging, but still they dallied and dithered.

Perhaps they hope the heat will kill me. Xicotencatl laughed half-heartedly. He had always assumed he would die a warrior's death, but the *teteo* seemed determined to give him a death that was neither glorious nor quick.

Xicotencatl tried to interlace his fingers. No luck. The rope had cut off circulation in his hands, and his sweat-covered fingers had gone cold as ice. He registered little sensation below his wrists and hung his head in despair.

It would have been better if Chichi had killed him when they were still in Tlaxcala. Instead, Chichi had bludgeoned him unconscious and bound him as if he were a prized carcass. When Xicotencatl finally came to, he discovered that he had been stuffed inside a hammock and was being transported to an undisclosed location by unfamiliar people.

Xicotencatl closed his eyes. He had never been so thirsty in all his life, and it hurt just to think. His head felt as if it would soon split open, and he doubted he could stay on his feet much longer. He craned his head backward and stared up at the thick network of branches overhead. The *teteo* had slung the noose over one of the low-hanging branches. When they were finally ready to hang him, they would hoist him upward.

The fir tree was old and strong; he was confident most of the branches could support his weight. So what were the *teteo* waiting for?

He could not begin to say. He had never understood their ways, nor would he ever. *Was that ignorance my undoing?* He pressed his chapped lips into a thin line. It didn't matter anymore. Soon, his suffering would be over.

The clop of horse hooves reached his ears. He tilted his head forward and turned toward the noise. A group of mounted men, led by Pedro de Alvarado, were heading his way.

Disgust curdled in his stomach. He hated few men as he hated Pedro and wished he could have killed the vile lecher before he ever set foot in Tlaxcala.

Pedro dismounted and handed the reins of his horse to a squire. He marched toward Xicotencatl with a translator in tow, the one called the Boy Conquistador.

"How fare you, Xico?" Pedro asked, his question translated by the Boy Conquistador.

Xicotencatl gave Pedro a searching look.

"Christ on a cross, do you ever smile? I've seen lepers with more cheer than you." Pedro squeezed his shoulder affectionately. "Doña Luisa asked me to intercede on your behalf. Tell me truly, did you ever imagine I might be your savior?"

Xicotencatl clenched his teeth. After a pause, he shook his head.

Pedro laughed. "I would not have expected it either. God works in mysterious ways, though. That's what the priests say, leastwise."

Xicotencatl pursed his lips. The *teteo* never missed a chance to talk of their accursed priests. They had fouled his ears with one of their sermons earlier in the day, and he hoped he would not have to endure another one of their nonsensical homilies.

"Alas, I must inform you that I failed to render the result your daughter hoped for. I tried to reason with Cortés, but he insists upon a hanging." Pedro sighed dramatically. "Is there anything you wish for me to tell your daughter?"

Xicotencatl stiffened. There was so much he wished to say to her. But he would not entrust his hopes and his worries to a brute like Pedro, not if it was the last thing he did.

"Tell her that I wish her good health," Xicotencatl said. "And that she deserves a better husband."

Pedro's face darkened once he heard the translation. Eventually, however, his serious expression gave way to a mincing smile. "Oh Xico, you have Lucifer's wit. I am curious to know: would you have intervened on my behalf, if the noose were around my neck?"

Xicotencatl stared into the distance. *I would have, Pedro, but only to make sure you weren't given a quick death.*

Pedro tutted and reached for Xicotencatl's braid. "I must say, your people have very strange customs."

Xicotencatl tensed. Would Pedro take his braid from him? *I cannot stop him if he tries to.* Anger welled in his stomach. The *teteo* could never be contented with what they already had, and their greed threatened to destroy the One World. He wished he could have done more to frustrate their aims, but he was only one man. Despair and exhaustion overcame him, and he swayed on his feet.

Startled, Pedro let go of his braid and took a step back. He eyed Xicotencatl the same way an eagle would look at a half-dead snake. "Well, I suppose there is no reason to delay the hanging any further," Pedro said. "I'll tell the men to get to it."

Pedro turned away from him. As he walked away, Xicotencatl realized he had something he needed to ask. "What happened to Noyollo?"

Pedro glanced back at him. "Noyollo?"

"The woman—"

"Ah yes, Chichi did mention a woman. She seems to have disappeared. Your father is bitterly disappointed. He hoped to make a good trade for her."

A flood of relief swept over Xicotencatl. Noyollo had escaped. She could not use a bow as well as him, but he trusted that she would be able to forage for food on her own.

Xicotencatl sucked in a deep breath. He had many regrets, but he would go to his death easier knowing that

Noyollo would survive him. She would find her way to a friendly village, he was sure of it. Even if it meant traveling far outside of Tlaxcala, she would find a way to reach safety.

He turned his gaze to the crowd one last time. The *teteo* were staring at him with undisguised contempt, but the faces of his own countrymen were decidedly less hostile. Some of them gazed upon him with pity, others with fondness.

Xicotencatl puffed out his chest. The *teteo* had maligned him as a traitor, as had many of his people, and he prayed their assessment would not stand the test of time. He loved his people and wished only the best for them. He recalled his last conversation with Chichi. His one-time subordinate was convinced Tlaxcala stood to gain a great deal from the alliance with the *teteo*.

I hope you are right, Chichi. I hope for all of us you are right.

A vicious tug hoisted him into the air, and the noose tightened around his neck like a piece of twine. He wriggled like a captured eel, but it did nothing to relieve the pressure on his windpipe. Darkness began eating away at the edges of his vision. His kicks grew weaker, his breathing shallow. Slowly, the pain gave way to an all-consuming numbness. By the time he breathed his last, the pain was nothing more than a distant memory.

Part Three
June-August, 1521

Chapter 16

Cortés rubbed his aching knees. He had not been kneeling on the hassock all that long, but his joints often gave him trouble these days. Owing to a recent injury, even writing was painful. Much as it displeased him, he now had to rely entirely on his notaries to maintain communications with court officials in Spain and the West Indies. He spent many a night slaving over carefully-worded missives, only to have them go unanswered and unacknowledged.

The hassock creaked loudly, reminding Cortés of his present troubles. It was a rather uncomfortable piece of furniture, not that Father Urrea cared. Matters of joy and pain meant little to the hard-bitten friar. None could accuse him of a surfeit of compassion, but he made up for it with an abundance of piety. He took his duties as a priest most seriously and had erected a confessional in the middle of his tent, even though it left precious little room for anything else.

Father Urrea did not seem to mind the cramped conditions and had been immensely pleased when Cortés entered the confessional. *Will he still be pleased once he hears all of my sins?*

Only one way to find out. Cortés crossed himself and said, "Bless me, Father, for I have sinned. My last confession was…" Cortés ran a hand through his beard. He could not remember the last time he made confession. He rubbed his eyes. Keeping track of the days had become difficult as of late. Embarrassed by his lapse in memory, Cortés whispered, "My last confession was some time ago."

"What sins do you mean to confess?" Father Urrea asked.

Cortés tensed. He did not lack for sins. In months past, he might have made light of his transgressions, but he could not bring himself to do so now. The siege of Tenochtitlan was stretching on much too long and could continue well into autumn. Perhaps next spring if the Indians were truly obstinate. "I have violated God's sacred commandments."

"That is a most serious sin," Father Urrea said, his voice laced with censure. "Do you mean to suggest you have violated all ten of His commandments?"

Cortés shook his head. "No, Father. I did not mean to suggest that." Cortés rubbed his temple. Why did his tongue fail him so often these days? He had suffered some debilitating head injuries during the course of the campaign, and he sometimes felt as if he had never truly recovered all his wits. "Father, I fear God is wroth with me. I have violated His Sixth Commandment many times over. I fear He will not be able to forgive me."

Father Urrea mulled his answer in silence. "Murder is a crime of the highest order. Killing a Christian is an offense to God."

"Is the same true of heathens?" Cortés asked, his voice strained with worry.

"No," Father Urrea said. His tone brooked no disagreement and Cortés waited for him to say more. Almost half a minute passed before he added, "They are a people sunk in vice, and God does not love them as he loves Christians."

"I pray that is true, Father. I have put many heathens to the sword, and I sometimes fear for my soul. Sleep no longer offers me the reprieve it once did, and I am afflicted with the most terrible dreams."

"Do you accept Jesus as your Lord and Redeemer?"

"Yes, Father."

"Do you recognize the Church is supreme in all matters and conduct yourself as a Christian?"

Cortés fidgeted on his hassock. "Of course. My own kin fought in the *Reconquista*."

"Fear not, then. God will look after you," Father Urrea said.

Cortés began to object but stopped himself. Who was he to disagree with a friar? Father Urrea had dedicated his life to the study of Scripture and was far more fit to wear a miter than him. Surely it made more sense to put stock by his word than the occasional pang of conscience.

"Sleep does not come easy to the man with many burdens," Father Urrea added. "What is it that vexes you most?"

"I would that I knew where to begin."

A long silence followed. "Are you worried for your safety?"

Cortés rubbed his shoulder. He had received a nasty injury during a battle with the Indians a few weeks prior and struggled with recurrent bouts of pain. Nonetheless, it was his pride that hurt most. Had it not been for López's skillful swordsmanship, the Indians might have taken him captive. López had too much tact to remind him of such, but he did not doubt that López would call upon him once his Majesty Don Carlos recognized Cortés as Governor of Mexico. "No, Father. I trust that God protects me."

"Then what is it that vexes you?"

So much, Father. Cortés rubbed the wooden screen that separated them. As a child, he had been scared of confessionals. It seemed so easy to become trapped inside, so easy to become locked away forever. He had long since outgrown the fear, but a certain apprehension still lingered.

"Father, we have been fighting the Indians a very long time now. I know I have much to be thankful for. We have won many victories—all the settlements in the southern rim have fallen to us, and López's brigantines have been a godsend. The Indians cannot hope to match our strength on the lake…" Cortés trailed off.

He wished he could say that he had gained total control of the lake, but the lie tasted false in his own mouth. He had assumed López's brigantines would grant him complete control of the lake and half-expected the Indians to surrender once they sighted the lofty sails.

By all rights, they should have. The canoes were no match for the brigantines; any sensible foe would recognize that. But instead of surrendering, the Mexica had learned how to evade and sabotage the brigantines. In the space of a few weeks, they had destroyed almost a third of his fleet, and constructing new ships would take months. Meanwhile, the Mexica would use that time to hoard food and lay traps.

Father Urrea coughed. Cortés remembered himself and continued, "The Indians are weakening by the day. They cannot hold out much longer—"

"And this troubles you?"

"Of course not!" Cortés hissed. "But it vexes me greatly that they continue to fight us. They must know their cause is hopeless, so why do they refuse to make homage to us? We could offer them so much, if they just accepted our rule." Cortés sucked in a deep breath and added, "I worry we cannot make conquest here, not when we must contend with so much hatred. Even the Indians who break bread with us care little for our company. Our own allies despise us."

"Not all the Indians are like Xicotencatl," Father Urrea said. "Some of them will always cling to barbarism, but many can be guided to the righteous path. Do not give up hope. God has granted you many victories, and He will guide you to many more."

Cortés snorted. "Our Indian allies have stolen my victories. Ixtli and his warriors do whatever they please, strategy be damned. Had we but focused our attentions on Tenochtitlan, we could have captured the city by now. Instead, Ixtli sends out his warriors all throughout the countryside so they can seize bird feathers and silly beads from hapless villagers. And instead of censuring him, our own countrymen help him. All so they can grab a few more slaves, a few more baubles they'll fritter away in a game of dice. Do they not understand the folly of their actions, Father?"

"You must do more to make them think of you as their liege—"

"They honor no liege," Cortés spat. "God as my witness, the self-seekers will ruin this campaign if they are not brought to heel. I would that I had soldiers like Caesar for I could conquer the world if I had soldiers that could keep faith!"

Cortés stopped. He had let his temper get the best of him. He could not control it the way he used to, back when he still lived in Cuba. Two long years since he had last set foot on that beautiful island. Whether he won or lost his campaign against the Mexica, he would never be able to return. His *encomienda*, his friendship with Governor Velazquez, all of it was forsaken. All so he could wage war against the Mexica. *A war I might not win.*

"Father, I do not know how to bring this war to a close," Cortés said. "We have cut off food and water to the Mexica, but they are no more interested in suing for peace than when I first landed on these shores. Victory continues to elude us, and I am told there is but one way to prevent calamity. But the costs involved would be most steep."

Father Urrea scoffed. "You are laying siege to a city richer than any in all of Spain. Surely you will recoup the costs."

Cortés laughed quietly. "You need not remind me of the riches of Tenochtitlan. I assure you, they are ever on my mind. But if the Mexica do not soon surrender, I will be forced to raze Tenochtitlan to the ground." Cortés sighed. Thanks to López's brigantines, and Tenochtitlan's extensive system of canals, he could sail ships directly into the heart of the city. With enough time, he could level every building of note. Only a few weeks ago he torched Motecuhzoma's zoo. The screaming of the animals still haunted his dreams. "Do you think God could forgive me for destroying a city as beautiful as Tenochtitlan?"

"Was Canaan not a beautiful country before Joshua sacked it?" Father Urrea asked. "God demands that we make war against the heretics, and you must carry out the war against the Indians with the same fervor as the blessed Crusaders who freed Iberia from the Moors. If a few excesses are committed along the way, do not fret overmuch. God forgives all."

"It heartens me to hear you say that, and I thank you for your wisdom," Cortés said. "I sometimes feel as if I am a ship adrift—" Cortés' voice broke. Could he tell Urrea of his nightmares? That terrible, gnawing dread that he might be forced to spend eternity with the very same heathens he had killed? He cleared his throat. "Thank you, Father, for being my crutch in my time of need. Without you, I would be lost."

"I am but a servant of the Lord," Father Urrea said. "Cortés, the path to righteousness is a narrow one. No good Christian avoids confession and you have put your soul at great risk by not seeking me out sooner."

Cortés' pulse quickened. "I have?"

"I fear it is so. God would have all of us enjoy His love, but do not forget that He is a stern master. Fortunately, God has provided His flock with a powerful means of atonement in the form of papal bulls. Please allow me to grant you an indulgence. It could help save your soul from the ever-lasting fires of hell."

Relief washed over Cortés, but it soon gave way to disappointment. Why should he put any stock by Father Urrea's papal bulls? He never needed those expensive indulgences when he was poor, when he was an undistinguished hidalgo from Medellin. Father Urrea just wanted to use him, same as all the others.

The crew was infested with self-seekers, and they seemed to multiply with unholy speed. None of his dependents, not even Doña Marina, cared for his well-being. They only cared for what he could give them, what he could do for them once Don Carlos recognized him as Governor of Mexico. They would hound him without mercy if he thought to keep a single maravedi for himself...

He sighed. It was better to be rich and hounded than poor and ignored. Even if he wished to return to the simple life he once knew, he no longer could. He had made too many enemies, broken too many vows. Victory would provide him protection against reprisal. Failure would cost him his life. Much as Cortés wished it were not so, he did not have any other options.

"Call upon me when the war is won," Cortés said. He stared at the indentations his knees had made in the hassock's thin cotton padding. Unable to bear the ache in his knees anymore, he pushed himself to his feet. Cortés had no choice but to tolerate the self-seekers in his crew, but he did not have to tolerate Tenochtitlan's continued defiance. He had given the people of that wretched city every chance to surrender. If he needed to tear down every building in the city to make them sue for peace, he would do so without question. God would forgive him. Perhaps most importantly, so would Don Carlos.

~ ~ ~

Cuauhtemoc, careful to keep his calves tucked under his thighs, stretched forward to pick up a cup of hot water. Formal occasions usually called for something more exotic, pulque or hot chocolate, but such items were in short supply because of the siege. Even fresh water was scarce these days.

Despite being surrounded by lake on all sides, Tenochtitlan depended upon aqueducts for fresh water since the lake water was not fit for consumption. The barbarians understood this dependency all too well and had sabotaged the aqueducts a few months prior. Were it not the return of the rains and the willingness of his people to dig new wells, the city would have run out of water long ago.

Cuauhtemoc shuddered and let his gaze wander toward the horizon. The Wind God's Pyramid offered an excellent vantage point, and he studied Northern Tenochtitlan's profile in silence. The major structures were mostly intact, the twin pyramids and the Calendar Temple had sustained little damage, but the market square had been cleared of all people in case the barbarians decided to launch a surprise attack. For the most part, the barbarians had done little to harass the people of Northern Tenochtitlan, but he knew that could change at any moment. The barbarians were as unpredictable as they were ruthless.

He took a sip of his water before placing his cup on the reed mat in front of him. Ecatzin, an envoy for the *pilli* of Northern Tenochtitlan, sat across from him, and he gestured to the drinking cup with an open hand. For the sake of his host, Cuauhtemoc tilted the cup back and drained the cup of all its contents.

"Would you like some more?" Ecatzin asked.

"Perhaps later," Cuauhtemoc said.

Ecatzin nodded. "Would you care for food?"

The mention of food made his mouth water, and his empty stomach ached with a newfound intensity. When the siege first began, food was still easy to come by. Not only were many of the causeways safe to travel along, the lake was safe for fishermen and traders. These days, only the barbarians could travel along the causeways. Enterprising boatmen could evade the water-houses and their terrible weapons, but they did so at great risk.

Cuauhtemoc shot a quick glance at his attendants. Most of them had not eaten anything the entire day; Ollin had not eaten more than a morsel the past two days. He could not disrespect Ollin, or the others, by eating in front of them. Not when they had gone without food for so long.

Perhaps Ecatzin has enough food for everyone? Much as Cuauhtemoc wanted to ask, he could not bring himself to do so. If the answer was no, he would embarrass himself and Ecatzin.

"I must decline," Cuauhtemoc said. A brief look of surprise flashed across Ecatzin's face. "I am fasting in preparation for battle," Cuauhtemoc added.

A small smile graced Ecatzin's lips. "Your piety is commendable. There was much rejoicing in Northern Tenochtitlan when you were elected Great Speaker."

The glib compliment did little to impress Cuauhtemoc. His lineage counted for a great deal with the people of Northern Tenochtitlan, but he understood he had been chosen as Great Speaker because of necessity rather than personal fondness.

"My heart turns white to hear that," Cuauhtemoc said. "I consider it an honor and a privilege to lead our people to triumph over the barbarians."

"Do you expect this victory to soon materialize?"

Cuauhtemoc bristled. "Now that the rains have returned, Cortés will lose many of his allies. The Tetzcocans and the Tlaxcalteca will return home with their spoils, and there is little Cortés can offer them to stay."

Ecatzin quirked an eyebrow. "You do not think our treasures offer a suitable enticement?"

"The Tetzcocans and Tlaxcalteca are interested in slaves above all else, and there are plenty of those to be found outside of Tenochtitlan. They know the rains will make it easier for us to withstand the siege. Once we remind them that we will not soon surrender, they will lose heart."

"And if their allies abandon them, you believe the *teteo* will abandon the siege?" Ecatzin asked.

Cuauhtemoc shook his head. "They hanker after our gold too much to quit the field so easily. But when they can no longer rely on their allies for protection, we can rally warriors for a counter-strike. If we can take them by surprise, we can eliminate most of their forces the way we did during the Night of Glory."

Ecatzin scratched his chin. Many months had passed since the Night of Glory, but it was that crushing victory which gave Mexica the strength to fight on. Recreating the circumstances that culminated in the Night of Glory would be nigh impossible, but Cuauhtemoc knew better than to admit as much. He could not deprive his countrymen of hope, not when they had been deprived of so much already.

"Once the war is over," Ecatzin said, "some will urge a return to the familiar. If you wish to have Northern Tenochtitlan's assistance in the battles to come, you must resist those pleas. We cannot return to the old division of power."

Cuauhtemoc's heart quickened. Without the assistance of Northern Tenochtitlan, defeat was a certainty. The water-houses had proven terribly effective, and it was no longer possible to wage an effective resistance from Southern Tenochtitlan. "Please elaborate."

Ecatzin's voice took on a more serious timbre. "For generations, Northern Tenochtitlan has made tribute payments to Southern Tenochtitlan. If we are to aid you in the campaign against the *teteo*, we must be exempted from all tribute payments in the future. And from now on, all Great Speakers must hail from Northern Tenochtitlan."

Cuauhtemoc blinked. The terms were far more reasonable than he had expected. They were almost too good to be true. Whether or not they knew it, the people of Northern Tenochtitlan were taking a great risk by agreeing to a pact. Once the *teteo* learned of the pact, they would be sure to turn their wrath on Northern Tenochtitlan and would do their utmost to reduce the city to rubble. Did Ecatzin not understand that?

Cuauhtemoc studied Ecatzin's features. To his surprise, the envoy did not shy away from his gaze. He seemed to welcome the scrutiny, and his warm expression never faltered.

A bead of sweat trickled down Cuauhtemoc's back. Ecatzin genuinely believed the barbarians could not prevail against the Mexica forces. Despite the shameful setbacks, despite the humiliating defeats, Ecatzin trusted that Cuauhtemoc would lead the Mexica to victory.

The blind faith touched Cuauhtemoc as much as it shamed him. Ecatzin, and so many others, were counting on him to deliver peace and security. Thus far, he had failed them. He had to do better. But could he?

"We can agree to those terms," Cuauhtemoc said, his voice tight as a drum. He cleared his throat with some difficulty. "With your permission, I would like to begin moving warriors into Northern Tenochtitlan tonight."

"Of course. We are honored to open our homes to your brave warriors."

Cuauhtemoc forced a smile. He cast his gaze toward the horizon. Had he better eyesight, he might have been able to pick out the *teteo* camp. It was located on the other side of Lake Tetzcoco, so close to the water's edge the barbarians had been forced to dig ditches to divert flood waters.

In times past, the camp had been guarded by three water-houses. No longer, though. The barbarians were now using those same water-houses to lay waste to Southern Tenochtitlan. Once thriving neighborhoods had been reduced to rubble and dust, all to make sure the warriors could not use the buildings for cover.

"I would like to choose a redoubt close to the water's edge," Cuauhtemoc said. "Would you be so kind as to help me choose a location?"

"I would consider it a great privilege. May I ask why you prefer a redoubt close to the water's edge?"

Cuauhtemoc tensed. He did not wish to share battle strategies with anyone he had not fought alongside, but he could not permit himself such a luxury. He had to take his allies where he could find them and had to trust that Ecatzin understood the value of discretion. Cuauhtemoc dropped his shoulders and did his best to appear relaxed. "Once the barbarians learn that I have chosen a redoubt close to the water's edge, they will try to take me hostage. Few of their soldiers are familiar with the layout of Northern Tenochtitlan, so they will send in a very large force. If we lay a proper trap, we could win a great victory."

The promise of a great victory did not produce the warm smile Cuauhtemoc had expected. If anything, Ecatzin appeared a touch disturbed. After a long silence, he said, "It seems you intend to use yourself as bait. Is there not risk in that?"

"Enormous risk," Cuauhtemoc said. "But since when does victory go to the timid?"

Chapter 17

Cortés stepped off the gangplank onto the Tepeyac causeway. He still needed to walk a quarter length of the causeway and cross over a canal before he reached Cuauhtemoc's redoubt. He glanced at his guards. Most of them wore light armor and moved with far more purpose than him. Anxious as they were to reach Cuauhtemoc's redoubt, they kept their eyes fixed on the lake's surface.

Owing to the recent rains, the water level had risen so high that a man could hang his arm over the edge of the causeway and snatch a fish. Not that any of his men would try. They were a superstitious lot and many were convinced the lake was haunted. He understood their apprehension well. A great many Christians lay at the bottom of Lake Tetzcoco, buried beneath muck and refuse.

A lump formed in his throat. So many of his soldiers had drowned during the Sad Night, and he would have traded all that he owned to have them back again. But God would never countenance such a trade, and the lake would never relinquish them. They were forever gone to him, like the innocence Adam and Eve once knew.

I can still avenge them. Cortés took a deep bracing breath. First he had to bring the war to a close, and he could think of no better way to do that than capturing Cuauhtemoc.

Alderete had concluded the same and led a contingent of two thousand men into Northern Tenochtitlan to take Cuauhtemoc's stronghold. Cortés admired his audacity and hoped he succeeded in his efforts. Nonetheless, Cortés had no intention of letting the ingrate keep

Cuauhtemoc. If need be, he would force Alderete to hand him over.

Cortés was only bringing twenty men into Northern Tenochtitlan, but he trusted all of them to keep faith with him. Alderete had powerful friends at court, but he had joined the expedition much too recently to cultivate any real affection amongst the company men. He had men who fought with him, not for him, and Cortés was willing to wager his own life that Alderete's men would not intervene if Cortés demanded Cuauhtemoc.

Cortés stared ahead. The end of the causeway was in sight. If they kept pace, they would reach Northern Tenochtitlan's first canal in a minute or two. Once they crossed that, it would not take long to find Alderete's men.

An eerie grating filled the air, shrill as a whistle and keen as a bird's cry. His pulse quickened. He knew that sound. It was a death whistle. The Mexica used them primarily during ceremonies... and coordinated attacks. He ordered his men to prepare for an ambush.

In an instant, every man assumed a fighting position. Olea hoisted his shield above his head and ran to Cortés' side. Cortés crouched and prayed to God for safekeeping. He braced himself for a volley, but the expected attack never materialized. Confused, he looked upward. The sky was clear. He glanced at the lake's surface. Not a single canoe, no matter where he looked.

Cortés ordered Olea to lower his shield and took stock of his surroundings. His line of vision was unobstructed on both his flanks, and he could see nothing that gave him cause for alarm. No swarm of Indian canoes rushing toward them, and no volley either.

More of the death whistles sounded. Cortés cast his gaze ahead. Off in the distance, a dark form was coming into view. He tightened his grip around his sword. A glimmer of steel caught his eye, and he let out a deep breath. The dark form wasn't a band of Mexica warriors; it was a group of Spaniards.

"That must be Alderete's contingent," Cortés said to no one in particular.

Still uneasy, Cortés advanced a few paces. A distant din reached his ears. It almost sounded as if the men were shouting the word retreat over and over again. His stomach dropped. Alderete was nothing if not proud. He would never call a retreat, not unless it was absolutely necessary.

How it could be necessary, Cortés did not understand. Alderete's contingent, including the Indian allies, numbered two thousand. To overpower such numbers, the Mexica must have laid a truly terrible trap.

"Alderete's men need help," Cortés shouted.

He broke into a run, and his guards hurried to keep up with him. If Alderete's men had been set upon by a large force, there was little Cortés could do to help. He had only twenty men with him, and they had no weapons other than lances and swords. Still, they had to try. To do nothing was unconscionable.

As they drew closer to the commotion, the din of battle grew louder. What Cortés saw was even worse than what he heard. The buildings on both of Alderete's flanks were still intact, and his men were being attacked from both sides. Many tried to return fire, but the thick wooden beams and thatched roofs provided ample protection to the Mexica warriors. Perhaps most concerning of all was the situation with the canal, however.

Alderete's men must have used some kind of makeshift bridge to cross but whatever they had used, it no longer existed. Stymied by the canal, Alderete's men were effectively trapped inside the city. Many huddled in place and hid underneath their shields. The others tried their luck with the canal. It was only fifteen strokes across, but it was much too deep to wade across and many sank to their death. Those who did not sink were pelted with arrows and spears and darts. Some of the Mexica warriors were so crazed by bloodlust they threw themselves into the canal to give chase to the fleeing soldiers.

Another blast of death whistles sounded. Cortés stopped and whipped his head to the side. Canoes full of Mexica warriors were heading toward the melee. Struck dumb with horror, he watched as a group of warriors nocked arrows and fired at the defenseless swimmers. A wave of screaming let him know their arrows had flown true.

Seized by rage, Cortés sprinted forward. He was only twenty paces from the canal. He could not save all the men, but he could save some of them. His guards shouted something, but Cortés did not pay him any mind. He had to help Alderete's men.

He registered a dull thump in his leg and collapsed to the ground. Confused that his body would fail him so suddenly, he glanced down. A light spear eight handspans long was sticking out of his thigh.

His eyes widened. If the spear had lodged itself in bone, he might never walk again. If the spear had nicked an artery, he would be dead before nightfall. He reached for the shaft. He had barely wrapped his hand around it when a group of Mexica warriors hauled him to his feet.

A thick-set man with a pox-scarred face grabbed the spear.

Cortés stiffened. "Please don't. Please—"

The warrior twisted the spear and yanked it out with a vicious tug. The sudden eruption of pain was so consuming, so over-powering it blocked out all his other senses.

Unable to make words, unable to think, he gasped and sputtered incoherently as the Mexica carried him away. The pain, the pain, God it was terrible! It felt as if a burning lance had been plunged into his flesh. Nothing he had ever experienced had prepared him for such an ordeal, and he prayed to God for relief. The warriors hauled him toward the canal. He did not try to fight them, tried to stanch the sudden flow of blood instead. Another bout of pain seized him once he put hand to wound, and he cursed God and Jesus and all that was holy.

Somebody shouted his name. He tried to turn. Couldn't. More shouting. Closer now. One of the warriors who had been helping carry him collapsed. So did another one. Unbalanced, Cortés dropped to the ground like a sack of powder.

The impact drove the air from his lungs, and he groaned in pain. New hands grabbed hold of him, dragged him away from the canal. These hands felt more familiar, less rough. His head lolled backward, giving him a brief glimpse of his captors. The faces, they were familiar—his guards had rescued him!

A wave of elation rolled over him, and tears welled in his eyes. His men had risked their own lives to save him. *They have truly forgiven me for the Sad Night.* A stab of pain reminded him of his wound, and he glanced at the Mexica warriors who had tried to take him captive.

They weren't giving chase. Why weren't they giving chase? He blinked the tears from his eyes, and his vision came into focus. Olea was the reason. He had placed himself between the mob and Cortés and stood erect as a stone tower, slashing through flesh and bone with a two-handed broadsword.

Awed by the stunning display of power and swordsmanship, Cortés watched as Olea rent a stomach open and severed an arm at the elbow. His heart swelled with pride. If he ever had a son, he hoped he would be as brave as Olea. The guards pulled Cortés to his feet and turned him away from the melee. He lost sight of Olea.

He tried to walk on his own. Still couldn't. He glanced backward.

Olea had fallen.

Cortés' breath caught in his throat. The Mexica warriors had surrounded him on all sides and assaulted him with every manner of weapon. One used a *macuahuitl*, another used a spear, one used a club, another used his feet.

The sheer senselessness of it made him seethe with righteous indignation. He ordered his guards to go to Olea's aid, but they ignored him. Instead, they dragged him farther away from Olea, toward safety. He raged and he shouted, all for naught. A puddle of blood formed around Olea's head.

Cortés tore his gaze away, looked in front of him. He was on the causeway again. A mounted soldier raced toward him. He dismounted as he neared and shoved the reins toward Cortés. The man tried to shout something, but an arrow burst through his throat and he dropped the reins.

Cortés' guards rushed forward and grabbed the horse before it could bolt. A flurry of hands pushed Cortés onto the horse. He ducked to avoid a spear and tried to pivot the horse toward Olea.

A soldier, Quiñones, grabbed the bridle. "Save yourself," Quiñones shouted. "If you are killed, we are all lost!"

Cortés tried to object, but the guards turned the horse and smacked it on the rear. It charged forward like iron shot from a cannon, and Cortés grabbed onto the saddle horn to keep from falling off.

Each jolt of movement made his leg hurt anew. He had made a grave mistake by following Alderete's men into Northern Tenochtitlan. The fool had led his men right into an ambush, and Cortés had almost died trying to help him. He cursed himself for being so careless and swore to never again let his pride, or a misguided sense of compassion, guide his actions.

From now on, he would wage a war of attrition and privation. A quick victory was hopeless; too much of Northern Tenochtitlan was still intact, and too many of the warriors were still willing to fight. Better to bombard the city with his brigantines and focus on piecemeal attacks in the months to come. Only when every neighborhood had been razed and every canal filled would he send a large body of soldiers into Northern Tenochtitlan. And when that day finally came, he would make sure the Mexica paid dearly for their insolence.

~ ~ ~

Cuauhtemoc stared at the mutilated heads. They had taken on a foul odor, and he gave thanks for the incense and the fan-bearing attendants. Were it not for them, the stench might have been unbearable. It was certainly pervasive. It felt as if every nook and cranny of his redoubt reeked of congealed blood and putrefied flesh. Nonetheless, a foul odor was a small price to pay for victory.

Even now, he had a hard time believing the battle reports. Seventy *teteo* had been killed in the battle, and one hundred and twenty had been taken captive. Two hundred Tetzcocan warriors had been killed in battle, and three hundred had been taken captive. Eight hundred Tlaxcalteca warriors had been killed in battle, and four hundred had been taken captive. It was a stunning victory, the likes of which his people had not experienced since the Night of Glory, and could not have come at a better time.

Not only had the barbarians lost a considerable number of fighters, they had lost another water-house. When they first put their water-houses on the lake, they had thirteen. They had only six now. If they lost just a few more, it would no longer be possible to blockade

Tenochtitlan. For the first time in months, victory seemed within reach.

Looking around the room, he saw that he was not the only one cheered by recent events. Ollin had a smile as wide as Lake Tetzcoco, and Ecatzin wore the smug expression of a triumphant gambler. Of those present, the attendants seemed the giddiest but that was to be expected. If the city fell, the barbarians would be sure to press them for information regarding Tenochtitlan's riches. They could be absolutely ruthless when it came to matters of gold, and Cuauhtemoc pitied all who fell into their possession.

A fly landed on the *teotl* head closest to him. It took a moment to surveil its surroundings, and then crawled toward the *teotl's* gaping maw. More intrigued than revolted, Cuauhtemoc watched as the tiny creature gorged itself on fetid flesh. Flies were dirty and impure, but so too were *teteo*. They deserved each other.

Cuauhtemoc waited for the fly to leave. When the hungry interloper finally took flight, he pulled the blood-stained mat closer. Thick sheaths of *amatl* paper had been laid underneath each head, a decision he considered questionable as he did not like to see *amatl* wasted. He did not speak his thoughts on the matter, though. Today was not a day to be blemished by complaints and petty asides; today was a day for celebration. And politicking.

As Great Speaker, he would have to decide what to do with the gruesome collection of severed heads. Some urged Cuauhtemoc to add them to the Great Skull Rack, but that seemed a terrible waste. For months, the *teteo* had terrorized the people of the One World with their lightning raids. Those who tried to fight or run away were maimed and disfigured in the most heinous ways. Many Speakers assumed the *teteo* could not be defeated in battle and concluded that surrender was the most sensible course of action. Cuauhtemoc was optimistic, however, that if those Speakers received proof—bloody incontrovertible proof—the *teteo* could be beaten in battle, more people would be willing to rise against them.

If there was any one item he was absolutely certain would spark interest amongst the foreign envoys, it had to be the head of the hornless stag. Everyone in the valley had heard of the terrible beasts that stood taller than most grown men and ran thrice as fast. To know that it could be killed, to see up close what a hornless stag looked like would be a privilege and honor for any Speaker.

Cuauhtemoc was tempted to keep the head for himself, but he knew better than to give in to such a selfish urge. The war effort took priority over all else, including his personal curiosity. Much as it pained him, he would have to let some other Speaker puzzle over the beast's startlingly large eyes and its whiskered snout. *If the gods are kind, they will give me a hornless stag of my own.*

He squared his chest and turned toward his attendants. "I want this head sent to the people of Xochimilco," Cuauhtemoc ordered. "They fought bravely against the barbarians and deserve a worthy prize."

Cuauhtemoc waited to see if anyone would object. Ecatzin, seated directly across from him, nodded his approval and Ollin, seated to his right, offered nothing besides a shrug. Either of them would have been within their rights to point out that the people of Xochimilco now fought bravely for the barbarians, and he was grateful they did not mention as much. Tenochtitlan was in desperate straits, and Cuauhtemoc could not afford to turn his nose up at any potential ally.

Seeing that nobody would object, Cuauhtemoc ordered an attendant to dispose of the head. Ugly scars covered the attendant's face and chest, and Cuauhtemoc turned away as he drew near. The Great Rash had left many of its victims with scars they would bear for the rest of their life, and he gave thanks the terrible scourge no longer stalked Tenochtitlan.

It was difficult, however, to feel all that grateful. The shortage of fresh food and potable water was ravaging the city the same way the Great Rash had. Some of his best warriors were taken with the bloody flux, and many more would succumb to hunger if he could not find a way to break the siege.

"Place the head in some kind of container," Cuauhtemoc said to the attendant. "We do not want it to spoil before it reaches our friends in the southern lake."

His comment prompted weak laughter on the part of Ecatzin and Ollin, but the others offered more hearty chuckles.

Cuauhtemoc turned his gaze toward the rotting *teteo* heads. Their pale skin had taken on a waxen pallor, and he did not want to imagine how grotesque they would look once a more advanced decay set in. Despite knowing they had suffered immensely in their final moments, he could not summon any pity for the dead *teteo*.

There had once been a time when he respected their audacity, but their penchant for depravity made it impossible to hold them in high regard, not to mention foolish. Given the chance, the *teteo* would force every man, woman, and child of Tenochtitlan into slavery, just as they had done with the people of Tepeaca.

He pulled out his knife and dug his hands into the dead *teotl's* beard. He sawed off a single lock of hair and stared at it closely. It was as red as a chili pepper and curled like a hook. He had never seen hair like it in all the One World, not before the *teteo* arrived. Cuauhtemoc turned his gaze toward the other *teotl*. He lacked a full-beard, but his mottled cheeks gave him an even more striking appearance.

Cuauhtemoc rubbed the hair strands between his fingers. The *teteo* were as ugly as they were dangerous.

He bid his attendants closer. "Send the bearded head to Chalco, and send the other one to Cuahnahuac."

In the flutter of an eyelid, both *teteo* heads were whisked away. Cuauhtemoc sucked in a deep breath. "With the *teteo* gone from the room, I already feel as if I can breathe easier."

Only the attendants laughed this time.

"To which Speaker should we send the Tetzcocan head?" Ecatzin asked.

Cuauhtemoc tapped his knife against his knee as he contemplated an answer. Tetzcoco and Tenochtitlan had a long history of friendship. They first entered into alliance generations before and waged countless campaigns together. Then the *teteo* came, and the Tetzcocans forget all their promises.

"We will not send it to any Speaker," Cuauhtemoc said, his voice as hard as flint. "This rotting lump of meat can serve no useful purpose."

A disquieting stillness settled over the room. Ollin fixed his gaze on Cuauhtemoc, a silent question on his face. Cuauhtemoc did not oblige him with an answer, and Ollin cleared his throat. "What would you have us do with it, then?" Ecatzin asked.

"Dispose of it as you would any other item of refuse," Cuauhtemoc said. Some of the attendants shuffled nervously. Sacrificed captives were often subjected to gruesome rites while they were still alive, but they were always accorded a certain amount of dignity in death. To treat a corpse, or part of a corpse, as refuse went against everything proper.

"Would you have us do the same to all the Tetzcocan captives?" Ollin asked.

Cuauhtemoc scratched his chest. "How many are still alive?"

"One hundred."

Cuauhtemoc blinked. *Have so many been put to death already?*

"The Givers hope to sacrifice the last of them during the Festival of the Great Lords," Ecatzin added.

The Festival of The Great Lords was one of the most important events in all the year. Cuauhtemoc understood why the Givers would want to sacrifice the last of the captives during the festival, but he could not allow it.

"The Givers will have to plan for five captives instead," Cuauhtemoc said. "From now on, we are never to sacrifice more than five people in a day. And we must sacrifice at least one captive every night from now on."

Ecatzin and Ollin shared a brief glance. Ecatzin broke eye contact first and bid one of his attendants over. "Great Speaker, could you please tell us why?" Ollin asked.

"We need to be mindful of battle considerations. Tetzcoco and Tlaxcala remain true to Cortés, but our recent victory has encouraged many of the warriors from the smaller settlements to defect. We need to do everything we can to encourage others to do likewise, and a mass sacrifice will not serve our goals well."

Ecatzin furrowed his brow. "Of course it would. A mass sacrifice lets us communicate our strength to all the nations of the One World."

"It is not enough to seem strong on one day," Cuauhtemoc replied. "Our strength comes from proving we can kill the barbarians any day and every day with impunity; in doing so, we can prove to all the One World that the gods still favor our cause."

Ollin chuckled and shook his head. "Great Speaker, surely you do not wish to humiliate Cortés for months on end? I hear he is not the forgiving type."

Cuauhtemoc shrugged, but Ecatzin did not bother to feign amusement. "You do not think the barbarians will try to retaliate?"

"I think they will," Cuauhtemoc said. "But we will beat them back, same as always. And if they are foolish enough to stage a rescue attempt, we will trap them in the city and win an even greater victory."

"Let us pray it is so," Ecatzin said. "For if there is anything we know about Cortés, it's his penchant for violence. Should he get the chance to retaliate, I fear he will not be merciful."

Chapter 18

Cortés stared at the map as he waited for his officers to file into the tent. The Tlaxcalteca had gifted him the map months prior, and he would have to commission a new one soon. With each new day, it became a tad more brittle, a tad more discolored. Worse yet, it was curling around the edges, and he had to use weights to secure it in place.

He tapped his thumb against the map. He used to pore over every detail of it, moving pieces wherever he pleased. But the pleasure it once gave him was no more, had been replaced with a dull sense of loss.

For two years and three months, he had dedicated all his energies to bringing Mexico under his yoke. In that time, he had achieved much. Not only had he formed pacts with Tlaxcala and Tetzcoco, Cortés gained control of numerous settlements throughout the One World. But the crown jewel—the beautiful floating city of Tenochtitlan—continued to hold fast for Cuauhtemoc.

A warm draft entered the tent, prompting him to look up. Ixtli, along with a small band of Tetzcocans, were making their way inside. Cortés muttered thanks under his breath. It would have been most embarrassing had Ixtli ignored his summons.

He surveyed the tent interior. Pedro and Tapia were on the other side of the table and hardly spared the map a glance. They were probably discussing carnal matters. They had a weakness for the flesh that could put any sultan to shame and could spend numerous hours recounting their sexual exploits. Chichi had significantly improved his comprehension of Spanish, but he made no attempt to take part in their conversation. He stared at the map instead, his gaze fixed on the island of Tenochtitlan.

Cortés shifted his gaze to Sandóval. Like Chichi, he made no attempt to converse with others. Unlike Chichi, he did not seem all that interested in the map and focused his attentions on Doña Marina.

A pit formed in Cortés' stomach. *Does he fancy her?* Cortés had always assumed Sandóval was not beholden to such base urges, but it was hard to know one way or another. He was not the type to volunteer private information and seldom made his dalliances public.

Sandóval turned his way, and Cortés quickly averted his gaze. He could not look him in the eye, not yet. Sandóval was taciturn by nature, but he could not abide failure. *Probably blames me for the debacle with Alderete's troops.*

Cortés ground his teeth together. He wanted to hang Alderete by his heels. The vainglorious fool had set the campaign back months, if not years. News of his failed attack had spread like Greek fire, and local allies were deserting the company in droves. The Tlaxcalteca and the Tetzcoco had stayed faithful, but the warriors and porters who hailed from smaller settlements were disappearing with alarming regularity. If he could not find a way to stanch the flow, the entire campaign could fail.

Doña Marina laid a hand on his shoulder. He started and the sudden movement made his injured leg ache anew. He winced. The wound in his thigh had finally closed, but it would be months before he could ride or run again without pain. All because he had been foolish enough to let the Indians stick a spear in his leg.

He cursed inwardly and glanced at Doña Marina. She smiled at him and gestured to the others in the tent. They were waiting for him to speak. How long had they been waiting? He cleared his throat. It didn't matter anymore.

"Thank you for joining me," Cortés said. "We have much to discuss and we do not have much time to spare, not when we are so close to defeating the Mexica once and for all."

He turned to his countrymen as he waited for Doña Marina to translate for Chichi and Ixtli.

"Did the Mexica send an envoy to say they will soon surrender?" Tapia asked.

Cortés doubted the Mexica would ever send that type of envoy, not while they still thought Cuauhtemoc could lead them to victory. "Not yet, but that matters for little. Circumstances will soon force them to surrender."

Once the Indians heard the translation, they started speaking to each other in Nahuatl. Cortés was about to ask Doña Marina for a translation when Sandóval said, "We lost many men during Alderete's attack. Might that not prevent the Mexica from soon surrendering?"

The room went quiet. Chichi and Ixtli could not understand Spanish as well as the others, but they had to recognize the mention of Alderete because they stared at him like hungry kestrels.

Cortés fought the urge to squirm. Why did Sandóval insist upon putting questions to him so directly? "The incident with Alderete was not... helpful. I wish to God it had never happened. But we must soldier on if we are to triumph. Did Ferdinand and Isabella not suffer setbacks in their crusade?"

Doña Marina translated his statement, but a nasty coughing bout forced her to stop. She wiped her mouth with the back of her hand, cleared her throat, and resumed her translation. Doña Marina was not in good health these days, but the same could be said for many in his company.

"When can we expect more reinforcements from the coast?" Sandóval asked.

"I cannot say with any confidence. But whether or not reinforcements soon arrive, it is important we remind the people of Mexico of the power we command. The vassals who have reneged on their commitments need to be punished, and those who have kept faith ought to be rewarded." Cortés paused to allow Doña Marina time to translate. He pushed his hair back and added, "Ixtli, your warriors have won important victories all throughout the valley. Where do you think the soldiers of Tetzcoco can do the most good?"

If Ixtli was pleased by the compliment, he gave no sign of it. Stoic as ever, he responded through Doña Marina, "We will stay close to Tetzcoco so we can extract more tribute from the local settlements and keep them from defecting to the Mexica."

Cortés knew there was little chance they would ever defect to the Mexica, but he forced a wan smile. Ixtli was his most important ally; he had to grant him a wide berth in military matters, even if his goals rarely aligned with his own.

"Excellent. The Mexica will be forced to surrender if they cannot get aid from the lakeshore settlements." Cortés turned toward Sandóval. He trusted him more than any of his officers, but he would never be able to confide in him as an intimate. Sandóval was too cold and too distant; he'd be better off trying to bed a nun. "I need you to gather a host in support of the Otomi. They are having trouble with Matalcingo and need our assistance. The Otomi have done a great deal to support our campaign, so I trust you will understand the importance of your mission."

Cortés held his breath as he waited for Sandóval to answer. Otomi territory was far from Tenochtitlan, and the march promised to be both long and grueling. After a long pause, Sandóval gave his assent in the form of an almost imperceptible nod.

Pleased that Sandóval had not objected, Cortés turned to Tapia and pointed at the map. "The *altepetl* of Cuahnahuac has decided to throw their lot in with the Mexica and have declared they will give us no more tribute. They must be punished severely if we are to prevent others from doing the same. Seize all the loot you can, and inflict however much suffering you see fit."

Tapia grinned. "It would be my honor, Captain."

"Captain, where would you have me go?" Pedro asked. He pulled out his knife and picked at the grime under his nails.

Cortés rapped his fingers on the table. Long ago, he had entrusted Pedro with independent command. The result had been an absolute disaster, one that almost sank the campaign. He could not strip Pedro of command, but he would never entrust him with so much power again. "We cannot allow the Mexica to regain control of the lake so I need you to stay. Together, you and I will carry out attacks with the brigantines. We have razed most of Southern Tenochtitlan, and we must do the same to Northern Tenochtitlan. Otherwise, the Mexica will never surrender."

Pedro stiffened as if he had been slapped. His color rising, he sheathed his knife. He looked up so he could stare Cortés in the face.

Pedro could be incredibly short-sighted, but he was no knave. He understood that razing Northern Tenochtitlan was a process that could take weeks, if not months. Not only would it be dangerous, there would be few opportunities for plunder. Tapia and Sandóval, on the other hand, would be free to pillage to their hearts content as they roamed the countryside.

"Do you not think I can be helpful in other ways?" Pedro asked.

"I think you proved how useful you could be with the Toxcatl massacre," Cortés said, an edge to his voice.

Pedro flushed and glanced at the other officers. None came to his support, and he glowered in silence.

Chichi said something in Nahuatl, and Doña Marina translated his words into Spanish. "Many of the Tlaxcalteca who assisted Alderete's attack were taken captive. What plans are being made for their rescue?"

Cortés furrowed his brow. Surely, Chichi was not so naive as to think he intended to dedicate significant energies to a rescue mission? Such a mission was unlikely to succeed and would only lead to more loss of life. He waited for Chichi to say more, but the surly Tlaxcalteca held his tongue. "The scouts say they are being held in a well-defended stronghold in the center of the city," Cortés said. "It will not be prudent to launch a rescue mission before razing the nearby buildings. Otherwise, the area will not be safe for foot soldiers and cavalry."

Chichi's expression darkened. "How long will this razing take?"

Weeks, you dolt. "I cannot say with confidence," Cortés said. "As soon as it is safe to launch a rescue attempt, we will do so."

He studied Chichi's face as he received Doña Marina's translation. An unmistakable flash of anger distorted his features. "The Mexica have inflicted a great hurt on us, and we ought to respond in kind. If a rescue attempt is too dangerous, we ought to launch a retaliatory raid. My warriors can be ready by week's end. When will your men be ready?"

Cortés fought the urge to roll his eyes. He shot a glance at his countrymen, confident they would share in his scorn. The expression on Tapia's face gave him pause. Was Tapia seriously considering Chichi's proposal? Surely, he understood there were more important matters at hand. If not, he was a fool of the worst sort.

"We must find the strength to resist our rash impulses, or the Mexica will win," Cortés said, forcing some civility into his voice. "Regaining the support of our vassals and filling in the canals takes priority over all other concerns. Rest assured the Mexica will suffer for their treachery, but we ought not waste our energies on a raid that will do nothing to hasten the end of the war."

Doña Marina stared at him expectantly as if she expected him to say more. When he did not oblige, she cleared her throat and passed on his words to Chichi. He narrowed his eyes once he heard the translation and quickly gave a reply.

"Chichi says he will carry out a raid himself, whether or not you and his countrymen help him."

Cortés flared his nostrils. He had always known Chichi was a touch too prideful, but he had never been so obstinate in the past. "Tell him I need him and his men to assist with filling in the canals. We cannot bring a large army into Northern Tenochtitlan until we have filled in all the canals, and it is essential that the Tlaxcalteca assist with this very important task. Victory depends upon his cooperation."

Doña Marina paled when she heard his response. "Chichi says he is not yours to command."

Cortés stared at Chichi in shock. The Tlaxcalteca had been stalwart allies, and he did not want to cause a breach in relations. Nonetheless, he could not give his blessings to Chichi's sortie. The company had lost enough men in Alderete's attack, and he had no wish to put more of his men at risk for the sake of Chichi's pride. He took a second to compose his thoughts. "I cannot deny there is truth in what you say. But the brigantines are mine to command. If you disregard my counsel and commit yourself to a raid, you will have to do so without my brigantines."

Chichi's stoic expression faltered once he heard the translation. Cortés suppressed his smile by taking a swig of his water. Chichi had far too high an opinion of his fighting abilities, but even he had to understand that attacking Northern Tenochtitlan without the aid of brigantines would be foolhardy.

"The Tlaxcalteca have made war without the aid of brigantines, and we can do so again," Chichi said. "We hope you will join our raid but if you do not, it is no great loss to us. The glory and the loot will all be ours."

~ ~ ~

Ollin peered into the hole he had dug in the middle of his courtyard. He still had his coa handy and could round out the edges more. Not that there was any point. The grave was more than deep enough for both the urns.

Could probably bury five in there, if I had to. Scraping out the dirt had given him a strange sense of catharsis, but the sensation had proven fleeting. He felt exhausted and hollow now, could not even bring himself to glance at the urns that contained his wife and daughter. He was not ready to bury either of them. *I need more time.*

Time was a precious commodity these days. His daughter and his wife had been so alive a few weeks ago, but he had lost both of them to the bloody flux a few days prior. No amount of rage or pleading would bring them back, and he had to accept they were forever gone. It was his duty, therefore, to bury their urns and marry them to the earth.

But now that the moment had come for him to lay the urns in their final resting place, he found himself drained of all energy. *Should I call on Zeltzin for help?* No, that would be dishonorable. His daughter and his wife deserved to be buried by him, not a house servant.

Tears welled in his eyes. For the life of him, he could not understand how or why they had succumbed to the bloody flux. He breathed the same air as them, drank the same water, ate the same food, and prayed to the same gods; the bloody flux should have taken all of them or none of them. But for some terrible reason, it had spared him and killed them.

He had asked the healers and the Givers for explanation, but the answers they gave him only confused him more. He wasn't the only one with questions. Only a few months ago, the bloody flux was considered a rare disease. These days, it seemed every family in Tenochtitlan had lost somebody to the accursed illness.

Some blamed the blockade, and some blamed the gods. Both seemed equally likely to Ollin. *Hopefully, it will all make sense one day.*

The sound of muffled footfalls reached his ears. He cocked his head in the direction of the sound. Had he misheard? It was still dark out, and he had assumed most people would not rise until later in the day.

A sense of unease stole over him. He was the only one in the courtyard, but the solitude unsettled him more than it comforted him. *Perhaps I should go back inside the house.* He stood and made his way toward the hallway, his hackles standing on end.

Ollin stepped inside the hallway. At the end of the hallway, a flash of red caught his eye. He blinked. His wife and his daughter both loved the color red. Had the gods taken mercy on him? Had they returned his family to him?

He rubbed his eyes. Whatever he had seen was no more. *Perhaps I imagined it.* A small creak grabbed his attention. He stopped in place, unsure if he could trust his senses.

Ollin glanced backward. The hallway was empty behind and in front of him. His eyes drifted to the obsidian mirror hanging from the wall. The dark reflection instantly sobered him. Two figures had entered the courtyard, and both were armed.

He pressed against the wall to hide from view. Only a few more moments before they entered the hallway, and he didn't have a single weapon. He glanced at a Toltec vase balanced on a nearby plinth. The vase was a priceless work of art and had been in his family for generations. Today, however, it would have to suffice as a weapon.

He grabbed the vase's neck and lifted it above his head. Just a few moments later, the first warrior entered the hallway. Ollin smashed down with all his strength as the warrior turned toward him. The vase shattered upon collision, and the warrior slumped to the ground like a felled oak.

The other warrior swung his *macuahuitl* toward Ollin, but the door frame obstructed his arc. Sensing an advantage, Ollin threw himself at the warrior.

Ollin landed atop the Tlaxcalteca raider and wrapped both his hands around the man's windpipe. He pinned the man's arm underneath his knee and pressed down with all his weight. The man's eyes bulged outward, and he raked his hand across Ollin's face.

His nails dug deep into Ollin's flesh, and he grimaced in pain. Blood dripped into his eye, and he shook his head to try to clear his vision. No luck. He closed both his eyes and pressed down harder.

The Tlaxcalteca warrior extended his arm outward. He was trying to reach for something. But what? Ollin rubbed his face against his shoulder. He opened an eye. The raider had grabbed hold of the coa!

Ollin tried to move, but it was too late. The Tlaxcalteca warrior plunged the coa deep into his side. The simple digging instrument was by no means a warrior's weapon, but the hooked head was plenty sharp enough to pierce his flesh. Deeper and deeper he pushed it in, and Ollin could do nothing but grit his teeth to withstand the agony. No matter what, he could not let go of the man's throat.

The man yanked on the coa. The eruption of pain was so intense it robbed Ollin of his breath. Still, he did not let go. Instead, he pushed down harder. The warrior gurgled weakly and pulled harder on the coa. Ollin's vision swam, and he bit down on his tongue. The taste of blood filled his mouth.

The sensation was so unexpected, so wretched he gagged. He coughed and blinked away tears. By the time his vision cleared, the Tlaxcalteca warrior had gone still.

A strange calm took hold of Ollin. Relieved but apprehensive, he slowly pulled his hands back. The Tlaxcalteca warrior remained still. *I have done it—I have killed a man with my bare hands.* He had taken many warriors captive in battle, and seen them sacrificed afterward, but never had he snuffed out a life in a manner so intimate. And brutal.

Ollin leaned to the side and retched. A loud groan grabbed his attention. He glanced backward. The man he had felled with the vase had risen, off-balance like a drunkard. Blood streamed down his face, and he clutched a dagger in his left hand. He leaned against the wall for support and stared balefully at Ollin.

Ollin shot a glance at the *macuahuitl* his slain foe had dropped. He could reach it before the other man. Probably. He adjusted his position in case he needed to dive for the weapon. The small movement sent fiery tendrils of pain shooting through his body, but he hid his pain behind a mien of anger.

A conch shell blared in the distance. The wounded warrior blinked as if he had woken from a dream and pushed himself upright. He retreated from sight and disappeared into the hallway. Ollin let loose a relieved sigh and pushed himself off the dead intruder.

Pain exploded in his side, and he yelled so loud his voice went hoarse. A servant woman, Zeltzin, came rushing toward him. He was tempted to dismiss her, angry that she had only come to help him now that the intruders were gone, but the pain was too great for that.

"Ollin, what can I—"

"Pull the coa out," Ollin said. "Now."

Zeltzin flushed. "Let me fetch you a healer. They will know how to help."

Ollin grabbed Zeltzin's arm. "I need this coa out of my side now, not later."

She glanced at his wound. "What do you need me to do?"

Ollin opened his mouth to answer, but a blast of conch horns interrupted him. *Why are so many going off now?* He had assumed Mexica warriors were behind the din, but every blast of conch shells was followed by a loud call to retreat.

His hand brushed against the coa, sending a bolt of pain through his body. He would have to figure out the mystery of conch shells later. He needed to focus.

"Zeltzin, how thick is the coa shaft?"

"Two fingers," Zeltzin said, her voice trembling.

Ollin cursed. If the coa were a little thinner, he might have asked Zeltzin to snap it in two. But if the shaft were two fingers thick, the coa would not break easily. Better not to try.

"How deep is the head?"

"Too deep. I can only see half of it," Zeltzin said. Tears flooded her eyes. "Ollin, you are bleeding so much. Let me find a healer to help you."

Ollin suppressed a flare of anger. "It is not safe to leave the house," he said, forcing his words out through gritted teeth.

Off in the distance, a Mexica man urged his countrymen to give chase to the retreating Tlaxcalteca. His command was taken up enthusiastically, and it was not long before the heavy tromp of feet filled the air.

Ollin lay flat on his back. The Tlaxcalteca had probably hoped they could take the city unaware, but they had made a grave error. Half the city was awake now, and they would chase the raiders all the way to the shore if need be. He intended to join in the chase, as soon as Zeltzin dressed his wound.

"Zeltzin, I need you to grab the coa near the head. Then pull… with all your strength."

Zeltzin shook her head. "I cannot—"

"You can and you will," Ollin said. He guided her hand to the coa. "I am going to count to five. Pull it before I reach five. It is very important. You understand what I have told you?"

Zeltzin nodded.

"One—"

Zeltzin pulled the coa out, and he gasped as flesh and skin give way. He pounded his head against the soft dirt and prayed to the gods for mercy. They answered his prayers, but not in the way he had expected.

His pain did not give way to relief, but to exhaustion. And numbness. He pressed his hand to his wound. A jolt of pain shot through his side, but then the numbness returned. He could feel something trickling between his fingers, something warm and wet.

My life water. He pressed down harder, determined to keep the exhaustion and numbness at bay. It worked for a time. But then it returned, accompanied by coldness. Pained shouts reached his ears. Something terrible was happening outside his house, something that seemed important. He wanted to investigate, but he was tired. So very tired.

Zeltzin shook him and shouted something he could not understand.

"I'm sorry," Ollin said, his speech slurred and his thoughts jumbled. His tongue was dry and thick, his eyelids heavy as stone. "Should have told you… need to press wound. Stop… bleeding."

Ollin turned his head to the side. The last thing he saw before he closed his eyes were the urns for his wife and his daughter. He smiled. Perhaps the gods would be kind enough to reunite them in the next world.

203

Chapter 19

Cuauhtemoc rubbed the golden armband between his thumb and his forefinger. Not so long ago, he would have worn it on his arm, but the simple adornment no longer fit him.

A quiet sigh escaped his lips. He had lost a great deal of weight during the past few months, as had everyone in Tenochtitlan. His arms used to bulge with muscle; now they were skinny as saplings. He stayed away from reflective surfaces as much as he could. His appearance, something he once prided himself on, did not provide him the same comfort it once did.

He placed the armband on a nearby stool. Even though it no longer fit him, he liked having it close. The armband was a reminder of how things used to be before the war, before hunger and sickness.

Cuauhtemoc glanced at Ollin. *Few have suffered as much as him.* Not only had Ollin lost his daughter and his wife, he had lost his health. The healers were optimistic he would recover from his stomach wound, but it might be weeks before he could walk unassisted. Months, if he was unlucky. By the time he recovered, the war could be over. And no matter how much time passed, he would never regain his loved ones.

Ollin stirred and mumbled something under his breath. After an extended silence, he opened his eyes and coughed, sending spittle flying into the air.

Cuauhtemoc grabbed a water gourd and brought it to Ollin's lips. He tilted it back and let Ollin drink at his leisure. He managed only a few mouthfuls before he began coughing again. Cuauhtemoc pulled his hand back and waited for Ollin to stop.

"How fare you?" Cuauhtemoc asked.

"It may not be long until I marry the earth," Ollin said.

Cuauhtemoc flashed a mirthless smile. "The healers tell me they expect you to make a full recovery."

Ollin grunted and tried to sit up. Unable to do even that, he exhaled loudly. "How many were killed in the attack?"

"Fifty warriors," Cuauhtemoc said, his voice clipped. He trusted Ollin as he trusted few others, but he saw no reason to burden him with a full accounting of the death toll. No need to tell him of the women and the children who had been killed, no need to tell him of the porters and the slaves who had been cut down like stalks of corn.

"What happened?"

"Tlaxcalteca raiders snuck into the city under cover of dark. They attacked your household, and many others, before they were discovered."

Ollin's hand drifted to his side. Hot maguey sap, mixed with herbs and salt, had been applied to the wound when he was still insensate, along with fresh bandaging.

"Once our warriors learned what was happening, they were quick to mobilize," Cuauhtemoc said. "The Tlaxcalteca tried to fight them, for a time, but they were unable to overcome our forces and called a retreat."

"Then why did so many…" Ollin whispered.

"It was a feigned retreat. A small contingent of Tlaxcalteca archers hid themselves near the causeway. The men who pursued the retreating raiders did not realize until it was too late."

While it gave Cuauhtemoc no pleasure to admit as much, the attack had been well-planned. Had he been present for the fighting, he probably would have given chase to the raiders and might have taken an arrow himself.

"How many of our warriors were captured?" Ollin asked.

"Twenty."

"I hope they will be given good deaths."

Cuauhtemoc said nothing. He doubted the barbarians would put the captives to death. More likely they would force them into bondage and give them ugly burns to mark them as slaves. Proud warriors who had won stunning victories for Tenochtitlan would spend the rest of their days cleaning out chamber pots and groveling before an unworthy people. He shuddered. Death was a far better fate.

"Will it be possible to rescue them?" Ollin asked.

Cuauhtemoc shook his head. Whether they were being held in Tetzcoco or the *teteo* camp, rescue would be impossible. The *teteo* camp was too well-guarded, and Tetzcoco was too populous. Even when Tenochtitlan had been at the heights of its power, Cuauhtemoc would have been wary of launching a raid against Tetzcoco. He certainly did not intend to order one now, not when so many of his men were dead or half-starved.

"What vexes you?" Ollin asked.

"Matters you need not concern yourself with," Cuauhtemoc said. "Focus on your recovery."

"You were not thinking of our previous glories, then?" Ollin asked.

Cuauhtemoc forced a laugh. "I must admit I was thinking of other matters. Perhaps I would be better off thinking about our past, though. It sometimes feels as if our brightest days are behind us."

"Which triumph are you most proud of?" Ollin asked.

"Our victory over the Tepanecs. Had it not been for that victory, we never would have gained our independence." Cuauhtemoc envied the warriors who had taken part in that campaign. Their bravery would forever be extolled by anyone of note. He could never hope for half as much praise. "What say you?"

"The campaign against the Huastecs."

Cuauhtemoc furrowed his brow. "Is that the truth now?"

"Trust that I am not trying to twist something," Ollin said. "I think there is much to be proud of when it comes to our victory over the Huastecs. They were not an easy people to conquer, and they have faithfully served us for generations."

Cuauhtemoc nodded. The Tepanecs were never given a chance to serve. Their bravest warriors had been put to death after the siege ended, and the women with the best blood were married off. The Tepanec children were taught to think of themselves as Mexica, and the city folk were displaced by an influx of Mexica settlers. In the course of a few generations, the Tepanecs went from being the mightiest nation in all the One World to being almost completely erased.

"Do you think we can prevail against the barbarians?" Ollin asked.

"Of course," Cuauhtemoc said. Ollin gave him a searching look. Cuauhtemoc sighed and turned away. "But I suppose the Tepanecs and the Huastecs also thought they would prevail."

~ ~ ~

Cortés put down the writing stylus and rubbed his eyes. He had been bent over his desk for nearly an hour, trying to compose a letter to his father. But no matter how hard he tried, he could not focus. It did not help that his candle light was poor and that he had to contend with an unrelenting cacophony of noises now that dark had settled.

He put a hand over his ear. Quieter, but not quiet enough. How could a man be expected to think when he had to contend with an army of frogs and fowl? So many of them had made a home in the lake it was a small wonder anyone could sleep come nightfall.

Cortés removed his hand from his ear, allowing the horrid din to envelop him once more. He sighed. Some battles could never be won. If God was kind, the Mexica would realize as much one day.

Despite the blockade, despite disease, despite dwindling numbers, the Mexica had yet to surrender. They would have to bend the knee at some point, even the most prideful of warriors could not subsist on puddle water and sun-dried bricks, but Cortés had grown tired of waiting. And he had grown tired of Mexico.

More and more, he longed for the charms of home. He missed the tolling of church bells, the sight of fresh-fallen snow, the taste of fresh milk. And he missed his family. His mother had such a beautiful voice, but he could no longer remember the hymns she sang under her breath. Cousin Maria had such soft eyes, but he could no longer remember if they were brown or green. Did Father still fret over his bald pate? Had Uncle Gonzalo sired any more bastards? Did any of them pray for him still?

He doubted it. Almost twenty years had passed since he had last seen any of them. Every now and then, he wrote letters to some of his family members. The words used to come easy to him, back when he was an unimportant hidalgo trying to manage an *encomienda* in Cuba. But much had changed since then. He no longer enjoyed Governor Velázquez's good standing, and he could never return to his *encomienda* in Cuba. He had forsaken all of that for the campaign, sure that the king would reward his sacrifice with royal favor. But the king had yet to respond to any of his entreaties. *Will he ever?*

Cortés stood and wiped sweat away from his brow. *Perhaps I should summon Doña Marina.* He dismissed the thought. Doña Marina was still important to the expedition, and the risk of getting her with child was too great. He had given in to weakness before, but he had sworn not to do so again. Much as she tempted him, he had to put the mission first.

He patted around in the dark for his boots. He shook the first one and turned it upside down. Cortés grabbed the other one, shook it even more thoroughly than the first one. He pushed his foot into the tight confines on his boot, confident he would find no bugs inside. Too confident.

Something clamped down on his toe, and he flung his foot outward. His boot went flying across the tent and collided with a chamber pot. Thankfully, it did not spill.

A guard outside asked after his welfare. Cortés assured him all was well and trudged over to the other side of the tent. He picked up the boot and shook it even more thoroughly. Nothing came tumbling out, so he smacked the sole a few times for good measure. Satisfied he had no more cause for worry, he carefully slipped the boot on. He let loose a relieved breath when his toes pressed not against writhing limbs but solid leather.

He grabbed his canteen, made his way to the tent flap, and started to undo the knots. His mind was abuzz, but his body was weary and his fingers did not cooperate as they should have. It took almost half a minute before he could peel back the tent flap and step outside.

The sky was dark and overcast, blotting out most of the night stars. However, owing to the torches, the camp did not lack for light. Nor did it lack for people. Cortés had assumed most of the men would have turned in by now, but a great many were still awake, entertaining themselves with dice and various other pastimes.

His gaze settled on a group of men playing cards by the light of a nearby fire. Cortés could not put a name to any of their faces, but he was curious to see what game they were playing. He made his way to them, careful not to announce his presence. They were so absorbed in their cards they did not notice his approach, and he stopped five paces short of the firepit. The game they were playing was utterly unfamiliar and if he came any closer, they would be sure to notice him. *I am too weary for conversation with strangers.* He retreated a pace. Better to stay in the shadows. The light revealed too much.

Too weary to stand, he made his way to a row of crates. He sat down on the nearest one and took a sip from his canteen. The lukewarm liquid did little to give him more energy.

"Is that you, captain-general?" a voice asked.

Cortés turned to the side. It took him a moment to recognize the disheveled figure as Pedro de Alvarado.

"Aye, it is me," Cortés said.

"Would it displease you, if I took a seat next to you?"

Only a few months ago he would have taken a seat next to me without asking. But much had changed over the course of the campaign. Cortés had never punished Pedro for the Sad Night, but he had never forgiven him either. "Not at all," Cortés said.

Pedro nodded to the men who had gathered around the fire. "Think they will keep at their game for long?"

"I cannot say with any confidence," Cortés said. "God as my witness, I am a poor prognosticator. Much that I have predicted has not come to pass, may never come to pass."

His thoughts flew to the catapult his engineers had erected in Southern Tenochtitlan. He had been so sure it would work, so sure its awesome might would finally cow the Mexica into submission. In the end, his certainty counted for little. The catapult failed to fire even a single load and had done nothing to hasten the end of the war.

"You still have my confidence, captain-general," Pedro said.

Cortés blinked. He had not expected such a heartfelt answer from Pedro. He cleared his throat and squared his shoulders. "Do you plan to put to sea, after the war is over?"

Pedro laughed. "I think not. Never cared much for the ocean."

Cortés nodded. He shared Pedro's aversion. Why any man would wish to spend his life on the sea was a mystery to him.

"You do not intend to take your gold back to Spain, then?"

"Never," Pedro said. The certainty in his voice surprised Cortés. Perhaps seeing the question on his face, Pedro added, "We're building a dynasty here, remember?"

Cortés smiled. An odd thing, to have Pedro use his own words against him. "Dynasties flourish only with the king's favor," Cortés replied. "Don Carlos has not responded to any of my missives, and I hear his heart may be set against us." He stopped to take a sip from his water canteen. *Was I wrong to send his Majesty so much of our gold?* He knew some of the men still resented the decision, not that he could fault them. Even he had come to regret his decision. "Circumstances might require that we travel to his court to secure a personal audience," Cortés added. "Otherwise, Don Carlos may never favor our cause."

Pedro clenched his teeth. After a long pause, he said, "Perhaps circumstances will require that we stay. We have given Don Carlos more gold than can be found in all the West Indies; he will favor our cause."

I would that I had your confidence. But months of silence had taken their toll on Cortés. He did not know if he could trust the king to make the right decision, did not know if the king had ever spared him a thought.

Cortés exhaled and turned toward Pedro. "What do you mean to do after the war is over?"

"The war will never be over, not for me," Pedro said. "Once the Mexica surrender, my brothers and I will find a new campaign. And when that one ends, we will find another one."

Cortés frowned. "Why fight if you do not mean to enjoy the spoils?"

"The battles are the spoils," Pedro said. "Cortés, we left home for a reason. Had we stayed in Estremadura, we'd be breaking our backs, tilling some fallow field. Had we stayed in Cuba, we'd be tending to our *encomiendas*, growing fat and lazy as our slaves worked the land. We came here to prove our worth as men, to bend the savages to our will."

Cortés tugged on his beard. The Sad Night had changed Pedro. For a time, it made him humbler. But the newfound humility quickly faded and had been replaced with something much uglier. Not only did he become more comfortable giving in to his most violent urges, he became more determined than ever to prove his gallantry. "Would you say the war is going well?" Cortés asked.

"I think we would do well to attack the Mexica on the morrow," Pedro said. "We cannot allow them any respite if we mean to win."

Cortés' shoulders sagged. Unfortunately, Pedro was right. By the time the war was over, Tenochtitlan would be as thoroughly destroyed as Jericho of old. "I am glad we are of the same mind," Cortés said. "I pray your next campaign will be different. Our victory has come at a steep price. A peaceful conquest would have been better."

Pedro snorted. "The Indians will never peacefully submit. They will fight us wherever we go but we will triumph in the end, just as we did with the Moors."

But if we cannot convince the Indians to love us, we will suffer the same reverses as the Moors. Cortés exhaled loudly. Pedro would never understand his worries. Men like him could only think of the next campaign, the next conquest. He could worry not ponder his place in history any more than a pig could read Scripture.

I would be happier, if I could be more like Pedro. He dismissed the thought quick as it came. Men like Pedro did not make old bones. Neither would Cuauhtemoc, so long as Cortés had his way. The vain fool had dragged on the war far too long, and Cortés meant to make him suffer for it.

Cortés took a swig from his water canteen. Most of the gamblers had retired for the night. *Time for me to do the same.* He said farewell to Pedro and returned to his tent. The campaign had given him many sleepless nights, but all his sacrifices, all his suffering would finally be worth it once Tenochtitlan surrendered.

Chapter 20

Cotton Flower stared at the ceiling of her wooden hovel. Despite the darkness, she could make out the individual beams if she squinted. She sometimes spent half the night staring at the ceiling, too anxious to fall asleep but too exhausted to rise from bed. Nights were always the worst. Almost a year had passed since she had been freed from barbarian captivity, but the memories of that terrible time haunted her still.

As long as she lived, she would hate the barbarians for treating her so foully. Owing to the siege, the rest of her people were learning to do the same. When the barbarians first put their water-houses on Lake Tetzcoco, she assumed the warriors would sink or capture them in a matter of days. Despite the valiant efforts of her countrymen, many of the water-houses were still intact. The blockade was practically impossible to circumvent these days, and any who ventured onto the lake to hunt or trade did so at great risk.

Cotton Flower sat up. It would do her no good to stay in bed any longer. She reached for her sandals, but a sound outside her room made her freeze. She strained her ears. A group of men were approaching her room. Her heart thumped against her chest. Had the barbarians come to steal her away again?

She looked for something she could use as a weapon and was about to leap from bed when a familiar voice reached her ears. The tension ebbed from her body. The voice belonged to Cuauhtemoc. She could not think of a good reason he would call on her so late, but she trusted he did not mean her any harm.

"Princess," Cuauhtemoc said, "may I enter your room?"

Cotton Flower tensed. *If I say no, will he leave me be?* She could not say for certain. He was her husband and the Great Speaker; her guards would not stop him if he demanded entry. A terrible thought occurred to her. What if Cuauhtemoc had come to claim his marital rights?

A knot of dread formed in her stomach. She was not ready to take anyone into her bed, not even her husband. Surely he understood that? He knew what the barbarians had done to her, knew how much she had suffered at their hands.

"I must speak with you regarding an important matter," Cuauhtemoc said.

Cotton Flower furrowed her brow. Cuauhtemoc would not disturb her sleep for a trifling matter, would he? She put aside her misgivings and told her guards to let Cuauhtemoc pass.

The sight of her husband shocked her. The open wounds on his arms wept blood, and his gaunt face made her breath catch. He looked as if he aged ten years since she had last seen him. She worried for a moment he had been hurt in battle, but she soon realized his wounds were self-inflicted. *Why would he choose to bleed himself at a time like this?* She knew the devout often did such things, but she could not imagine doing the same. Hunger made her dizzy enough; bloodletting would only sap her energy further.

"May I sit, Princess?" he asked.

Cotton Flower nodded, sure that he would seat himself on a stool or the floor. To her surprise, he seated himself at the foot of her bed. She pulled her feet back and retreated a handspan.

"My apologies for disturbing your sleep," Cuauhtemoc said, his gaze fixed on the floor.

"You are forgiven, Great Speaker," she said, trying her best to strain the worry from her voice.

Cuauhtemoc nodded and muttered under his breath. Her legs began to tremble. She knew her fear was unbecoming but could not help it.

"Is something vexing you, Great Speaker?" Cotton Flower whispered.

Cuauhtemoc sighed but stayed silent otherwise. Her chest tightened uncomfortably. What was wrong with Cuauhtemoc? He was never so taciturn, so lifeless.

"Cuauhtemoc, please tell me what's on your mind."

The mention of his name woke him from his strange stupor. "What do you believe we will leave in remembrance? After we are gone?"

Cotton Flower quailed. *Does he intend to ask me for a child?* She shivered and forced herself to make words. "What do you mean, Cuauhtemoc?"

"I fear we may not be remembered at all," Cuauhtemoc said, his voice thick with regret. "So much of what we have built has been destroyed. The skull racks have been toppled, the temples have been desecrated, and our warriors have been humbled... what is there to remember us by, besides broken bones and shattered spears?" Cuauhtemoc paused, took a deep breath. He cleared his throat and said, "The city can hold out no longer. I must surrender to the barbarians on the morrow."

The air rushed from Cotton Flower's body. She felt as if she had been kicked in the stomach and drawing breath became painful, almost impossible. "You can't," she sputtered.

"I must," Cuauhtemoc replied. "Too many of us have died to keep fighting."

Cotton Flower quieted. She did not dare deny the truth in his words. These days, the specter of death hung over Tenochtitlan like a dark storm cloud. It blotted out warmth and happiness in equal measure and pervaded every conversation. Some estimated the city had lost almost two thirds of its population in the past year, but she refused to put stock by such claims. The gods would never allow such a tragedy.

"But if we surrender, the barbarians will get everything they want," Cotton Flower said.

A choked laugh escaped Cuauhtemoc. "No, they will not. The warriors have made sure of that."

"What do you mean?"

"The barbarians have gained a great deal in their war with us, but they will not gain more of our gold, that I am sure of."

Cotton Flower averted her gaze. It mattered little to her whether the barbarians took possession of Tenochtitlan's gold stores. She knew all too well they had other interests, and her body would forever bear the scars of their terrible cruelty. The barbarians liked to think of themselves as mighty warriors, but they were nothing more than base scavengers.

Her throat constricted painfully. "Do you think the barbarians will be merciful?"

"Perhaps they will be relieved by the war's end, perhaps they will be outraged we fought for so long." Cuauhtemoc rubbed the calluses on his hand. "I suppose we will have an answer soon. At daybreak, I will assemble what is left of the Mexica leadership. Together, we will sail to the water-houses and formally surrender."

Tears flooded Cotton Flower's eyes. Never in all her life had she expected Cuauhtemoc to utter such awful words. Cuauhtemoc was supposed to fight for Tenochtitlan, not surrender. A terrible anger seized her, but it quickly dissipated. The barbarians enjoyed advantages the likes of which the Mexica had never known. Her countrymen had fought valiantly, and she could ask no more of them than that.

"Am I expected to come with you, Husband?"

Cuauhtemoc shook his head. "I have made arrangements for you to be smuggled out of the city. When you are ready, I will take you to a canoe. It might be possible to slip the blockade while it is still dark out."

Cotton Flower's eyes widened. The water-houses were constantly patrolling the lake, and trying to paddle for the shore was incredibly dangerous. She trusted that Cuauhtemoc would take every precaution to keep her safe, but the idea of trying to slip past the water-houses filled her with dread.

What would happen if Cuauhtemoc picked dishonest men? They might hand her over to the barbarians instead of sailing her to safety. Such treachery would have been unimaginable a few months prior, but she knew privation could do strange things to the mind.

"Would it not be better for both of us to leave?" Cotton Flower asked.

Cuauhtemoc stiffened.

"Together, I mean," Cotton Flower added. "As husband and wife."

Cuauhtemoc straightened his posture. "It would be dishonorable. I cannot leave the city I have been tasked with defending, not when so many have no choice but to stay."

Cotton Flower opened her mouth to object but could not bring herself to say the words. Cuauhtemoc had been raised to abide by the warrior code. He could not abandon the city anymore than he could grow a new hand. Even if she were as eloquent as the legendary Shield Flower, she could not hope to change his mind.

"Would it not be very dangerous to sail for the shore?" Cotton Flower asked. "The water-houses might intercept my canoe before I made landfall. And even if I reached the shore..."

Cotton Flower reflected on some of the stories she had heard. Common women captured by the barbarians were used in the worst of ways. She could not endure such a terrible fate, not again.

"Do you think the barbarians consider me valuable still?" Cotton Flower asked. "They have already had their way with me, and Tahtli is dead."

Tears spilled down her face. It still pained her to think about what they had done to Tahtli, Great Speaker before Cuauhtemoc. Tahtli had been nothing but kind toward the barbarians, and they had repaid him by imprisoning and torturing him.

"The barbarians know nothing of honor or decency, but they have become more learned in political matters," Cuauhtemoc said. "A few of them will be able to recognize you on sight. If they capture you, arrangements will be made so that you can take an important *teotl* as a husband."

A sour taste filled her mouth. The *teteo* were an uncouth, foul-smelling, unrefined people. She would not want a *teotl* for a husband any more than she would want a tapir for a bed stool. Surely death was better... Cotton Flower shook her head. Despair was dangerous, and she would not give in to it.

But what could she look forward to as a wife of somebody like Cortés? Or worse, Pedro? Cotton Flower pinched her lips between her fingers. She could think of only one *teotl* she would be willing to marry.

She closed her eyes, tried to picture Juan Cano's face. His mouth was round and small like a tomato, but his nose was large and bulbous. Most startling of all were his pupils. They were blue and soft, like Lake Tetzcoco on a pleasant day.

Might the *teteo* marry her to Cano? She knew she would not have the final say when it came to her intended, yet she hoped to at least influence the process. But if the barbarians caught her fleeing the city, she could expect little in the way of kindness. Perhaps it would be better to come to them as a supplicant. So long as the warriors recognized her, they would hand her off to Cortés or Ixtli.

Or they might ravage me instead. She knew all too well that not all warriors conducted themselves with honor. The ones who didn't recognize her would be the most dangerous of all. For if they did not recognize her, they might treat her as they would as they would any other captured woman: by burning her with an ugly brand and forcing her into bondage.

Cotton Flower touched her cheek. The pain was supposed to be unbearable, worse than childbirth even.

She sucked in a deep breath. Tonight would very likely be her last night as a free woman. The choice she made tonight could define her life for years to come. If she were truly unfortunate, it might be her last chance to decide her own fate.

She reached for Cuauhtemoc's hand and squeezed it. "If you cannot leave the city, then neither can I. Come what may, we will face the new future together."

~ ~ ~

Malintze tucked back a strand of hair with trembling fingers. It was finally over. The Mexica were surrendering. The terrible war was finally over.

She clenched her teeth to keep them from chattering. She had never felt so nervous. Not the day she first met the Spanish, not the day her family sold her. She ran a hand down the front of her dress to smooth the wrinkles.

In a matter of moments, Cuauhtemoc would climb the last of the pyramid steps and formally surrender. She glanced at the spread of foods spread across the table. Cortés had insisted upon a magnificent banquet to celebrate the occasion.

The blaring of a horn let her know Cuauhtemoc was close. She took a deep breath to steady her nerves. She had spent years dreaming about this moment. Ever since she had been a child, the Mexica had been the most powerful nation in all the One World. To see them humbled, and to know she had played a role in their downfall, was vivid proof the world had changed.

Malintze glanced at the other Spaniards who had gathered on the pyramid's summit. Pedro, Sandóval, and Aguilar were all nearby, along with a host of other Spaniards who had crowded underneath a flimsy canopy erected by the Spaniards. No warriors from Tlaxcala or Tetzcoco had been invited to the parley, and she was glad of it. The fewer Nahuatl speakers in the tent, the more the *teteo* had to depend on her.

Cuauhtemoc crested the last stair and stepped under the shade of the canopy, followed by a stream of attendants. The sight of the Mexica party made her breath catch.

They were emaciated and sickly and hollow-eyed as skeletons. Even Cuauhtemoc, ruler of the most powerful nation in the One World, had no more flesh on him than a fasting penitent. Most surprising of all, they smelled rancid. She rubbed her eyes. It was hard to trust her nose or her vision. The Mexica washed fastidiously, but the men standing before her were caked with grit and blood and all manner of foul substance.

Cortés seated himself in a high-backed chair and had a reed mat laid out for Cuauhtemoc. "Please make yourself comfortable. I am honored to speak with you today."

Malintze translated the statement for Cuauhtemoc. He glanced contemptuously at the mat and said, "I will not sully myself by sitting on your foul mat."

Malintze flushed. She glanced at those close enough to overhear and gave thanks none of them could understand Nahuatl. She cleared her throat and said to Cortés, "Cuauhtemoc prefers to stand and hopes you will understand."

Cortés rapped his fingers against his arm rest. "Ask him if any of his women will be joining us. We have such a beautiful spread of food, and it would cheer me immensely if we could share this bounty with his kin."

Cuauhtemoc's face darkened. "They are in the city, waiting for assurance of safe passage."

Malintze bit her lip. She was usually reluctant to translate statements verbatim, but she could understand Cuauhtemoc's concern. And since she could not think of a way to make his language more courteous, she passed on his words unaltered.

Cortés laughed once she explained Cuauhtemoc's response. "Cuauhtemoc, I give you my word as a Christian they have no need to fear for their safety. Our quarrel ends today. From now on, there will only be peace and love between our people."

"My heart turns white to hear that," Cuauhtemoc said. He puffed out his chest and straightened his posture. "There is much I would say to you, but you and your wicked countrymen know nothing of compassion or reason. Yet even if you do not have the sense the gods would give a drooling babe, know that I have done everything in my power to defend my *altepetl* and free it from your hands. Our gods have abandoned us to your cruel machinations, and I have none that I can call upon for protection. Know that it would be just if you took my life. You have already destroyed my city and killed my vassals so take my life and put an end to the Mexica nation."

Malintze's eyes widened. *Apparently defeat has not chastened this one.* She cleared her throat. Did she dare to translate his statement verbatim? No, she could not. Cortés would be sure to take offense. Still, she could not change it completely. That would be too suspicious. Better to leave out the insults and translate everything else.

Despite her efforts to soften Cuauhtemoc's words, Cortés glowered when he heard the translation. He turned to his attendants. Aguilar suppressed a snigger, but Sandóval and Pedro did not share his amusement. Color flooded Cortés' cheeks, and he whipped his head toward Cuauhtemoc.

"Do not place the blame for this destruction at my feet," Cortés hissed. "Had you the sense to surrender when I first sent peace envoys to you, this long and terrible war could have been avoided." Cortés made as if to stand, but a glance from Father Olmedo checked him. He relaxed in his seat and rubbed his knee. "Let's put this acrimony behind us. Many good Christians died at the hands of your men, and we must have peace from now on. Sit and enjoy this fine food we have prepared. We have much to discuss."

Malintze decided not to translate his angry rejoinder, choosing instead to focus on his desire for peace and amity. "What does Cortés wish to discuss?" Cuauhtemoc asked.

Cortés fidgeted in his seat when he heard the translation. Instead of answering, he glanced at the untouched food and picked at his dry lips. She knew he had been looking forward to this banquet all morning, and he seemed perplexed that Cuauhtemoc was so unwilling to break bread with him. He sighed and said, "His Majesty Don Carlos is a king unlike any other. Spain has prospered under his rule, and our country is envied by all of Christendom. He loves Jesus with all his heart and has involved himself in many endeavors to spread the One Truth Faith to barbarous lands. By surrendering, you have agreed to recognize Don Carlos as your master and to assist him in all matters. As I am his chosen representative in these lands, I must ask that you assist me in collecting gold for his Majesty."

Cortés sounded as if he were giving a memorized speech, and his lack of conviction surprised her. In times past, he had always spoken of Don Carlos with warmth and affection. *Why has that changed?* She was tempted to ask, but this was neither the time, nor the place.

Confusion was no reason to shirk her duties. She translated his statement for Cuauhtemoc. He nodded and whispered to one of his attendants. The man hobbled to the edge of the pyramid and made a signal with his hand. Three conch shells went off in short succession, and a small procession of porters entered Cortés' redoubt.

Each one carried a present of some kind. Some carried golden discs, some carried golden banners, and some carried golden labrets. Beautiful as they were, it did not amount to much in a material sense. By the time the *teteo* smelted it down, they would probably only have a few ingots.

"Is this all the gold they mean to present us today?" Cortés asked.

Malintze translated the question for Cuauhtemoc. "Yes," Cuauhtemoc replied, his voice grave but strong.

"When will they deliver the rest?" Cortés asked. "We wish to have the gold that Motecuhzoma kept in his palace, and the gold we lost during the Sad Night."

A grim smile touched Cuauhtemoc's lips. "We wish we could help, but we cannot deliver what we do not possess."

Malintze looked at him askance. Surely, Cuauhtemoc knew it was pointless to lie. The *teteo* would not hesitate to search every house and every person for hidden gold. She waited for Cuauhtemoc to say more, confident he would try to explain himself further. But he did no such thing, much to her dismay.

"Great Speaker, what do you mean?" Malintze asked.

Cuauhtemoc's smile widened. He glanced toward her, repeated himself, and turned back to Cortés.

Anger welled in her breast. *Cuauhtemoc's intransigence will ruin this parley.* She cleared her throat and said, "Cuauhtemoc would have us believe there is no more gold to be had."

Cortés thinned his lips. "I have no time for riddles and japes. We know there is more gold in Tenochtitlan. We have looked upon it with our own eyes. Where is the gold from the Sad Night? Where is the gold from Motecuhzoma's palace?"

Malintze passed on his words. She had tired of Cuauhtemoc's obstinance and adopted a tone not so different from Cortés. Cuauhtemoc did not seem to care over much. He did not even glance her way. Instead, he stared off into the distance, his gaze fixed on the distant shoreline. "The gold is gone."

Cortés tensed. "Gone where?"

"To the bottom of the lake."

Malintze blinked. Had she heard wrong? She studied Cuauhtemoc's features carefully. There was no fear on his face, no remorse either. Only defiance and anger.

Malintze's heart lodged in her throat. Cortés had made promises to her, so very many promises. And not just her. To everyone. To his soldiers, his allies, his kin, and his king. Those vows were built on the recognition he would be flush with gold after Tenochtitlan fell. If the gold was no more, Cortés' words amounted to null. *Including his promise to free me.*

Her gaze drifted to Cuauhtemoc and his attendants. She had assumed they had refused to surrender, even after it became clear they could not triumph against the *teteo* and their allies, because their pride would not allow them to admit defeat. But if it was pride that had motivated them, it was spite that had sustained them. It was spite that had given them the strength to endure when food became scarce, when disease became rampant. And it was spite that convinced them to dump their treasure in the lake.

A strange desire to laugh took hold of her. The Mexica must have decided months prior to commit the gold to the bottom of the lake. The *teteo* constantly complained of the treachery of the Mexica, but never in their worst dreams could they have conceived of such perfidy.

Pedro shot her a concerned glance. She bit back a smile. He would never get the gold Cortés had promised. He would never rise above his modest circumstances, would never establish himself as a great lord for all to fear.

"Doña Marina, what did he say?" Cortés asked.

Malintze turned toward the captain-general. Pity almost convinced her to lie. But there was no sense in lying; she could not make more gold appear, nor could she undo what Cuauhtemoc had already done.

Cortés went pale as an eggshell when he heard the translation. "Surely…" He trailed off, unable to make words. Her lips twitched. Cortés had won thousands to his cause with the eloquence of his tongue, but even he could not make light of such a great calamity.

Malintze staggered toward the edge of the flat-topped pyramid. A strong gust of wind pushed her backward. Nevertheless, she persisted, even as the stench of death and despair came wafting toward her. She stopped a few paces short of the ledge. The sight below made her stomach clench.

The *teteo* and their allies had spared no section of the city. The beautiful wooden buildings of Northern Tenochtitlan had been put to fire, the stone buildings of Southern Tenochtitlan had been razed. The gardens had been stripped bare, the temples desecrated. Motecuhzoma's precious zoo had been reduced to cinders, and the Sacred Precinct had been defiled.

The wind was picking up, and a stench that was once faint became anything but. To breathe through her nose was to risk gagging, so she breathed through her mouth instead, filling her lungs with the noxious stench of putrefying flesh and acrid smoke. Her gorge rose, and she clamped a hand over her mouth.

She closed her eyes and waited for her breathing to calm. Had the destruction served any purpose? The *teteo* could never recover the riches of Tenochtitlan, and the city was no more than an empty husk now. *Just as the Tlaxcalteca and the Tetzcocans always wanted.* She shook her head. The *teteo* had won a great victory for their allies, but they had little to show for it besides rubble and ruin.

Aguilar laid a hand on her shoulder. Confused, she turned toward him. Why was he staring at her so expectantly? She looked at Cortés. He was staring at her the same way. *Have I done something wrong?*

"Doña Marina, we must put more questions to Cuauhtemoc," Cortés said. "Are you able to assist us?"

For the briefest of moments, she considered saying no. Reason, however, prevailed upon her. Much as she wished it weren't so, her fate was tied to the *teteo*. So, too, was the fate of Tenochtitlan.

Malintze placed herself between Cortés and Cuauhtemoc once more. The *teteo* had won the battle for the city, yet they had lost the battle for its riches. If they meant to win the peace, they would have to learn from the Mexica. Martial strength could build an empire, but it could not hold one together.

A deep sadness stole over Malintze. The *teteo* might not prove any different than the Mexica. Their imperial ambitions had ended in failure and blood and smoke and misery, and the *teteo* might very well follow in their footsteps.

Would there be any way to stop them from doing so? Malintze could not say. She knew, however, that Cuauhtemoc's decision to sink the gold would have enormous implications for Tenocthtitlan's future.

Even if Cortés and his countrymen forced every slave to muck for treasure, they would never be able to recover more than a few baubles and trinkets. The lake was too big, the Mexica too devious. For better or worse, the gold was forever lost. She shuddered to think of what would happen once the *teteo* realized as much.

They would not be merciful, that much she knew. They would be sure to punish the Mexica for failing to provide them tribute, just as the Mexica had done to countless other peoples. She closed her eyes and shook her head.

Perhaps one day the senselessness of it would become obvious to all. She hoped she would live to see that day. A silly dream, she knew. But one she could not put aside either. For if there was anyone who understood the power of dreams, it was Malintze of Painalla.

Not so long ago, she was a nameless slave. Now she was one of the most powerful women in all of the One World. She knew better than anyone that life did not have to be any one way. Malintze had forged her own path, and Tenochtitlan could do the same. For her own sake, and the sake of every innocent whose life had been upended by war and chaos, she hoped the city chose well.

Epilogue
April 1527

Bartolomé de las Casas seated himself on a wooden bench in the courtyard of Puerto de Plata and watched as a carmine butterfly flitted between the wild daisies. It moved with enviable grace and speed, bringing to mind a time in his life long since passed. Bartolomé suspected it would still be many more years before he met his Lord and Savior, but he knew he would never be able to move with the purpose and vigor he had enjoyed in his youth.

Bartolomé exhaled deeply. Both body and mind had slowed since he first arrived in the West Indies, and his writing had suffered for it. A text that might have taken him an hour to translate could now take an entire morning. Dictating his thoughts was no easier. If anything, he struggled more to capture his inner musings with ink and parchment.

As far as he was concerned, the infirmity was a blessing in disguise. God knew he had put words to paper in too great a haste in times past. He was not sure he could ever fully atone for the mistakes of his youth, but he certainly meant to try. He could not call himself a Christian otherwise.

Friar Jorge approached him from the other side of the courtyard. He had known Jorge only a few years, but he could read him the same way he could read Genesis or Proverbs. Judging by the frown on Jorge's face and his hurried step, he had something important on his mind. Nonetheless, Bartolomé remained seated and waited for Jorge to come to him. *I am the head of this friary; surely, I deserve a few more moments of leisure?*

Rare were the moments when he could be alone with his thoughts. All too often he was writing letters, reading texts, or conferring with other friars.

Jorge stopped in front of him. "A man at the front gate is asking for an audience with you. He says he used to soldier for Cortés and believes you would be interested in hearing his relations. His name is Vitale. Do you wish to speak with him?"

Bartolomé racked his brain. The name Vitale meant absolutely nothing to him. He could not remember ever having met somebody named Vitale, not in the West Indies or Spain or elsewhere.

"Should I turn him away?" Jorge asked.

Bartolomé scratched his beard. *Why would a soldier of Cortés seek me out?* Many of the conquistadors despised him for his advocacy on behalf of the Indians and would sooner put a sword through him than speak with him. But even the most depraved conquistador would not travel all the way to his remote friary just to disembowel him.

"Bring him to my study," Bartolomé said.

Jorge shuffled off to do his bidding. Bartolomé turned his gaze back to the daisies. The butterfly was no longer flitting between flowers and had disappeared to some place he could not see. *Would I recognize you, if I saw you tomorrow?* He could not say. God must have loved butterflies for He had made many of them.

Bartolomé stood and made his way toward the study. A chilly draft greeted him once he stepped into the hallway, and he suppressed a shiver. The transition from the sweltering heat of outside to the friary's frigid interior was rather jarring, and he despaired that he might never get used to it.

He stepped into his study, surprised to see a disheveled man seated at a table in the middle of his room. Jorge, ever one for formality, had not taken a seat himself and stood beside the man. Bartolomé smiled. *Jorge did not waste any time escorting Vitale here.*

He noted, with a touch of disappointment, Jorge had stinted on refreshments. Besides a stale loaf of bread and a modest serving of honey, no other refreshments had been laid out.

Bartolomé approached the table slowly, studying Vitale all the while. He was probably thirty or so, if Bartolomé had to guess. Lowborn, too, based upon his sun-darkened skin. And poor, judging by his shifty eyes and his threadbare tunic. *He looks as if he has not eaten in days and smells as if he has not changed in weeks.*

Bartolomé was certain he had never seen the man before, but he knew his type. Men like Vitale could be found in every colony. Too proud to beg, too strong to starve. They sold their swords and their consciences to the highest bidder and drowned their sorrows in killgrief and vice. He had taken confession from many such men, but none of them ever had the temerity to seek him out at his friary.

"Greetings, son," Bartolomé said. He took a seat across from Vitale. "Forgive me for being so bold, but you look as if you traveled a great many leagues. Would you care for any other refreshments?"

Vitale shook his head. He dug his fingers into the bread, tore off a large hunk, and slowly brought it to his mouth. He kept his eyes fixed on Jorge the entire time, staring at him as if he were a vendor who had demanded payment. Bartolomé sighed. Dire circumstances seldom brought out the best virtues in a man.

Jorge shot Bartolomé a pleading look. Bartolomé motioned to the door, and Jorge saw himself out. Vitale's gaze followed him all the way to the door. A half minute passed before he finally tore his gaze away from the door. But instead of turning toward Bartolomé, he focused his attention on the shelves that lined the walls.

"Did you come to admire my book collection?" Bartolomé asked, half-jesting.

Vitale gave no acknowledgment he heard him, his gaze fixed on the leather-bound tomes on the far side of the room. "Did it take long to read all them books?"

Bartolomé smiled. "A very long time. And it will take even longer to transcribe them. But we do what we must."

Vitale wiped bread crumbs from his lips. "I hear you called the Protector of the Indians."

"Yes, I have been called that. And other names." Bartolomé reflected on the slurs that had been hurled at him by the *encomenderos*. God as his witness, they hated him more than they hated the Moors, all because he refused to condone their slaving and murdering. "Did you seek me out on your own volition?"

Vitale huffed. "Volition—you talk like somebody I used to know." A wistful look passed over his face. "You ever spent any time in Mexico, Father?"

Bartolomé shook his head.

"But you heard about what's going on there?" Vitale asked. "The wars, the…"

"Atrocities?" Bartolomé finished.

Vitale nodded.

"Yes, I have heard a great deal about the mistreatment of the natives there," Bartolomé said. The battle for Tenochtitlan had ended five years prior, but the battle for the New World raged on. If anything, it had become worse. Since Cortés had not been able to make good on his promise of gold and silver for his soldiers, he gave them land and slaves instead. But there was never enough of either, so the war continued to spill into new villages and new lands. "News from the mainland can be hard to come by at Puerto de Plata," Bartolomé added. "I hear Cortés has received a coat of arms from the king. Is that true?"

Vitale nodded and stuffed another hunk of bread in his mouth.

Bartolomé pursed his lips. *If the king can look past Cortés' cruelty, he may be willing to do the same for others.* Bartolomé would have to write a letter to the court soon. Cortés could not be allowed to arrogate more power.

He focused his attention on the soldier once again. He had not expected him to be so taciturn. Bartolomé wondered if he had made a mistake by agreeing to speak with him. For all he knew, the man was a charlatan. He realized he had not asked the soldier his name, had simply trusted that Jorge had given him good information. "What's your name, son?"

"Vitale."

"Is there not more to your name?" Bartolomé asked.

Vitale stiffened. He cleared his throat and said, "Some of my compatriots would call me Eliseo Vitale, but my family knew me as Benelisha Vitale, and I hail from Pampaneira."

Bartolomé blinked. Benelisha was a Hebrew name. If Bartolomé were to report him to the Inquisition, the soldier might never see the light of day again. After a trice, he said, "I have a distant relation who hails from the same area. Perhaps your family is acquainted with her." Bartolomé leaned in close and lowered his voice a fraction. "She once went by the name Amada."

Vitale's eyes widened. "You mean—"

Bartolomé cut him off with a wave of his hand. One could never be sure of who was listening. *If the Inquisition ever learns of my family background... God perish the thought.* "As I said, a distant relation. It matters for little, anyway. God is far more concerned with our souls than our heritage. Tell me about your experiences in Mexico. Did you sail for the country after Tenochtitlan fell?"

Vitale stared at his dirt-encrusted hands. "I sailed for the country long before that. I was with Cortés for Tlaxcala and Cholula... and so much else." Vitale glanced up from the table. "Father, what I tell you won't be easy to hear. Great wrongs have been carried out in the New World. Are you sure you wish to hear my relations?"

Bartolomé nodded. "I would be most interested in hearing your relations, Vitale. Please, let me send for some refreshments. Make yourself comfortable. I wish to have a full accounting from you."

Vitale furrowed his brow. "A full accounting will take many hours. Do you not have other tasks to attend to?"

"None as important," Bartolomé replied. "I would have an explanation as to why you joined Cortés' crew, and what happened during the course of the campaign. Do not spare me any of the details. I wish to know all of it."

A curious warmth blossomed in Bartolomé's chest. He looked down at his hand. The itch to write, to advocate was sending tremors up his arm. He flattened his hand against the table. Now was a time to listen, not write. There would be time to write later. That he was sure of.

"Thank you, Benelisha Vitale, for seeking me out. Please give me a full accounting when you are ready. I think the information you mean to relate will be of great interest to Christians everywhere."

Historical Note

When I began the Tenochtitlan Trilogy, I had only a vague sense of how I would end it. I knew the fall of Tenochtitlan had to be included, but I wasn't sure how much else to include. Much as I wanted to explore the aftermath of Tenochtitlan's fall in this novel, I think the subject is a bit too expansive to cover in just a few chapters. Consequently, I decided to end the novel with the fall of Tenochtitlan since the aftermath is a subject that deserves a book all its own.

I understand some readers may find my decision frustrating. Lest anybody accuse me of ending my work on too abrupt a note, I want to assure fans there is a chance I write a spin-off novel that covers the aftermath. A slim chance, but one within the realm of possibility. Nonetheless, I do believe closure is important so I want to take some time to explain what happened to some of the characters after the war ended.

Since many of my readers consider Malintze the most interesting character, I will start with her. Cortés did eventually make good on his promise to free her, and they conceived a child after the war ended. They named the child Martin, after Cortés' father, and he is considered to be one of the first mestizo individuals to be born in Mexico. Long after the battle for Tenochtitlan ended, Malintze took a Spaniard for a husband, a soldier named Juan Jaramillo, and had a daughter with him. The daughter, Doña Maria survived Malintze, as did Martin.

The circumstances surrounding Malintze's death are not all that clear. It seems likely that she succumbed to disease, but the specific disease is a bit of a mystery. Many scholars contend it was smallpox and while it's certainly possible, I think another disease is more likely: syphilis.

Stigma surrounds most STDs, so I can understand why some would be wary of making such a charge. Having said that, I do think there is a great deal of evidence in favor of the syphilis hypothesis.

First and foremost is her relationship with Cortés. Based upon DNA samples, we know Cortés did contract syphilis at some point in his life. The exact time frame is a little bit hazy, but historical accounts indicate he probably contracted syphilis long before he sailed for Mexico. Of course, it's possible he never passed on the disease to Malintze, but it would be a minor miracle considering they had a child together and could not avail themselves of modern-day contraceptives.

Besides her relationship to Cortés, there is also the issue of timing. Syphilis is a slow, and often silent, killer. This is particularly true for women as it is generally easier to misdiagnose female victims as opposed to male victims. Undiagnosed and untreated victims often die within a decade of contracting syphilis. We know for certain that Malintze first met Cortés in 1519 and considering that she died somewhere around 1529, the timeline makes sense. Of course, syphilis is not always fatal and it's possible she may have been done in by some other disease. Small pox, after all, killed a great many Nahua people, but it is worth noting she survived the great wave of 1520 and would have been at far less risk for contracting it once she gained a household of her own.

As luck would have it, Cortés survived Malintze by quite a few years and died in 1547. The capture of Tenochtitlan was, in many respects, the highwater mark of his life. None of the other military expeditions he took part in netted nearly as great a prize, and life became significantly more difficult for him after Tenochtitlan fell. While he eventually received honors from the king, he was never granted the title he wished for most: governor of Mexico. Neither, for that matter, was he able to hold together the military coalition that helped him take Tenochtitlan. Many of his Spanish officers broke faith with him after the war ended, one did so at the express urging of Governor Velazquez, and Cortés' violent reprisals did not sit well with court officials. Accused of theft, murder, and various other crimes, Cortés sailed all the way to Spain to plead favor from the king. His pleas fell on deaf ears and the experience left him embittered and resentful. One should not feel too sorry for Cortés, however; he enslaved 287 human beings to manage his estate, and that's not even counting the many thousands who were enslaved as a result of his military campaigns.

Gonzalo de Sandóval, one of the few to keep faith with Cortés, joined Cortés on his journey back to Spain. Along the way, Sandóval contracted some type of illness and had to be sequestered to an inn after the crew made landfall in Southern Spain. Cortés assumed, correctly, Sandóval would not recover and left him at the inn to seek out the king. Sandóval was robbed on his deathbed, having been abandoned by his friends and his dependents.

Pedro de Alvarado decided to try his hand at leading a military expedition and journeyed south to make war on the Maya people. His penchant for brutalizing enemy peoples, as well as faithful allies, eventually backfired, culminating in a protracted, bloody campaign. He died in battle, crushed under his own horse. He had three children with Doña Luisa.

Bartolomé de las Casas never had any children and dedicated his life to the Church. He is widely considered to be one of the first progenitors of human rights and authored numerous works related to theology, history, and ethics. Many of his works, such as In Defense of the Indians and A Short Account of the Destruction of the Indies, are still in print today. A pariah in his time, Casas has come to be much better regarded these days.

Juan Garrido does not enjoy the same name recognition as Bartolomé de las Casas, but he was a pathmaker in his own right. He was very likely the first person to cultivate wheat in all the Americas and established a church in Mexico after the war ended. The church no longer exists, but it was one of the first to be erected in the New World. He spent the rest of his life in Mexico, as did Maria de Estrada and Cotton Flower.

Owing to her heritage, Cotton Flower became one of the most important women in post-war Tenochtitlan. She had a child with Cortés, but they never married. Had she any say in the matter, it is extremely unlikely she would have wanted him for a husband. Putting aside his philandering, it beggars belief she would have any romantic interest in the man who helped kill so many of her family and friends. After Tenochtitlan surrendered, Cotton Flower was married to Alonso de Grado. The marriage did not last long as he died about two years after they married. Some time later, she took Juan Cano as a husband. They had five children together.

Speaking of Cano, I should mention that the timeline for when they first came into each other's lives isn't technically accurate. We can't know for sure they had any interactions in 1520 but if they did, it would have been a few weeks later than I suggested in The Bend of the River.

Ixtli, better known as Ixtlilxochitl, joined numerous military campaigns after the fall of Tenochtitlan. He converted to Christianity at some point and forced many of his countrymen, including his own kin, to convert. Elder, Father to Xicotencatl the Younger, also converted to Christianity and continued to be an important figure in Tlaxcala politics up until his death.

Cuauhtemoc did not fare well at the hands of the Spaniards. The Spaniards tortured him for information regarding the gold and subjected him to all manner of degradation. Cortés, never one to forget a grudge, had him burned at the stake a few years after Tenochtitlan fell. Nevertheless, his spirit lives on, and statues have been erected in his honor all around Mexico.

Pozon is a character I created for this novel. He endures a great deal of abuse in the story, but he at least can look forward to the prospect of freedom thanks to Malintze. The same was not true, however, for most of the people captured by the Spaniards or their allies. Owing to a combination of disease and mistreatment, most of the captives did not survive all that long. The labor shortage became so severe that the Spanish looked abroad for a solution, leading to a dramatic expansion of the Trans-Atlantic Slave Trade.

From an accuracy standpoint, it might have been better if I had given Pozon a trajectory truer to the experience of most captives. I decided against doing so primarily for two reasons. First, it would have been depressing. Most of the characters in the Tenochtitlan Trilogy do not enjoy a "happy ending." Plenty of the recurring characters, the historical figures and the fictional creations, meet violent ends so I felt it would be nice to give one a chance at happiness. Second, historical records do indicate Malintze took a Nahua boy into her household after the war ended and became a surrogate mother to him.

Little is known of him, he is referred to in historical sources as Don Diego de Atempanecatl but he seems to have cared a great deal for Malintze. When some of her detractors tried to sully Malintze's character post mortem, he came forward to testify to her good character. We know very little of Don Diego, but I like to think it could have been somebody like Pozon. Wishful thinking on my part, Don Diego probably came from an important family, but that's allowed every now and then in historical fiction.

On the subject of accuracy, I should also mention there is a great deal that I omitted from this book. The final months of the Spanish-Mexica war were bloody and dramatic, and I did not consider it practical to try to cover all the events leading up to the fall of Tenochtitlan. For the most part, I focused on the events I considered most important to the story I was telling and that means I left a decent amount on the proverbial cutting board.

Readers interested in gaining a fuller understanding of the war, and its aftermath, do not suffer for a shortage of materials. In no particular order, I recommend Camilla Townsend's "The Fifth Sun," Ronald Wright's "Stolen Continents: The New World Through Indian Eyes Since 1492, Caroline Dodds Pennock's "Bonds of Blood," ABC-CLIO's "Conflict in the Early Americas," AJPA's "The Genetic Impact of Aztec Imperialism: Ancient Mitochondrial DNA Evidence from Xaltocan, Mexico," David Thomas Orique's "The Life, Labor, and Legacy of Bartolomé de las Casas," Barbara Mundy's "Mapping the Aztec Capital: The 1524 Nuremberg Map of Tenochtitlan, Its Sources and Meanings," Christopher Morehart and Dan T.A. Eisenberg's "Prosperity, Power, and Change: Modeling Maize at Postclassic Xaltocan, Mexico," CarnivalNoblesse's "Ginetta Spanish Horse Riding," Manuel Aguilar-Moreno's "Question for September 2008," Karl Taube's "Aztec Religion," Gizmodo's "Hear the Aztec Death Whistle That Mystified Scientists," Robert Goodwin's America: The Story of Spanish North America: 1493'1898," Latin American Antiquity's "Egalitarian Ideology And Political Power In Prehispanic Central Mexico: The Case Of Tlaxcallan," Al Sandine's "Deadly Baggage: What Cortés Brought to Mexico and How it Destroyed the Aztec Civilization," C Harvey Gardiner's "Naval Power in the Conquest of Mexico," Brigit Katz's "14th Century Steam Bath Found in Mexico City," Alan Yuhas'

"Conquistadors Sacrificed and Eaten By Aztec-Era People, Archaeologists Say," Christina Warinner's "Mixtecs, Aztecs, and the Great Cocoliztli Epidemic of AD 1545-1550," History on Fire "The Conquest of Mexico: People of the Sun," Richard Herzog's "How Aztecs Reacted to Colonial Epidemics," Tristan Siegel's "The Environmental and Cultural Effects on the Conquest of Mexico, Doñald Chipman's Moctezuma's Children: Aztec Royalty Under Spanish Rule," This Podcast Will Kill You "Episode 36: Shades of Syphilis," CDC's "What is Syphilis," C. Harvey Gardiner's "Martin López: Conquistador, Citizen of Mexico," Alva Ixltixochitl's "The Native Conquistador, James Lockhart's translation of "We People Here: Nahuatl Accounts of the Conquest of Mexico," Keitlyn's Alcantara-Russell's "The Diet of Sovereignty: Bioarcheology in Tlaxcallan," Angela Herren Rajagopalan's "Reading Between the Lines: An Indigenous Account of Conquest on the Missing Folios of Codex Azcatitlan," the "Codex Laud," the "Codex Aubin," Susan Kellog's "Law and Transformation of Aztec Culture," and Si Sheppard's "Tenochtitlan's 1519-1521."

The list includes a mix of academic articles, primary sources, non-fiction books, short blurbs, news articles, podcasts, and YouTube videos. Some sources had numerous authors, and I listed only the publisher's name in these cases. It is by no means a definitive list, but it is a useful jumping-off point. For the sake of clarity, I should mention that I omitted mention of works I referenced in the first and second book in this series.

Note to Readers

To avoid confusing readers, I should mention which names I have changed. As I mentioned in the historical note, Ixtli is short for Ixtlilxochitl. Likewise, Chichi is short for Chichimecatecle. Elder is short for Xicotencatl the Elder. I worried keeping track of two Xicotencatl's would be difficult so I referred to Xicotencatl the Younger as Xicotencatl and referred to his father as Elder.

On that note, I should also mention that I used English and Spanish translations for many Nahuatl terms. Coa, for example, is a Spanish translation of the Nahuatl word, uictli, and Willow Grove is a translation of Huexotla. Additionally, I decided to use the term Northern Tenochtitlan in place of Tlatelolco. Because I used the term Northern Tenochtitlan, I was also obligated to use the term Southern Tenochtitlan to refer to the rest of Tenochtitlan even though Tenochtitlan proper was not called Southern Tenochtitlan to my knowledge. Of all the translations, Snake Den is probably the least kosher since the English translation for Coatlinchan should have more along the lines of "in the home of the snakes."

Should you have questions about anything you came across in this book or simply want to share your thoughts regarding my work, please do not hesitate to post them to the review page on Amazon or Goodreads. The reviews are enormously helpful when it comes to improving my craft and increasing the visibility of my work.

Acknowledgments

If it takes a village to raise a child, it takes a town to develop a writer. I owe thanks to a great many individuals and I would like to give thanks to those who have been particularly helpful.

My mother has been nothing but supportive of my writing habit and I owe her great thanks. Additionally, I also owe thanks to my godparents, to Cailin, Martha Leonard, Lawrence, Lilly, Alura, Joe, Ligia, Robert, Nathan, and Robbie. The encouragement, and the reviews, really do help.

I also owe thanks to Matthew Restall, Kathleen O'Neal Gear, Andrew Rowen, N.D. Jones, Casey Robb, Revered Kathryn Haueisen, Ronald Wright, Reverend Javier Alanis, C.T. Mexica, K.M. Pohlkamp, Aaron Booth, Jim White, Zoe Saadia, authors and academics who were kind enough to provide me advanced reviews for my work. I also owe thanks to academics who were able to help me with research matters, such as John Schwaller. The painting featured on the cover of my work, The Conquest of Mexico, comes from the Kislak collection.

Lastly, I would like to give a special thank you to Ms. Patterson. I first went to her for writing help in elementary school and she never hesitated to put aside time to help me edit my work, even when I made a habit of coming in every week.

www.ingramcontent.com/pod-product-compliance
Lightning Source LLC
Chambersburg PA
CBHW072006210726
48294CB00013B/1675